THE GORGON DESOLATION 1E194-199

KELSON HAYES

EDITED BY COURTNEY MCCALL

THE SERIES SO FAR:

THE NORTHERN WARS

1E75-80

THE GORGON DESOLATION

1E194-199

UPCOMING TITLES:

GROETSHVEN

1E144-199

TAURO THE TITAN-SLAYER

1E15-23

THE GORGON DESOLATION

PRINTED BY CREATESPACE

FIRST EDITION/ November 2015

SECOND EDITION/ April 2016

ALL RIGHTS RESERVED

©2015 by Kelson Clarke Hayes

FRONTCOVER DESING BY CREATESPACE

THE COPYWRITTEN PORTIONS OF THIS BOOK MAY NOT BE REPRODUCED OR TRANSMITTED IN ANY FORM OR BY ANY MEANS, ELECTRONIC OR MECHANICAL, INCLUDING PHOTOCOPYING, RECORDING, OR BY ANY INFORMATION STORAGE AND RETRIEVAL SYSTEM, WITHOUT THE EXPRESS PERMISSION OF THE AUTHOR, EXCEPT WHERE PERMITTED BY LAW.

If you purchased this book without a cover you should be aware that this book is stolen property. It is reported as "unsold and destroyed" to the publisher and neither the author nor the publisher received any payment for this "stripped book".

Manufactured in the United States of America.

TABLE OF CONTENTS

Map Of Southeast Aerbon

Prologue..p.1
Chapter One...p.8
Chapter Two...p.21
Chapter Three...p.35
Chapter Four...p.49
Chapter Five...p.59
Chapter Six...p.70
Chapter Seven..p.77
Chapter Eight..p.84
Chapter Nine...p.93
Chapter Ten..p.102
Chapter Eleven...p.111
Chapter Twelve..p.121
Chapter Thirteen......................................p.131
Chapter Fourteen.....................................p.141
Chapter Fifteen..p.149
Chapter Sixteen.......................................p.159
Chapter Seventeen..................................p.170
Chapter Eighteen.....................................p.179
Chapter Nineteen.....................................p.187
Chapter Twenty.......................................p.195
Chapter Twenty-One................................p.201
Chapter Twenty-Two...............................p.208
Chapter Twenty-Three.............................p.216
Chapter Twenty-Four...............................p.223
Chapter Twenty-Five...............................p.233
Chapter Twenty Six..................................p.240

Epilogue..p.248

MAP OF SOUTHEAST AERBON

PROLOGUE
SUMATRAN OCEAN
Summer, 1E 194

Surrounded by the darkness of the night, clouds swathed the sky, blotting out all light from the stars and the moon in the depths of the heavens above. Eight great Nardic ships sailed the rough waters of the Sumatran Ocean that separated the Nardic Isles from the Gorgon Desolation in the mainland of Aerbon to the North. Thunder boomed and lightning cracked, shattering the silence of the night whilst the sea rumbled and roared as foamy waves crashed upon the warships. The Nardic fleet sailed from the port of Baiern on the northern coast of Dusseldorf; the largest of island of their Isles in the South and closest to the orc-lands they sought out. The ships had been sailing for nearly a week and each of the men aboard fought their hardest to make it as far as they had in those rough waters. Two ships had already been lost to the sea-god, Urasmus, and the weather threatened to take even more sailor's lives with the ships they manned.

Men shouted orders back and forth all along the decks of the ships and others raced along to do the bidding of their superiors. Hail pelted the sails as they continued to plough through the surging waves with difficulty. The going was slow and arduous but they continued to make headway even as the hail occasionally tore holes in the hemp sailcloth. Ulrich looked up to see the sails struggling to break free of the masts that bound them with the help of the heavy storm that assailed the Nardic ships relentlessly. Rain washed over the main decks and men slipped and slid as they raced from bow to aft and back again. Some men had already been dragged overboard by the enormous waves that sprayed arrogantly over the survivors of the onslaught.

An ominous wave surged towards the Nardic fleet in slow motion and two more ships further port-side were swallowed whole upon contact with the towering wall of seawater. Ulrich felt his gasp of shock as it was sucked away by the strong winds that blew all around, helplessly watching from the starboard as his comrades death shrieks were drowned by the thunderous storm and raging ocean. Each of the sailors aboard the remaining ships of the Nardic fleet felt all hope drain from within them as the rain washed it away into the infinite depths of the ocean they battled for their very lives. If any amongst them could have found the time to take in their surroundings, they would have found that there were no landmarks or signs of anything remotely signalling the end of their wretched misadventure. It was instead their luck, however, to maintain the course of their great war vessels and devote every ounce of their being to keeping those wooden whores afloat, lest the sea crush their hopes of landfall as it dragged them all to their watery graves.

Men shouted and swore, fleeing as a bolt of lightning struck the centre-mast of one of the ships nearer to the middle of their formation, splitting it in half and setting the deck aflame all around where it struck. Another ship, on the outside towards the port-side, had the misfortune of being capsized by a giant wave and the cries of its occupants could easily be heard over the raging storm and wind that buffeted them as they faced their impending deaths. A third ship rode the crest of a wave and the wave suddenly broke beneath it, sending the ship crashing down straight towards the ocean surface head-first where it dived under like some sort of submarine. When it resurfaced the remains of the ship were upside down, it sank slowly as water filled up the cabins and cargohold through the giant breach in the hull on either side. Of the five remaining ships, few amongst their survivors held any faith that they would live to see land.

Ulrich felt the water sweep him off his feet. His heart felt as though it were about to burst out of his chest, beating rapidly as he slid across the slippery wet surface of the ship deck. He reached out for anything that would hold him until the wave passed over but his hands grasped at empty air and sea spray. His back crashed into the railing that ran all along the sides of the ship and he rolled off the side into the ocean below. Making one final grab at salvation before he was swept away never to be seen again, Ulrich closed his eyes and prayed as his hand wrapped around the railing. Water rushed over and around him and he could feel it pulling him away from the wooden rod he clung to for dear life. Once the wave had swept over and the ship had readjusted itself, Ulrich pulled himself up and over the side. He clambered over the railing and thanked the Nardic gods for allowing him to keep his life amidst the rampant death and destruction that engulfed his fellow countrymen at sea.

His only thoughts were of his wife Aeryn and his two boys; Frank and Hans. He thought of his home in Baiern and of his friends in the town that he left behind for national duty to his country. Some had even joined him on the voyage North, a few of them were already dead by the will of the Urasmus. Each of the ten ships had originally held five thousand warriors of the Nardic Isles; a grand total of 50,000 men began that accursed journey to the Gorgon Desolation. Now there were only five ships and maybe twenty thousands, at the most, still aboard. Out of that number even fewer were fit enough to travel and there was a broad range of injuries and maladies of the sea afflicting them. Counting the living was useless aboard the ships, however; there was no way of knowing who was still alive and who was fish fodder in the chaos of the storm. They would have to wait until they were safely ashore if the time ever came before they could count their losses.

Upon returning to the semi-solid ground of the ship deck, Ulrich returned to his duties in attempting to keep the ship afloat and on course. The pilot was still at the wheel and his captain was away at sea, drowning in the choppy waters of the Gorgon Gulf. Ulrich damned the ship, his captain, the elves, orcs, and everything else that he could find to blame for his current predicament. The ships continued to fight their way through the rough currents and crashing waves. Men held on for dear life on the rollercoaster ride across what they'd affably referred to as a leap over the pond prior to boarding the ships. It had quickly earned itself the title of "Voyage To Hell" throughout the course of the weekend storm that assailed them even now. The first four days of their voyage had been smooth sailing until the storm hit.

Lightning flashed and thunder boomed; Ulrich nearly jumped out of his skin with each crack of lightning that echoed resonantly in his ears. The wind howled and sometimes he felt himself being lifted off his feet by the gale-force strength of the winds that buffeted him and his kinsmen. He was drenched from head to toe in seawater and he was shivering in the cold rain. Parched by all the seawater he'd swallowed, Ulrich's mouth was parched and swollen and his lips were cracked, dry, and blistered. His eyes were red-rimmed and burned with a growing intensity every second that he kept them open. Sleep was all Ulrich wanted; he welcomed its warm embrace in the icy chill of that stormy night.

He longed for his bed at home, but he'd even settle for his seamen's bunk in the cabin space below. It was his duty to remain on the main deck however, and that's where he stayed. All that was left of the main mast was a splintered wooden beam no higher from the deck than his head. The frayed ropes swung about helplessly as the ocean waves surged over the deck and gusts of wind gave them life as they blew wildly. In the distance rows of cruel jagged teeth were visible, barely protruding above the ocean's surface. They peeked out of the depths of the sea eagerly anticipating the approaching Nardic warships like the sinister bristles of a whale as it swallowed plankton whole.

 The ships headed directly towards the rocky teeth on the great ocean waves they rode. The rock mouth opened its jaws wide as the water shrank back before waves came crashing down upon it, bearing ships full of Nardic seamen. Barnacle-encrusted stalagmites tore into the wooden frames of the warships like human teeth sinking into an apple; seawater came pouring into the vessels through the fresh tears in the hull of the mighty vessels. Ulrich and those nearby him were flung helplessly across the deck by the force of the impact. He felt his back make contact with the cabin door and he fell through it. The door splintered and cracked, giving way to his superior weight and the combined weight of his fellows who came crashing through with him.

 Water had already filled the cabins and there were corpses floating up to meet them even as the survivors fought to make their way out. The ship leaned forwards again and they all tumbled back out of the temporary safety of the passageway. As the men all slid across the slippery main deck water sloshed over the and some of the men joined their lost brethren at sea. The waves continued to collide and break upon the ship, sending foamy sea spray over those who found themselves fortunate enough to still remain aboard the sinking ships. Some amongst them sought out the few life boats that had survived the whole ordeal and fled in an attempt to escape the wreckage.

Those who'd been thrown overboard tried to make their way to the lifeboats and many failed. Some amongst them did reach the boats, however, and found themselves holding on for their lives in the ten-man vessels, caught in the waves like a tuber in harsh rapids. The unfortunate majority who found themselves unable to reach the boats could be seen from afar, even in the warships; a single outstretched hand, grasping at empty air before disappearing beneath the rough ocean's surface. The men still aboard the ships prayed to their gods or wept, some even commit suicide after seeing the futility of it all.

The Nardic Tribes had seven gods; Urasmus, God of the Sea, Nova the Sun-Goddess, Stein the Earth-God, Hasst, the God of death, Benzin, the God of Life, Onanieren, the Goddess of Fertility, and Ein; the King of the Gods as well as the God of War. The gods ruled over all that fell under their dominion and Ein ruled everything else, as well as the gods themselves. Their gods were not physical in nature, but more or less like the strands of fate. They were beyond time and space and were made up of another fabric entirely in another dimension of existence. The gods were a part of everything around them and the belief of them caused everything to exist by their will. Without faith, nothing was real and because everything is real it had to be believed, otherwise there would be no point to existence. This was what the people of the Nardic Isles believed and these were to gods to whom they prayed.

Ulrich spoke silent prayers to Urasmus as did the majority of the seamen, some prayed to Stein to bring them to land, and a few even reached out to Nova, pleading her to end the storms. Ulrich began to wonder if he would ever live to see his family again and his thoughts wandered back to his final farewell. He remembered holding Aeryn in his arms, looking into her beautiful brown eyes and telling her that everything would be alright, and of telling Hans to keep his mother safe while he was away. The confused look on Frank's face when he watched his father kiss him upon the brown before leaving them. Hans was 13, a young lad in his own right, and Frank was just a toddler. They were both far too young to be without a father in their lives and the burly Nardic warrior fought back tears as he fought to remain aboard the damned vessel.

    It had nearly been an entire month since the elves had first sent their emissaries from their capitol city in Graenor to the Nardic island of Auchtung via elvish ships borrowed from the port town of Aereil. The elvish messengers spoke to the chieftain of the island who organised a meeting with the Nardic Council in the fortress of Sehnshult, capitol of the Nardic Isles in the South. Sehnshult was situated in the heartlands of Dusseldorf, the largest island of the Isles and home to the Warlord of the Nardic Tribes, to whom all the individual chieftains pledged their undying fealty. The Warlord declared the Nardic Tribes at war with the orcs of the Gorgon Desolation after hearing all that the elvish messengers of King Hassän had to say. He mustered a host of 50,000 men and sent them North to aid the elves of Gilan in their campaign.

    Ulrich still remembered sitting at the dinner table on the night that the courier had arrived on his doorstep bearing news of a draft. He and his fellow men had been ordered to take up arms and fight for their country abroad. Suddenly Ulrich was brought out of his thoughts as the ship lurched forwards in a spray of seawater. It rode the crest of the wave even as the water dragged it down and With a crash the fo'c'sle was swallowed whole beneath the water's surface and the last thing Ulrich remembered before he fell unconscious was flying headfirst across the deck before the ocean swallowed him whole.

CHAPTER ONE
SYTHIN, GORGON DESOLATION
Winter, 1E194

The sun rose on the horizon, across the barren flatlands of the Gorgon Desolation, and the light penetrated the light cloudy sky that loomed overhead above the elvish legions amassed on the border of the orc country. The elvish army had encamped itself upon the dead plains outside Sythin for the night and currently prepared for the final day's march, even as the midday sun rose above the black skies of the Gorgon lands. Their shining silvery armour gleamed in the sun as they broke fast in merriment, with little thought towards what laid ahead. They laughed and joked among themselves as if they were still in the comfort of their homelands in Gilan. The host consisted of three separate divisions; a division each from the outpost towns of Graenor and Eden, as well as a contingent of elves from the Aush Woods.

Their forces were 35,000 strong, opposed by an estimated twelve thousand orcs. The elves of Graenor were armed with scimitars and wore the traditional woven steel mail of their people beneath heavy steel-plate armour. Eden's troops consisted mainly of a lighter-armed cavalry, outfitted with just a simple coat of the chainmail, weaved by the elves of their town skilled in the art of blacksmithing. Their horses were attired in a similar fashion; the majority of horsemen were armed with long lances, though some officers amongst them brought their swords with them to the battlefield. The Aush Wood elves did not wear any metal armours to protect themselves, but rather clothed themselves with the grasses, leaves, and bark of the woods they so dearly loved. The leaves and grasses provided them with clothes and they crafted armour out of the bark of the sacred birch trees that grew throughout their domain.

The elves of the Aush Woods were very unlike their kin, if they could even be considered kin at all. Whereas the elves of Gilan were all blue-eyed and each elf had flowing golden hair, the elves of the Aush Wood were silver-haired at birth and their hair fell flat and went far past their shoulders. Unlike the elves of Gilan, they limited themselves to the bow and arrow and crafted whatever nature couldn't provide for them out of nature itself. The elves of the Aush Woods were also considered to be immortal, even by elvish standards. It was true that the elves lived unnaturally long lives, though they did inevitably come to an end. The same did not seem to prove true for the elves of the Aush Wood however, who were seemingly immune to the passage of time.

They were the keepers of the Aush Woods, the sacred ancestral burial grounds of Gilan. Entrusted with the task of tending the dead, they put the spirits of their dead kin to rest in that holy wood to return to the earth that brought them into the world and sustained them through their lives. The spirits laid to rest under the enchantment of the wood fed the life that sprung from the burial ground and the magic of the spirit wood was great. Flowers, trees, and fruits grew in that country the likes of which couldn't be found anywhere else in the world. They were radiant with the light of the spirit fire that burned and flowed within them. The Aush Woods had been the ancestral burial grounds of Gilan since the times of Myth, before recorded history had yet been developed.

The joint forces of Eden and Graenor made up the frontline whilst the Aush Wood elves formed a vanguard in the planned assault against the forces of the Gorgon Desolation. The orcs were a foul race; the majority of the Gorgon population as well as a tribal and warmongering breed. Destruction and consumption was all that their people knew. No fair things grew in their desolate wasteland and all that they wrought was tainted and corrupt. They grew and produced foul drugs that polluted the skies through the vile factories that refined the substance. Production of the drug was causing the skies to grow dark from the pollution that was steadily engulfing the land in darkness. The skies were dark grey and faded to back further towards the eastern horizon where Istul lay, hundreds upon hundreds of leagues away from where they currently stood.

    The elves could even taste the pollution in the air from where their current position in the westernmost reaches of the orcish country. Rather than heed the evil of the orcs that was apparent in those lands, the elves continued on their quest to free the world of their foul existence. The elvish host had been on march for nearly a fortnight and they were already upon the sqal* of Sythin. The orcish outpost was within sight; a dark smudge on the horizon that steadily grew in size until they were finally outside its walls. The ramshackle walls had spikes that jutted out, sharpened logs from the trunks of trees long gone from the land the orcs had taken as their own. The orcish outpost consisted of thatched huts made out of mud and spiked logs like those that lined their defensive wall. The elvish host continued to march without hesitation and they came to find the sqal teeming with orcs readying themselves for war.

    The orcs of the sqal were all attired in bone armour atop black leather cuirasses and their boots were iron shod. Thick bone horns protruded grotesquely from their fearsome helms, wrought like the jowls of some terrible beast. Their spiked pauldrons and gauntlets were also forged of iron and the metal of their outfit was all thickly coated in a resinous black tar. A couple orcs scrambled to and fro, abandoning their last-minute preparations against the elvish

---

*Orcs are a nomadic race, often travelling between more permanent settlements, similar to shanty-towns. These constructions, referred to as sqals, act as outposts, towns, gathering points, as well as a place to resupply between destinations on a march.

assault that was nearly upon them. When the elves had drawn within firing range, construction ceased whilst the orcish archers upon the battlements took aim with their bows and fired a volley of their poisoned darts into the heart of the elven host.Some of the arrows met their mark whilst the greater majority were repelled by the enchanted armour of the elves.

The orcish warriors within the settlement prepared themselves for the first wave of the incoming onslaught. Horses neighed restlessly and shock their armoured heads in the ranks of Eden's cavalry and the swordsmen of Graenor eagerly anticipated the order to charge. Captain Vasil of the First Swordsman Company of Graenor issued the command to charge and the host let forth all of their fury as they closed the distance between themselves and the outer wall of the sqal. Orcs poured out into the surrounding wastelands from within their outpost to meet the elves on the field of battle. Others leapt down from where they'd stood atop the ten-foot tall parapet that encompassed the perimeter of their town.

A second cloud of darts rained down upon the elves; the archers of the Aush Wood responded in kind with a volley of their own arrows, crafted from the holy wood of their land. Silver death rained down upon the orcs; the feathered Aush Wood shafts penetrated the sickly armour of the orcs and slaughtered them by the hundreds. The orcish armour was no match for the enchanted arrows crafted from the fair silvery wood of the birch tree, grown from saplings until they were grown enough to produce bows and arrows as well as armour.The birch wood they produced was stronger than metal, along with being more flexible, and it could pierce through most types of armour with ease.

The mounted cavalry of Eden charged through the ranks of the orcish forces that ran out to meet them and mowed them down, slicing through their host like a knife in warm butter. The swordsmen of Graenor followed behind in pursuit of their comrades in arms and they engaged the orcs as they came across them. Archers on both sides continued to rain down death from above, firing volley after volley into the midst of the battle. Death shrieks of orcs and elves alike intermingled with the battle cries of the living and the air was thick with the scent of blood and sweat. Steel clanged against iron and the sounds of war echoed throughout those plains as the companies of elvish warriors pushed the orc host back, against the walls that separated them from the dilapidated huts and shacks that made up the sqal of Sythin.

The orcs outside the walls who'd unsuccessfully attempted to repel the elvish invasion all turned and fled back within the safety of their outpost town. Out of the few remaining survivors of the initial skirmish, the majority were shot down by the keen-eyed elven archers; silver shafts protruded from their backs where they laid the the base of their outer wall or stuck, tangled in the spiked logs that randomly jutted out of the wall every 3-5 feet or so without any real order or pattern. Some of the orcs had managed to scale the walls and return to the temporary safety of their refuge, climbing the spiked logs to the top of the ten-foot tall parapet, nearly two times their height. Upon climbing the wall, they quickly hopped down into the streets of the sqal below before they were picked off by the Aush Wood elves who were well-known for their deadly accuracy with the bow and arrow.

The cavalry of elvish horsemen were hot on their tail however; only minutes after the escape of the fleeing orcs, the elvish horseman had already penetrated the outer defences of the wall. The horses all charged at the eastern gate entrance into the sqal and the wooden door gave way to their might, along with the debris of whatever the orcs had used to barricade the entry into their sqal. Orcish archers fired down into the streets, felling the horsemen as they charged through into the streets of Sythin from behind. Silver arrows pelted their undefended backs and seeing the futility of it all, Sythin's archers jumped down into the streets below and fled deeper into the heart of their city even as the elvish swordsmen company rushed in from behind, filling the western outskirts of the town.

Regrouping, the orcish archers ambushed the elvish cavalry deeper in the streets, closer towards the heart of the sqal. They popped out of the cover of the alleys they hid in to fire indiscriminately into the ranks of the horsemen who fought to push them back. The ambush had successfully taken its toll on the elves of Eden; those whose mounts were slain recovered themselves and some took up the riderless horses of their fallen comrades. The rest took up whatever weapons they could scavenge to replace their lances and joined the swordsman companies who were beginning to pour into the squalid streets of the orc settlement a ways behind them. The sqal of Sythin consisted of thatched huts and makeshift shacks, built out of mud, wood, and whatever scrap metal the orcs could salvage.

The streets were cramped and there was no order to them whatsoever; they streets were simply the area of land between the disarrayed rows of buildings. Sythin was a guaka-guaka farm, the orcs of the sqal thrived on the cultivation of the foul drug of their people, Guaka-Guaka. A black flowering plant similar to the rose bush in its appearance, Guaka-guaka was an amphetaminous drug that caused orcs under its influence to become blood-thirsty and its effects mimicked psychosis of a schizophrenic nature. Thorny wilted vines of the foul drug grew on orcish grow-houses. The vines spindled their way along the round thatched huts, weaving their way between the spiked logs that jutted out and wrapped around them, producing blooms of black flowers that secreted an oily resinous tar. A sickening odour wafted from in the air from its bulbs that mingled with the scent of death and it was enough to make some of the nearby elves gag and choke.

Stifling back their disgust, the cavalry renewed their assault upon their ambushers and chased the retreating orcs deeper into the heart of their sqal. The orcs banded together in their town centre and made a stand against the elves who assailed them, however, they were slaughtered by the dozens as the elvish cavalry mowed them down yet again. Elvish swordsmen engaged in battle with the more courageous of the tribal warriors even as their lesser kin turned and ran. The Aush Wood elves found their way into the sqal as well and took their marks, slaughtering any orcs who found themselves misfortunate enough to be turned into elvish pin cushions. Orcish warriors regrouped and surged forward in a wave of rage and desperation that quickly engulfed the forces of Gilan.

The remnants of the orcish host broke upon the swordsmen of Gilan and orc archers challenged the Aush Wood elves from afar. In the heat of the battle swords clashed and blows were parried; shields splintered and soldiers fell on both sides. The orc mass fell back and regrouped to break upon the elvish host, but it was to no avail; the elves of Gilan were far superior to the might of the orc tribes. Their scimitars and arrows felled their adversaries by the hundreds and their steel mail repelled the threat of death at the hands of the orcish tribals. The orcs crashed through the chaotic streets haphazardly in their futile attempt to escape the wrath of the elves. Corpses filled the cramped squalor of Sythin's streets and heaps of bodies laid in piles in the outlying wastes of the Gorgon plains. The black blood of the orcs coagulated on the bare grey earthen soil of the desolation and flies were already beginning to decompose their bodies.

The elves hewed down any fleeing stragglers as they passed them by on the hunt for bigger game. They were hot on the heels of the fleeing orcs and they continued to slaughter them with ease in their pursuit of Sythin's remnants. Fires were fed and spread throughout the outermost reaches of the sqal and soon a ring of fire encompassed the town that steadily burned their settlement to the ground. The elves set the outpost ablaze even as they took it and the remaining survivors amongst the orcs saw that they had no hope in escaping their demise. Each elf had vowed before undertaking the campaign that they would rid those eastern lands of the wretched creatures that inhabited them, polluting and defiling the world. The elves would purify and cleanse those forsaken lands of the orcish menace.

Some of the orcs turned around and laid down their weapons to surrender to the elvish army, pleading for mercy and begging for their lives. The elves ignored their pleas and killed them indiscriminately without the slightest hint of remorse. Though the elves of Gilan abstained from the taking of life, they slaughtered the orcs pitilessly. The infantry was hot on the heels of the retreating orcs and the archers continued to let loose their arrow volleys into the fleeing crowds of orcs. The host of Gilan would allow none to escape their wrath and no one would know of Sythin's fall by the will of the elves who exterminated its residents. The few orcs who'd been lucky enough to make it this far survived just long enough to witness the remnants of their kin slaughtered before their very eyes.

Still they resisted the might of the elves, fighting even in the face of defeat. They slaughtered as many of the elven warriors as they could before each orc was inevitably hacked down by the swords of their adversaries like trees in preparation for the lumber mill. It was not a glorious battle that would be passed down from orc to orcling as a ballad to be revered throughout the sqals of the

Gorgon Desolation. This battle against the elves would bring them no renown; it was the genocide of their people, the fall of the orcs, and there was nothing heroic or magnificent about it. The orcs were a race who hungered for battle and in the orc tribes, war was all that they knew.

Reputations were earned through bloodshed and respect was found on the battlefield; their chiefs were chosen from amongst the best warriors of a tribe or sqal. An orc chieftain could only be replaced by defeat in battle and the natural death of a chief had the potential to engulf tribes and even entire sqals in a civil war for dominance. The orcs only respected power and power was found in the excess of physical strength. The legions of Gilan had already killed Sythin's chieftain and their shamans were all dead too. The orc masses had lost their desire to fight and several had given up altogether, silently awaiting their death at the hand of the elves. Their best warriors were dead, their friends and family had all been eradicated, and their home was steadily burning to the ground; fear consumed their weak minds of frenzied orcs as the gathered themselves in a last ditch effort to escape.

It was useless; the victors ran their blades through the spines of the fleeing remnants and the battle was won, if such a bloodbath could even be called a battle at all. The orcs were demon-worshippers who followed gods of death, darkness, and destruction. In the few records they had of their people in Gilan in the times of Myth, it was said that Sythis, the God of Chaos had once reigned in the East before the Fall of the Gods. The orcs worshipped their wretched gods out of fear, kidnapping elves and taking their victims to the Tuhk of Istul to sacrifice as offerings in their Church. They served the dark beings and built altars for them at their command, growing guaka-guaka and distributing it amongst their people for religious and recreational use. Their gods spoke to them through the drug even as the burning hatred coursed through their veins, driving them insane.

    The elves of Gilan didn't see the fear that bound the orcs in their subservience to the demons, or the psychoactive and addictive nature of the drug they consumed on a daily basis. They only saw the result of their enslavement; the death and destruction that was spreading out of their lands. It was for this reason that the elves sought the destruction of the Gorgon menace. Their King had finally declared a much-needed war against the orcs of the East. His forefathers, King Hasäd (1E116-178) and King Hamäss (1E42-116), had been more economically-incline and preferred to ignore the problem of the orcs in the East after King Hamäss founded the Kingdom of Gilan in 1E42. After the Fall of the Gods the former kingdom of the elves in the times of Myth, Gorgorannon, had been razed by the orcs. Their demonic hosts drove the Southern elves from their homeland, forcing them to flee West into what was now Gilan.

    King Hamäss was a trader from Giessen who'd made a very successful empire off of the Gilan Wildberry trade with Rome. He constructed himself a castle in the elvish city and declared himself the King, so was the Kingdom of Gilan founded. After that he focused the majority of his power on controlling the wildberry trade, ignoring the threat of the orcs in the East, allowing them to form a kingdom of their own for the dark gods they served. Over the passing decades the Gorgon desolation only continued to spread whilst the elves of Gilan ignored the problem. They were experiencing an economic boom as trade flourished between Gilan, Rome, and the Kingdom of Legion to the North where they fermented the berries into the most expensive and desirable wine in all of Aerbon. After the death of King Hasäd in 1E178, King Hassän took over and after 16 years upon his taking up the throne, the new King had finally convinced his country to take up arms against the orcs of the Gorgon Desolation. He sent emissaries South to seek assistance from the men of the Nardic Isles and immediately deployed a force of 35,000 elves as an initial assault whilst he mustered a main host to reinforce them on their eastern travels. The Nardic men would rendezvous with their forces in the sqal of Gorgor before their combined forces marched upon Istul, the orcish capitol of those lands.

With the orcs defeated, the sqal continued to burn steadily to the ground and the corpses of the fallen orcs were eaten away by the fire along with their town. The prison, a great wooden cage that spanned ten feet by twenty, was smashed open and the prisoners were all freed. As for their fallen comrades, the elves of the Aush Woods took them away to the wagons and loaded the dead, treating the living as they were able. The healers crushed up trundle* leaves and boiled them in water before applying them to injuries. Other Aush Wood elves performed the last rites for the fallen before sending them away in the caravan that ambled along on its way back to Gilan. The slaves and prisoners went along with them as many needed treatment and few were in fighting condition.

*In Aerbon, there were many variations of the Trundle plant, dependent on the region of the continent. In the Southeast of Aerbon, around Gilan and the Nardic Isles, Southern Trundle grew throughout their lands and could easily be identified by its long thin sets of three serrated leaves. It is believed to be a relative of the *cannabis* family and is often mistaken for some sort of ivy. It is well-known by the elves for its minor medicinal qualities when applied to wounds and injuries.

Once the dead had been carted away along with the recently freed captives, the remaining elves turned their attention back to smouldering pile of ashes that Sythin was becoming. The leaders of the elven battalions convened and spoke amongst themselves of what was to be done. The rest of their victorious legions busied themselves with the cleaning of their weapons and equipment. Aush Wood elves went about seeking out any unbroken arrows as they could find them to replace those spent in the battle. Their birch arrows had the advantage of flexibility over arrows crafted out of other woods. The bent shafts could easily be straightened out in their fingers compared to the iron orcish bolts and pine arrows of the Nardic Tribesmen.

The gathered band of officers spoke to themselves of the Nardic Tribes in the South; the assault on Istul would require their aid if there was to be any hope of a victory. The sqals throughout the desolation were relatively open outposts whereas their capitol city of Istul was a Tuhk; a heavily fortified tower-temple that couldn't be taken by sheer force alone. In the centre of the fortress there was a hulking citadel that stretched up to the heavens above, spewing flames and fumes alike from the great exhaust chimneys that protruded from it. They polluted the skies throughout the Gorgon Desolation and covered them in dark clouds of black smoke; the clouds blanketed the orc country and prevented the sun's light from shining through.

It was here that the elvish campaign was to end, for better or for worse, if they truly hoped to conquer the Gorgon lands. If they were successful, they would rid the world of its orcish infestation and cleanse the lands of their foul pollution once and for all. The fate of Aerbon was in the hands of the gods and in the speed of the Nardic host. It would be an undertaking to cross the Sumatran Ocean and traverse the Dead Wood. Once the Nardic forces were clear of the wood they still had to span the vast Gorgon plains before meeting the elven host in Gorgor. If the elves were too slow in their travels they would be found out and eradicated before they drew anywhere within sight of the great Tuhk of Istul, however, if the Nardic host was not quick enough the elvish legions would be forced to fight without their added assistance in the final battle and they would be wiped out anyway.

CHAPTER TWO

Bruh was the orcish word for Bear. In this case, it was the name of an exceptionally larger orc who journeyed the Gorgon Desolation in the profitable venture of guaka-guaka peddling. Bear was a travelling merchant whose livelihood revolved entirely around the purchase, sale, and distribution of the drug. Guaka-Guaka was a black thorny vine similar in appearance to the rose bush, whose resinous black bulbs secreted an oily tar that could be extracted from the plant and synthesised in factories to produce a highly addictive psychoactive substance. Bruh bought the raw guaka-guaka flowers in bulk where it was farmed in the outer sqals scattered throughout the Gorgon Desolation before selling it to larger refineries in the larger sqals, Gorgor and Ishtan. Very rarely, Bruh made the long and dangerous journey to the orcish capitol, the Tuhk of Istul; home of the largest guaka-guaka refinery in the entire desolation.

The path to Istul was one seldom walked by Bear. Istul was a might tower-fortress, home to the Masters who ruled those lands, and Bruh was afraid of them. Most sensible orcs feared the Masters, as the demons who resided within the Tuhk of Istul called themselves. The orcish merchant could never understand how any living creature could bear to live in such a horrid place. The Church of the Masters was located in the heart of that city and formed the base of the towering citadel that was home to the gods they served. The Tuhk also served as a prison for the captured elf slaves before they were sacrificed in the highest reaches of that monstrous tower. In addition to being the church, prison, and home of their dark gods, the Tuhk also housed the largest guaka-guaka refinery in the Gorgon Desolation and the stuff that it produced was of the highest quality.

The Masters took residence in a large oval antechamber that sat upon the top of the citadel, like a satellite dish, and it was wreathed in fire and smog. In order to sell his product in the capitol, Bruh was forced to interact with the Pah'ka; the orcish priests of the Masters who also acted as a secret police in the capitol. The Pah'ka bought up raw guaka-guaka flowers in bulk before sending it to the factory midway up the great citadel to be extracted and refined into guaka-guaka tar so that it could be consumed by the orcish masses. Guaka-Guaka tar was smoked in special filtered pipes and had effects that resembled that of both opium and methamphetamine when ingested by the orcs and it strengthened the Masters hold over their minds. When under the influence of the drug they could hear the uncouth voices of the wretched demons whispering softly in their ears. The schizophrenic nature of the Masters influence under the intoxicating effects of guaka-guaka grew in strength the closer one was to their residence in the heart of the orc capitol.

As the orcs had discovered in the elven prisoners they captured on a daily basis to sate the bloodlust of their unholy gods, the drug caused a brief spell of insanity before the user experienced death by fatal overdose when ingested by non-orc creatures. Men were especially low-tolerant of the drug, driven into a hyperactive schizophrenic state for just a couple minutes before they were struck by seizures and epilepsy, foaming at the mouth and bleeding out of their eyes until finally suffering a cardiac arrest. The longest recorded survivor of a guaka-guaka overdose was a young elf, only seventy years of age, who lasted a total of seventeen minutes before ripping off the flesh of his face and laughing himself to death. The orcs discovered the toxicity of guaka-guaka in the other races very quickly after attempting to speed up the transport time of slave runs between Sythin and Istul.

Bruh took a drag from his thick clay guaka-guaka pipe and inhaled the sickly-sweet smoke into his lungs. He felt the drug stretch its spindling fingers over his mind and his eyes glossed over, lids drooping and eyes buzzing with an intensity. He could hear the echoes of the whispers of his dark lords from where he currently was in the outermost reaches of their domain. Time felt as if it had slowed down all around the orcish drug dealer and for a brief moment he felt clear-headed as if he could fully focus his attention on the will of the Masters. Their desire for him to buy up and distribute the guaka-guaka of that land was also his desire and as he smoked it he could think of nothing he wanted more at that moment.

He thought of the elves briefly and recalled a slaver he'd met in Ishtan where he'd recently met a slaver after selling a shipment of raw guaka-guaka flowers ready to be synthesised. With the money he'd made from the Sythic harvest, he bought fifty kilos of the highest quality Gregorian Guaka-Guaka tar that could be found anywhere outside the unholy Tuhk of Istul. He chatted with the slaver after selling him an ounce of the stuff at a lower price than he would have gotten away with outside the city limits of the second largest manufacturer of the drug in the orc country. The slaver was waiting to depart from the sqal with his slaver company, but in the downtime he spoke with Bear of his adventures as a slaver. He said he'd once been the captain of his own slave caravan until his crew was slaughtered in an elvish ambush on their way to Sythin.

They stumbled across an elvish scouting party who'd drawn up nearby reinforcements . The elves had killed off his entire crew and freed his shipment, returning them to the lands they'd been snatched up from. Penniless and without a crew, he made his way back to the safety of his own lands and enlisted in the ranks of a rival slaver as his apprentice in Istul. The whole ordeal was rather humiliating for the former slaver captain and Bruh offered the unfortunate orc his condolences. The slaver concluded the deal and was soon on his way to regroup with his outfit to prepare for their departure. The crew he was apprenticed to was on their way to pick up a shipment of slaves in Sythin to be brought before the Masters to offer up for blood sacrifice in their antechamber at the very top of the unholy Tuhk of Istul.

After bidding the slaver a blunt farewell, Bruh returned to his business. He liked slavers about as much as he liked the Pah'ka who served the Masters, and he didn't like the orc priests at all. They acted as a secret police along with their duties as religious prophets, reporting any and all acts of blasphemy and heresy within the borders of the Gorgon Desolation. They were the mouthpiece of their Masters and they spread the unholy word as law throughout their domain. Pah'ka were also notorious for kidnapping young orclings from their homes to perform their duty to the Masters, which normally involved either being initiated into the Pah'kan priesthood or offered up as a sacrifice to the gods. The latter usually only occurred in times of a slave drought where no new sacrifices had been made for some time. The Pah'ka did this to satisfy their gods bloodlust in order to save their people as a whole from the undying hunger of their Masters.

Bear's fear and disdain of the orc priests stemmed from childhood memories. He'd been selected to serve as the blood sacrifice to satisfy the Masters one particularly dry year. The Pah'ka invaded his family's tiny shack with armed soldiers at the ready to take up their son one day and his parents fought back, desperate in their futile attempts to defend their only child from the hungry jowls of their dark overlords. Bruh's father rose against them in protest and was quickly cut down by the orcish soldiers of the Tuhk who greatly outnumbered the family of three. The Pah'ka dragged his screaming mother away and ordered Bear to be exiled to the Desolation to live out the rest of his days in excommunication as repentance for his crimes. The young orcling begged the Pah'ka to end his life; they'd already killed his father and were taking his mother to the Tuhk to be sacrificed even as they spoke.

"My life has no purpose, end my suffering... Please." Bruh was only ten years old at the time.

"You shall live out the rest of your days in exile to repent for the crime of your birth; your father was a disgrace to his people and you are *murghat-khet* for being born of him." an orc priest replied in response to his pleas.

The same soldiers who'd only just taken his family from him escorted Bruh through the outer slums from where his family lived in the Market District. They guided him safely to the outer wall, where he was forced to depart from the Tuhk of Istul forever more, by the law of the Masters. He wandered aimlessly for some time in the desolate plains for time beyond his reckoning before finding himself in the Southern sqal of Gregor. The orcling took up an apprenticeship on a guaka-guaka farm past the outskirts of the town in the South, outside the Dead Wood. Gregorian Guaka-Guaka was notorious amongst the orcs for its aggressive high; it was very potent stuff, tainted by the influence of the Dead Wood in the South. Over time he found a point to his existence and he devoted his life to Guaka-Guaka. He forgot his hatred of the Gorgon priests as he found success in his craft. Bear began smoking guaka-guaka at the age of eleven and he worked at that farm for 5 years.

---

*Roughly translates to "maggot spawn". One of the most offensive terms in the orcish language, used to describe something that is so despicable that it is less than nothing.

At the age of fifteen he took off with a travelling merchant who'd bought a supply from the dying farmer Bear was apprenticed to. Bruh quickly conformed to the travelling drug dealer's lifestyle and learned as much as he could from the wise orc about the drug he'd been practising the cultivation of for the past five years. He treated the merchant, U'gra-hal, as a second father and discovered everything there was to know about the plant and drug that guaka-guaka was. He was already learned in the horticulture of the plant, but his mentor taught him also of the extraction, synthesis, refinement, and distribution of the drug itself. Bruh came to know the current street price of the drug as well as how to calculate its fluctuating value based on the supply, demand, and overall quantities available. U'gra-hal even taught his young apprentice how to differentiate the pure tar from the cheaper stuff they sold out of the slums. At the age of sixteen, Bruh finally surpassed his master and he was given the gift of freedom...

"You have been like a son to me, Bear... Here... Take this as a parting gift..." U'gra-hal coughed up blood as he thrust a small satchel into Bruh's trembling hands; he'd been shot through the belly by an elvish arrow and they both knew he wasn't much longer for the world. Elves closed in on the pair as Bruh knelt over his fallen friend who bid him a final farewell.

"I'm so sorry to leave you Bruh, you must go now before they capture you. Worse things await you if you stay." U'gra-hal spoke those final words to his last dying breath and then he was no more.

Bruh had tried as best he could to stop the bleeding and save his master, telling him everything would be alright and not to worry. The masterless orc looked up and stumbled to his feet, *blinking back tears. Elves were closing in on him and his master and soon they would be upon him; Bear turned and fled east away from the elvish border and back to the safety of his homelands. Bruh left the corpse of his dead mentor behind and fled from the wrath of the elves, chasing after his own absolution. His dearest friend had given him everything he needed in that pack; it contained several kilos of pure guaka-guaka tar as well as enough ears* to start a new life however he saw fit. The free orc chose to follow in the footsteps of his mentor and continue his former friend's trade of peddling guaka-guaka throughout the Gorgon Desolation. He became so successful over time that he was now currently one of the largest distributors of the drug in the Desolation.*

Bruh smoked another bowl of guaka-guaka and continued on his journey to Grishtan to sell his wares to the peasants, warriors, and nomads that usually convened around his stall in the cramped streets of that sqal. Upon selling his current stash of the drug he would make a detour home before continuing on his way to Sythin to buy up the flowers of that sqal. Sythin grew some of the most potent guaka-guaka in all of the orc country, probably were the farming outpost was so close to the elf kingdom of Gilan. Everything that sprouted from the elvish soil grew miraculously and it even extended into the guaka-guaka farms in the West upon their border. The refineries in Ishtan that Bear frequented were second-best only to the Great Refinery in the Tuhk of Istul. The Ishtan-synthesised Sythic Resin was some of the most expensive and highest-quality tar available outside of the premium strains, exclusive to Istul's Market District.

*Ears are the universally accepted form of currency in the orc lands; two orc ears have an equal value to one elf ear , and an elf ear is worth five ears of a human.

Bear continued on his westward trek through the wastelands on the back of the warg he'd purchased with some of the profits of his last dope run. It was liken to the cross between a wolf and a horse; the beast stood a hulking five feet from the ground and was large enough to carry two orcs comfortably throughout the Desolation. The monstrous beasts were the result of the demonic influence in those lands that tainted and corrupted the residual inhabitants of the land, long after the fairer native life had all died off or fled. Bruh travelled with the fifty kilo satchel of guaka-guaka strapped to the war's right flank and his assortment of weapons slung across his mount's left side. He rode with a broad-bladed cleaver, an orcish hatchet, and a goblin-forged iron shortbow crafted out of iron ore mined from the goblin mines in the Iron Teeth themselves. Along with his weapons there was also a pack containing enough food and supplies to last the orc as long as he needed it to on his travels .

At twenty-two years old, Bruh was considered old in the orcish lands where few made it past their eighteenth birthday. Life in the Gorgon Desolation was rough. Fighting was rampant throughout their race as a whole and there were several hundred rivalling tribes scattered all across the desolate plains to make matters worse. Orcish society was not entirely consumed by chaos however; they were divided by a caste system that was universal in those lands. In the order of lowest to highest, the peasants were at the bottom rung of society along with the farmers and labourers, followed by warriors, soldiers, slavers, merchants, chiefs and chieftains, and finally Pah'ka; the holy and protected mouthpieces of the gods who ruled over everything within their domain. The Pah'ka relayed the message of their foul gods from where they took up residence in the Church of the Masters in Istul.

Out of the hundreds of orcish tribes scattered throughout the wastelands, some of them joined together to form powerful alliances. For the most part however, each tribe openly rivalled their neighbours and fought constantly for minor territorial disputes. Clans and tribes fought amongst one another and even within their own ranks for food, slaves, territory, power, respect, supplies, as well as a simple means of resolving even the most petty of arguments. The main factions of the Gorgon Desolation were the Pah'ka who were led by the Masters, the Bhah'kulkha, Bhurghal-khan, and the Zhurgha'khet. The Pah'ka and their army of religious fanatics held control over the Tuhk of Istul and all orcs of the Gorgon Desolation were subject to their divine authority. Outside the walls of the Tuhk however, the rival tribes and clans fought between themselves for dominance in the wastelands.

The Bhah'kulkha, orcish for "Black Flesh", were a western alliance of tribes centred around the sqals of Sythin and Grishtan. Their tribe was named aptly for their noticeably darker skin compared to the orc tribes situated deeper in the heartlands of the country, where the sun never shone. Their alliance consisted mostly of farming tribes and roaming slaver bands and they thrived mostly on the guaka-guaka and slave trade between their sqals and the eastern refineries. Their main threat was from the central-based Bhurghal-khan tribe, situated in the midlands of the orc country in te broad expanse of land around Grishtan Ishtan, Istul, and Gorgor. The Bhurghal-khan were a marauding tribe who made a living off of slave caravans and lone merchants who travelled to and fro between the outermost sqals and the capitol, attacking in force and preying on the weak.

Lastly were the Zhurgha'khet, an eastern alliance situated in the South around the border of the dead wood in Gregor and the outlying plains. They were mostly farming tribes but there were also warring clans in the northern reaches of their territory who were quick to engage roaming bands of Bhurghal-khan raiders. Bruh had no tribe personally, though his father had ties to a small nomadic clan in the West. His clan was called the Bruhwumpscut, the Near Warriors, and it was the clan from which Bruh's name derived. His mother had come from the Bhurghal-khan and her reputation was high within their ranks. She met his father after he'd been ambushed on his way to Istul with the last survivors of his clan after they'd loss a battle of great proportions against the Rah'kulza. They were a larger tribe who were later overthrown by the Bhahghet clan who united the Western tribes to form the present alliance during the Bhah'kulkan wars.

During the ambush he'd slaughtered a great many of her fellow tribals before they yielded to his superior might. He was the sole survivor of the ambush and after failing to capture him, they brought him before their chieftain as a guest. Bear's father was given the daughter of the chieftain's brother's son and he was awarded the highest honours an outsider could attain within their tribe. Seeking a more peaceful life, he spirited his wife away to Istul where they gave birth to Bruh and lived out the rest of their days happily before the fateful day Bear's idyllic life had been shattered by the Pah'kan Priesthood. His father had died at the cautious old age of 36 and his mother was 28; they'd been married for twelve years before they were mercilessly slaughtered by the orcish soldiers of Istul in the name of the Masters.

After some days had passed in his travels, Bruh finally reached the outskirts of Grishtan and made his way through the eastern gate that granted him entry within the fortified walls of that sqal. It was less defended that the sqal of Sythin; being further from the elvish border, they had less of a risk of being attacked by an elvish force and they could easily fend off a roaming scout or company without difficulty. He made his way to the heart of the sqal and set up his stall in the centre of its chaotic network of roads. Within an hour his man-skin purse was filled up with the value of twenty elf ears and business showed no signs of slowing up. He filled several pouches up with the ears of his customers and a few even killed each other for the ears of their dead opponents, as well as whatever ears they carried on them.

Bruh was well-known throughout the Desolation and his popularity was mostly due to having grown up on a guaka-guaka farm as well as a network of people in the west who knew him from his own father's reputation, as well as being a direct relative to the leader of the Bhurghal-khan. Once he'd finished up for the day he closed shop and packed his things to prepare for his departure back home to Gorgor in the morning. He would return home and sell the remaining fifteen or so kilos to the residents of the sqal. Gorgor was a poorer sqal that focused mainly on weapons production, working bombs and other explosive devices out of the gunpowder they mined from the Iron Teeth as well as swords from the metals they also found within the depths of those mountains. There was also a minor guaka-guaka refinery within the sqal and it contributed to the majority of the Southern pollution around Gregor and the Dead Wood.

The drug dealing orc had a breakfast of man-flesh with a side of dog meat after spending the night in a thatched hut he'd rented on the town's western outskirts. He downed his meal with a drink from his waterskin containing the brackish water of the River Zum, where it pooled in a fetid lake on the banks where Ishtan was situated. The water was still fresh, having only been filled less than two weeks ago when he'd last visited the sqal. He prepared to depart as soon as he was finished with his meal; Bruh didn't like to linger too long in any given place and he was especially against hanging around in the sqals where he conducted business. There was always a risk of being robbed or killed in the orc lands by thieves, drug addicts, warriors, or worse.

The Thru'ahkuk Huang, or Thieves Guild in the Common Tongue, had a strong presence in the wealthier sqals of Grishtan, Istul, and Ishtan. There was little that could be done against them. In the Tuhk of Istul and also in Ishtan the soldiers of the Master's army acted somewhat as a police force, however, they would often accept bribes and in most cases the Pah'kan priests would overlook the matter entirely. They refused to acknowledge the Thieves Guild except in extreme cases which usually ended in public executions at the capitol to send a direct message to the guild. The underground organisation had even placed a price on Bruh's head once, though they later terminated the contract after he killed half a dozen of their finest assassins. Two of his victims were vampire mercenaries from the Northern Wastes; after their deaths no assassins were willing to take up the contract of a man with six confirmed attempts on his life successfully thwarted.

His father had once told him as a young orcling that the key to a long fruitful life was keeping your head down and picking your fights wisely. Even though his brains were addled by his constant consumption of guaka-guaka, Bear followed his father's dying advice. He never started fights with his neighbours and always kept his distance from the eye of the public, hanging around in the background out of the spotlight and away from attention whenever he was at home or abroad on his travels. Bruh was a travelling merchant, a drug peddler; he was no warrior and under no circumstances did he ever pretend to be. He avoided military service and national duty whenever he was able to and never pursued a fight in situations where it wasn't his only option.

The more aggressive orcs amongst the general population occasionally challenged their peers in times of peace when they could find nothing better to do and Bear did his best to dodge these occurrences as they arose. In the Gorgon Desolation there was always an orc quarrel going on or about to arise in any given place at any given time and the trick to avoiding these situations entirely revolved around staying out of the spotlight. Bruh was very talented at blending into crowds and deterring attention away from himself long enough to escape a fight before it had the chance to manifest itself in his presence. Compared to most orcs he was not nearly as loud or obnoxious as the majority and he was far less bloodthirsty than most. He always kept to himself and kept his eyes on the prize as he routinely went about his day to day life.

Suddenly a warg rider charged through the westernmost entrance into the sqal bearing news from Sythin. His mount raced through the streets on its journey to the heart of the sqal and orcs raced out of its way as the warg-rider screamed out news of an elvish assault en route to Grishtan at that very moment. The warg slid to a stop at the town centre and his orc rider leapt from the saddle, grabbing the chieftain of the sqal to tell him the news before collapsing from exhaustion. The rider was a warrior out of Sythin and upon hearing the news of its fall, Grishtan's chieftain ordered all orcs present within the city's walls to take up arms in the defence of their homeland. Bruh cursed himself for his late morning start and wished to himself than he'd departed from the sqal sooner, rather than become entangled in the battle that his fellow orcish kin frantically prepared for all around him.

CHAPTER THREE

Egorin walked along the outskirts of the elf camp in what was formerly Sythin and stared off into the distance. The Augen Mountains spanned the Northern horizon like a great wall of broken blunted hills that stretched thousands upon thousands of feet into the sky. The rolling plains that led up to the feet of the mountains were dead, barren, and foul. Where trees and bushes once sprouted from the ground there was now emptiness. The few trees that still stuck out of the ground after all that time were black and charred stumps; burnt and withered as if they'd been struck by lightning or died of an excessive heat and lack of water. The orc lands were significantly hotter than the rest of Aerbon from the excess of greenhouse gasses that trapped the sun's heat and prevented it from leaving their atmosphere. Nothing grew or survived in the Gorgon Desolation outside of the wretched abominations that thrived in the eternal darkness of that country.

As he patrolled the ruined outskirts of Sythin's former lands where the elf host was currently encamped, Egorin's silver hair laid flat against his back in the breezeless wastelands. His silvery birch armour glowed, radiant with the spirit fire that burned within it, and in those bleak grey lands he shone with all the beautiful serenity of a full moon as it glowed in the night sky. His grass underskirt protruded from beneath his cuirass as was the traditional attire of the Aush Wood's archers. He was tall (nearly six feet in height), slender, fair-skinned, and beautiful in the way that all elves were. The green raiment he wore, crafted out of the grasses of his homeland, was radiant with the spirit fire in the same manner as his cuirass, shining like stained glass under the light of the sun.

Alongside his fellow elven warriors, Egorin and his kin looked like gods in those forsaken land; come to cleanse the country of its parasitic orcish legions. As he wandered along the border of Gilan's camp, situated on the wreckage of the ruined sqal of Sythin, the elvish archer took up a goblin arrow into his hand and wondered to himself in thoughtful silence. He questioned his people's chance of victory and thought to himself of how the upcoming events of the near future might play out. In his mind's eye, Egorin roamed under the leaf and bough of the many birch trees that comprised the Aush Woods, hundreds of miles from where his physical body wandered the desolate orcish wastes aimlessly searching for arrows.

Presently, however, he was in the orc lands; fighting in the hopes of ridding those lands of the evil that infested them so that life could return to them once again. Egorin mused in his solitude on what would grow in the Gorgon Desolation when the orcs who populated it ceased to exist. Would there be great birch trees like there were in the Aush Woods of Gilan after the eradication of the orcs, or would grand firs and glorious oak trees? Or what of the beautiful rowan and majestic willows? Perhaps even the towering pine tree would choose to settle down in that country once it was purified of its foul inhabitants; only time would tell. These things Egorin thought to himself to keep his mind busy, lest his thoughts turn to darker things where they tend to dwell and linger in the solitude of one's own company.

Looking around, Egorin observed the other elves as they ate a hearty meal or drank merrily from their wineskin. Together they laughed and joked with the fellows of their company or spoke amongst themselves of their ventures thus far in the Desolation. Other elves within the camp tended to their horses or sharpened the blades of their scimitars in preparation for the next time they'd be needed. Many spoke of the campaign at hand, foreboding the final outcome in their war against the orcs. The majority of the elves were hesitant in trusting the Nardic Tribesmen. They doubted the abilities of the Southern men against the might of the demonic hosts of their opposition, though they had no other options in the war they waged against the East.

At midday, the elves set out, stowing away their gear and packing up their things before departing from the camp site. It had nearly been an entire day since their assault on Sythin and already they were underway in their journey to Grishtan. Egorin marched alongside his fellow archers and they made up the rear of the host; ahead of them were the forces of Graenor and Eden, the wagons drove in a convoy in the centre of their ranks, dividing them into two columns in their easterly travels. The elvish host stumbled across several roaming orc bands and camps along the way and eliminated them without slowing or deviating from their course. In his quiver Egorin counted twelve silver arrows of the enchanted elvish birch trees along with thirty long iron orc arrows. They were hollow and barbed, though still in usable condition. The orcish shots were made of the same resinous tar-like metal as their armour and they burnt the skin of the elves whenever they made contact with the putrid metal.

The arrows were hard and firm to the touch, though they appeared as if they'd melt in the hand if allowed. Egorin had looked upon the foul shots with disgust as he plucked each one individually from the corpses of the fallen. He gathered as many unbroken arrows as he could scavenge to replace those spent in the battle and now the wretched orc shots tainted his quiver with their repulsive appearance as he marched along through the barren grey lands. The orcs wore blackened iron armour wrought of some putrid substance that rubbed on whatever it came into contact with. It caused minor skin rashes and burns upon the fair skin of the elves as Egorin took note earlier in the camp after collecting several of the foul arrows.

In the eyes of the elves, orcs were nasty disgusting creatures. Though they were like to wretched humans, the elves saw no resemblance whatsoever in the short, squat, ugly creatures. Men were tall, proud, and beautiful in their own right whereas orcs were warped and twisted, fiendish in their nature and tainted by the demonic evil that flowed through their veins, corrupting them as was the nature of dark energies. The elves of Gilan did not worship gods, but rather worshipped the land and the earth as their god. To the elves, everything was made up of a spiritual energy that took up residence in each and every living creature and divided itself amongst the living and non-living organisms of the world, as well as the very earth itself. Everything was united by one consciousness and the elves worshipped this spiritual energy as their god; the elves of Gilan worshipped this energy in the form of Mother Nature and they loved the trees and plants above all else. They tended to the trees and raised them from saplings with as much love as a mother has for her newborn child and it was for this reason that the elves were granted their gift of unnaturally long life.

Where men generally lived a lifespan of forty or so years, the elves generally lived past their hundredth birthday and so they were blessed to see the fruits of their labours as the keepers of Nature. Burying their dead in the Aush Woods to feed the magic of their land, the elvish country was enveloped in enchantments and time ceased to exist within their domain. The orcs sought to lay waste to all that they loved and held dear; this was why the elves marched to war. For too long had the King's predecessors has sat idly by and allowed the orcs to muster their forces, but King Hassän had finally done what his forefathers failed to realise and declared a long-needed war against the orcs who were steadily snatching up their people and intruding upon their lands relatively unopposed.

Where the towns of Eden and Graenor had once been open villages in the fair and fertile hills of Eastern Gilan, they now stood as lone outposts against the slaver bands that roamed their lands. The orcs burned down their forests and encroached upon their lands, killing off the life of the land and defiling it like they did to their own homeland. To the elves, one did not own the lands they lived in. No one could lay claim to any portion of the earth, simply because it was not an object subject to ownership. The earth was a living being and to the elves boundaries did not exist; one was only borrowing the body they manifested for the brief moment in time that they inhabited the earth. Nature kept everything in balance.

The fox was given food in exchange for keeping the population of lesser plant-eating creatures in check, taking it's reward in the form of rabbits and other small animals. Termites existed to break down dying trees, devouring their remains as they withered away to provide nutrients in the soil for the next generation after their remains were broken down by earthworms. Flies broke down dead decaying corpses along with fungus and so the world remained in balance. The earth swallowed up the bones of the dead and returned their energy to the world to feed the new life that grew.

Orcs did not follow the path of existence, but instead burned and destroyed all they came into contact with. They killed for the glory of their gods and consumed demonic drugs. The elves harboured no pity for their race, felt no sense of understanding towards them or their cause, and knew no remorse as they eradicated the eastern plague once and for all. There had once been a time in the world long ago where elves had dwelt in those desolate wastes and they were once majestic woodlands. Those elves were closer in blood-ties to the immortal elves of the Aush Wood than the blonde-haired elves of Gilan, though the majority of elves in that present time were far too young to remember the fall of the eastern elves. Egorin knew of the Rise of Sythin, formerly the easternmost elvish outpost town of Syrein, though he'd spent the entirety of his life within the heart of the Aush Woods. He'd never travelled outside of the wood's reaches, not until the day King Hassän declared the Kingdom to be at war.

The orcs had poured westward across the once-fertile Gorgon plains and slaughtered the elves of that land, burning the beautiful forested lands as they went. Those lands had once been known as the Kingdom of Gorgorannon before the rise of the orcs. After the destruction of their people and the extinction of their race, all that was left of the former elvish kingdom was the Dead Wood, now rumoured to be haunted by demons, wraiths, and spirits of the undead. Egorin knew of the great tragedy, though it was many long decades before his birth. He knew of the countless corpses that never got the chance to return to rest in the peaceful tranquillity of the Aush Woods. A cold bitter rage burned in his his heart like an icy dagger in his frostbitten heart when he thought of the orcs and it was a common sentiment amongst the elf host.

As the elf host passed by yet another orc camp, the smell of burning hair and flesh was all too apparent where it emanated from a cooking pit in the heart of the small camp. There were three tents in a triangle perimeter around the fire pit, each large enough to accommodate four orcs. The campers were a mix of orc and goblin hunters; probably nomadic tribal hunters with no ties to any major clans or factions, but a threat nonetheless. Egorin and a handful of his fellow archers let loose a magnificent volley that fell with the tinkling ring reminiscent of a wind chime as each arrow penetrated the metal armour of the gathered orcs and goblins. The small orc band put up little opposition against the ranks of elvish soldiers and before long the elf host was passing by the former camp as they resumed their travels without a moment's pause. The corpses of the deceased hunters were piled around the smouldering slab of their half-cooked mystery meat, silver elvish shafts neatly sticking out of their backs like the many spines of a porcupine.

The journey to Grishtan was long and arduous, lengthened further by the chance encounters and brief skirmishes with roving bands of orcs and goblin raiders. Egorin took a swig from his wineskin and noted the dwindling supply that remained. He'd need to replace it at the wagons at some point with a fresh wineskin from their vast store of supplies. There were several wagons in their convoy, each laden with wine, food, and medical supplies. There were even a few wagons with empty cabins reserved for carting away the injured, as well as the dead when needed. He returned his attention from his wineskin back to the elf host in their travels; his company continued to follow steadily behind the ranks of horsemen of Eden. They were led by the First Swordsman Company of Graenor with Captain Vasil taking the lead upon his majestic white Eden-bred stallion.

Aush Wood elves were not warriors under normal circumstances, though in desperate times they were known to take up arms to defend their country alongside their fellow countrymen. They did not hold any jobs or duties outside of tending to the woods they called home, however, when summoned up for military duty they allowed themselves to be drafted into their own unified rule. Each elf of the Aush Wood in the Gilan ranks led himself into battle as a free individual under his own command. They formed no other companies, ranks, or divisions other that the Aush Woods Company as a whole and there were no ranks or titles awarded to any within their ranks. Once the war was concluded they would return to their homelands to perform the holy burial rites before returning to their normal daily routines. Even though the elves of the Aush Woods weren't inherently warriors, they were a mighty force to be reckoned with and not one to be taken lightly.

In the pitch-black of nightfall, the elf host stopped to set up camp to rest until dawn when they would break fast and depart in the morning. After a meagre meal of fruits and wine the forces of Gilan departed from their makeshift camp and continued to traverse the desolate wastelands on their eastern journey through the orc lands. The days passed by and no one spoke as they marched in utter silence. During the night they kept watch and no one made small talk during their travels past Sythin. Where the elf host had once been full of mirth and merriment they were now cautious and alert, ready for the slightest sign of trouble. Danger lurked just out of sight, waiting for a moment's lapse in their guard to snatch up the unwary amongst the elves in their ranks.

One night as Egorin sat keeping watch over his sleeping companions, thinking to himself how useless it was in the blinding darkness of the night, he spotted the slightest pinprick of red light. He took aim with his bow and fired in the direction of the floating red dot and didn't even bother to strain his ears as a squeal signalled to the arched that his shot met its mark; a lone orc scout smoking a bowl of his sickly drug to himself. As the hours of the night passed him by, Egorin could hear no sound of living creature or otherwise as he fought against the soothing cajole of sleep that beckoned to him. The rest of his shift at the night-watch passed him by uneventfully and before he knew it, the elf was already being shaken awake from his seemingly brief slumber. In the morning he spotted the dead body of the orc scout he'd killed during the night, an arrow jutting out of his chest in the distance where he laid clutching the pipe that betrayed him tightly to his chest in a death grip.

The elvish host left the body there to rot and departed from camp at the morning's first light. The sky was a dark grey and even when the sun reached its peak at midday it was still not much lighter than it had been that morning when they'd set out on the day's march. Lighting was minimal under the darkened cloudy skies of the Gorgon Desolation and it only grew dimmer the further into the country they travelled. The sun was shrouded in darkness and the air was repugnant with the taste of the foul odours that freely wafted in the air of that place. In the North the Augen Mountains were beginning to recede on the horizon as they furthered the distance between themselves and their homeland hundreds of leagues behind them in the West. To their right, the flat grey plains rolled all the way along to the Southern shore of Aerbon where the waters of the Sumatran Ocean broke upon the coastline. Somewhere in that direction, far over the horizon, the Nardic Tribesmen were making their way across the Sumatran Ocean in their voyage to the Dead Wood, even as the elf hosts made their way to the sqal of Grishtan in the East.

Egorin looked over his shoulder to the South and wondered to himself how the men of the Nardic Tribes fared in their voyage. Had they yet crossed the body of water that separated them from mainland Aerbon to the North, or were they already trekking through the Dead Wood even as the forces of Gilan marched East to war? Perhaps they were still mustering their forces; were they even mobilised as of yet? These things Egorin pondered, though the questions and contemplations only made him uneasy and there was no way of knowing for sure the answers to the questions that ate away at his subconscious. *I am no tactician,* the elvish archer thought to himself, *let them bother themselves with such worries.*

Putting his fears aside, Egorin marched alongside the fellows of his company without thinking and let his mind drift through timeless memories of a more peaceful life before the war of the orcs that they waged upon the elves. It was only within the past twenty years that the orcs had began to trespass and intrude upon Gilan's eastern border, running amok in the elf lands as they kidnapped their unfortunate victims willy-nilly in the broad light of day. Egorin still remembered the days before the orcs had made their return to power; there had always been dissent against the previous Kings of Gilan's joint decision to ignore the orc problem, though now it was too late to point out the mistakes of King Hassän's forefathers. Doing the only thing they could, the elves finally marched to war at long last against the repopulated legions of orcs in the eastern lands.

Suddenly, even as Egorin and the elvish host marched through the vastness of the desolate wastes, a shout went up from further ahead in the frontline. Approaching them from ahead to the Northeast a group of Sikhas* could be seen plainly in the distance as the led a convoy of slavers along, making directly towards the elf host where their paths would inevitably intersect one another. The slaver caravan was most likely on its way to the sqal of Sythin to gather up the assorted collection of slaves, snatched up from their native homeland in the eastern reaches of the Kingdom of Gilan. They would bring the captive slaves from Sythin to the Tuhk of Istul

---

*Bone Sprites; Sikha were demonic warriors who possessed and corrupted the skeletal remains of fallen warriors. They were challenging adversaries due mainly to their unnatural strength, as well as the long reach of their blades, that made getting close enough to deliver a killing blow nearly impossible.

where they would be sacrificed to the loathsome Gorgon gods that reigned in those lands. The wagons were dragged along by warped demon hounds, whipped incessantly by the goblin drivers of the dilapidated slave carts, and led in tow by the commanding Sikhan troop. At the sight of the elvish legions in the distance, however, the slavers diverted from their undertaken journey to engage to unwelcome intruders of their land in battle.

Egorin fitted an arrow into his bowstring and pulled it back with exceedingly powerful speed and agility. The arrow was lost in a sea of silver and a second later several dozen of the charging orcs crumpled to the ground, arrows protruded from their chests where they snapped like twigs under the heel of the blood-crazed orcish warriors. Taking aim with his second shot, Egorin fired his arrow off straight and true at blinding speed as it raced to meet his mark. The arrow bounced off the skull of a Sikhan warrior and both the skull and his arrow shattered into hundreds of tiny splinters. Each of the demonic creatures had an inverted pentagram etched into the forehead of their skulls and bone horns protruded from both sides of their head. The majority of archers found themselves unable to slay the Sikhan forces with their arrows, however; the only way to destroy a Sikha was by disrupting the demonic flow of energy they channelled throughout their bodies by severing the spinal column or through the destruction or decapitation of the skull from their body. In either instance, the energy would implode upon their annihilation like the super-nova of a star.

The swordsmen of Graenor ran alongside the cavalry of Eden as they charged forth to meet the slavers and their commanding demon overlords on the field of battle. Within no time at all, the demonic forces of the East were already upon them; elves, orcs, and Sikha clashed in the barren emptiness of the plains that engulfed them and blows were exchanged, countered, and parried. Whenever one of the gargantuan Sikha swung their horrendous two-handed cleavers it severed the victims in half and sent any nearby opposition fleeing for their lives from the deadly sweeping blows. The elves put up about as much resistance as a child against a full-grown adult in their encounter with the slave caravan and Sikha slaughtered them effortlessly. The orcish slavers cackled and laughed as they fought alongside their masters from the sight of the supposedly unstoppable might of the elvish warriors as they fled from the Sikhan troops.

In the defence of the elves, Sikha were a terrible foe and the sight of one was a horrifying sight indeed. The skeletal warriors morphed the remains of the fallen warriors they took up residence within to better represent the wretched nature of the demonic beings that manifested themselves within their bones. The Sikhan skeletons were liken to that of a normal humanoid skeleton except in the fact that horns protruded from the base of their skulls. Each of the demonic warriors was an average of six feet tall and they carried long, broad-bladed, Gorgon cleavers whose blades were nearly an entire foot wide and seven feet long. They swung the blades with mighty force and elvish archers challenged them from afar whilst the swordsmen sought out the numerous orcs and goblins who were starting to rush the company Aush Wood elves.

Although there was no armour or enchantment in their world that could protect one from the deadly blow of a Sikhan sword, several lucky champions amongst the elves found success in the killing of their gruesome undead adversaries. Arrows and darts rained down from both sides and the elvish infantry continued to push back the orcish forces away from the woodland archers who protected them from the Sikhan wrath. Taking aim once again, Egorin fired another arrow off at the approaching Sikhan forces even as the goblin slave drivers let loose their twisted hounds of hell to bound freely towards the elves. Some of the wretched beasts turned on their handlers, taking a bite of their vile saviours as an appetiser before the main elvish course. The elvish forces broke rank and fled from the hungry jowls of the monsters that pursued them.

Firing a shot at one of the wargs as it rushed him, Egorin skirted out of the way as it skidded across the bare wastes, crashing to the ground in a cloud of dust as it collapsed from the severity of its wound. The feathered silver shaft of his arrow stuck neatly out of the beast's left eye, barely protruding from the eye socket where it had plunged so deep inside the hound's enormous skull. Looking around, Egorin returned his attention to the battlefield after witnessing the horror of his fellow kin being tackled to the ground by the other wargs before they were brutally torn apart and devoured by the warped creatures. The archers fired their shots at the hulking wolf-beasts and the enchanted arrows continued to rain down on the eastern forces that assailed them.

Aush Wood archers still engaged the Sikhan troop as they were able whilst simultaneously defending their fellow elves from the wargs that descended upon their ranks. The swordsmen continued to push back the orcish forces and they were actually beginning to flee. At the sight of their glorious masters being struck dead, along with the hell hounds who were quickly falling to the superior might of the archers, the orcs gave up any hope they'd previously maintained of decimating the elf host and they fled from that place as far as they were able before they were smitten down by the divine retribution of Aush Wood arrows. With their combined might, the elvish archers and swordsmen finally overthrew the slaver caravan and slaughtered whatever survivors were left of the attack. Though they'd laid down their arms, it was too late for the orcs and goblins to surrender and the elves killed them all without mercy.

The battle was won, albeit at the cost of heavy casualties amongst the elf host. There were countless injured and numerous slain, the unfortunate result of their encounter with the slavers. The elf host was in no condition to continue onwards in their current state; an assault against Grishtan in their current form would decimate their remaining forces. Counting out their losses, the host came to find that of the 35,000 soldiers they'd started with, the elf host now numbered 22,000 still fit to fight. The captains and officers convened in the desolate wastes again and upon reaching a decision they parted ways to relay the tidings to their subordinates. Captain Errol, commander of the cavalry of Eden, sent a rider away back West to deliver tidings of the battle to the reinforcing host from Aereil and Giessen. They were already underway in their travels to rendezvous with the initial forces deployed in the orc country at the sqal of Grishtan upon their acquisition of the region.

The joint forces of West Gilan were originally meant to meet the main host outside of Sythin, however, due to delays they were only just crossing the elvish border into the westernmost reaches of Gorgon Desolation. Where their departure had been delayed, the main host had deployed without the assistance of the Western half of their military sooner than they'd expected. Now, however, there was a greater need for strength in numbers and so the forces of East Gilan anxiously awaited the aid from their western kin. East Gilan was a series of outpost towns and there was a greater necessity for military strength compared to the aristocratic western half of the elvish kingdom whose lives revolved around the wildberry trade between themselves and the Roman merchants who frequented their western cities.

CHAPTER FOUR
THE GORGON DESOLATION
Autumn, 1E195

Almardi of the Fourth Swordsman Company of Aereil laughed merrily and took a swig from his wineskin as he approached the outskirts of the elf camp. He marched in formation alongside his fellow soldiers within the ranks of the reinforcements sent from Western Gilan. As they passed through the rows of tents that made up the elf camp, the forces of East Gilan stopped in whatever they were doing to stare after the merry Westerners in silence with stony faces. Some of Almardi's companions poked fun at the veteran elves, calling them "statues of anguish" and "tombstone soldiers". They didn't respond to the jokes and continued to stare after the newcomers to their camp in solemn silence. Almardi continued to march alongside the ranks of his fellows, uncomfortably in an awkward silence, as his companions laughed and joked amongst themselves beside him. Almardi's dearest friend, Namroden, called out to an elf who approached them from where he marched beside Almardi, attracting the stranger's attention for a moment.

"What's wrong? You all look as though your wine has run dry, yet I see that it still flows amongst your people! Why then are the mighty forces of Gilan stricken dumb as if turned to stone by the most powerful Gorgon witchcraft?" he spoke loudly for all to hear, laughing to himself alongside his fellows all the while.

"Speak not of what you can't comprehend!" the elf replied harshly with a tone of authority, "Where were you at the assault upon Sythin? Where then were you and your forces when we were waylaid on the road to Grishtan? How many dead friends have you loaded into the wagons to be carted away to the Aush Wood? You were sitting in the comfort of the lands we die to protect sipping on the wine you haven't earned that's obviously gone to your head."

Namroden did not offer a response and the elf hadn't expected one as he awaited the elvish captains amongst their host. The affronted elf glared at Namroden as he looked down upon his own feet as if something interesting were happening deep underground, beneath him. The rest of the recently arrived reinforcements ceased in their merriment at the rebuke of their brazen comrade. Though they may not as of yet fully understand the great undertaking they'd become a part of, there was still plenty of time for them to witness the harsh realities of war. The elf whom Namroden had offended presently convened with his fellow captains throughout the united host of Gilan and he came to discover that the elf he'd spoken to was no less than Captain Vasil of the First Swordsman company himself. Rather than comfort him, the news had a rather opposite effect; he blushed red with embarrassment as his commanding officer apologised to the great Captain for Namroden's insolence.

The newcomers were dismissed to busy themselves throughout the camp as they assisted the veterans in packing away their supplies and gear. Whilst he helped a handful of his fellows to take down a tent, Almardi spoke with some of the veterans amongst them of what life was like on the frontline. The news and information he was able to gather was not heartening, nor was it encouraging, though it did provide the young elf soldier with a vague idea of what to expect along with advice to prepare him for the upcoming battle in Grishtan. His company had not yet been tested on the field of battle. Before the brief encounters they'd experienced with orcish raiding parties in their journey to rendezvous with the forces of East Gilan, none within the ranks of Almardi's company had ever raised a sword in true combat. As of yet, they hadn't suffered a single casualty, though they'd slaughtered several goblin raiders in their travels; prior to their arrival they'd begun to believe they were natural-born warriors with unrivalled prowess on the battlefield.

Almardi hoped he would not live to witness his friends dying all around him as some of the elves he spoke to described to him in their conversations. Praying that he would never experience the terrible tragedy of loading the corpse of a fallen friend aboard the wagons to be laid to rest in the Aush Wood, Almardi fought to keep the dark thoughts at bay. He avoided making eye contact with the Aush Wood elves and avoided them as much as possible, as did his fellow kin of the West. The elves of the Aush Wood were revered by the elves of East Gilan for the Keepers of their Kingdom that they were, though in West Gilan they viewed the undertakers of their people as one would a vulture or carrion crow. To the elvish legions of Western Gilan present in the elf camp, the Aush Wood archers were the harbingers of death and they hoped to never see the face of one in the heat of battle, lest they be cursed with misfortunate luck.

Once the reinforcements had settled in with the ranks of the main host and all was prepared for their departure, they disembarked, resuming their journey to the sqal of Grishtan. Almardi followed in rank under the lead of their captain who was under the command of Captain Vasil of the First Swordsman Company, answerable only to Prince Rässan; the recently arrived commander in chief of Gilan's army in the stead of King Hassän. The original force of Eastern Gilan rejected his rule as their true commander and pledged their loyalty to Captain Vasil. Their captain had delivered them from the shadowy ensnare of death and led them to triumphant glory in the midst of an impossible war. The forces of Eastern Gilan resented the rule of the newcomer; a royalist whose aid was come late and whose forces suffered no losses. They saw the reinforcements as a host of glory-hunters seeking to take credit for the efforts of their fallen brethren.

    Marching alongside his company, Almardi was totally unaware of the politics within the ranks of the elf host and he was entirely ignorant to the reality of war. Having no real experience on the battlefield, Almardi was anxious to prove his worth at the sqal of Grishtan. He desperately desired to show his kin of the East that he was not the aristocratic nobleman they believed him to be. The swordsman companies of Aereil that marched in formation behind those of Graenor made up the right-hand frontline of their host; across from them, on the upper-left hand side of their formation, the spearmen companies marched alongside them, past the wagons that divided the two halves of Gilan's army. Behind them, the cavalry of mounted lancers and archers trotted along on both sides of the wagon convoy and in the rear, the Aush Wood archers made up the vanguard.

    As they continued to traverse the dreary forsaken landscape a small pinprick of light loomed upon the horizon, steadily growing in size until the elf host could distinctly make out the torchlit battlements that surrounded the perimeter of the Grishtan. Where at first only the keenest-eyed amongst them could barely make out the tiny dot of light in the eternal darkness that surrounded them, but over the passing days it became radiant like a beacon of light as they drew nearer. It was the only source of light as far as they could see all around in any direction; they were deep in the orcs country and the sky was already pitch black in the middle of the day. They lost track of time and marched onwards endlessly for days without halting. When they finally came upon the sqal they broke to to make camp and rest before waging war on the residents of the sqal in the morning.

The veteran soldiers slept peacefully without worry, they'd grown accustomed to the ever-present threat of danger and no longer feared or cared for their lives. They lived on a day by day basis; to the elves of Western Gilan this seemed absolutely insane. Even with the additional sentries where they were so near to the sqal of Grishtan, the reinforcements couldn't sleep and were kept up by their paranoia of being spotted by the orcs. The night was uneventful, though uncomfortably tense and dragged out in the opinion of the newcomers. When Prince Rässan emerged from his luxurious and spacious pavilion after an extravagant breakfast, served by his own personal culinary staff brought along with him from his father's castle, he gave the orders to all of the gathered elves of the host to deploy and assail the sqal of Grishtan.

They reached the outer wall of the sqal without interruption or incident and found the outpost heavily manned and fortified in preparation for a siege upon their arrival at its western gate entrance. While the forces of Gilan marched upon them, the orcs of Grishtan had busied themselves in war preparations against the invading host of elves. Somehow they knew of the elvish campaign, though whether it was through a Sythic survivor or an elusive scout was unknown to the elves and they were unsure to the extent which the enemy knew of their presence in the Desolation. With no other option but to continue on their plight, the elves advanced upon the orc settlement and their woodland archers began to fire volleys of their deadly arrows within the walled safety of the sqal. Shrieks and cries informed them that at least some of their arrows had met their marks and embedded themselves in the corpses of the unlucky orcs-turned-pincushions. From within the crudely constructed walls orcish archers returned fire, sending a black cloud of their darts in retaliation. The elvish cavalry burst forth and the swordsmen and spearmen raced forward with them, against the cloud of death that rained down to meet them, their shields raised to protect themselves from the foul shots as they ran.

The horsemen broke upon the dilapidated battlements of Grishtan like the waves of the ocean breaking upon the shore and their horses came crashing through the fortifications. The wood yielded to the superior might of the horses and the elvish host pushed its way through the splintered cracks in the orcish defences. Many of the horses and their riders had fallen in the effort and those remaining were joined by the swordsmen and spearmen as they charged through the openings and quickly filled the streets of the sqal. Almardi ducked through a broken portion of the wall alongside Namroden and his fellows and they took to the cover of the wall as orcish archers fired down upon the elves within their sqal. The captain of his company made a signal and together Almardi and his comrades climbed up the ladders onto the parapet above and took to slaughtering the archers upon the wall.

Namroden extravagantly beheaded an archer as Almardi gutted another nearby orc atop the battlement. The Fourth Swordsman company raced along the length of the western wall, securing it as they went to protect their fellow soldiers below. Swordsmen and spearmen continued to pour into the city beneath them through the broken bulwark of the sqal and orc warriors met them in the streets, fighting for their very lives as the elves sought to eradicate all of their kind in the eastern lands. There were men, women, and children alike in the multitudes of orcish warriors fighting in the streets of the sqal and the elves killed them indiscriminately. Almardi and Namroden leapt down from the liberated battlements and joined the tide of elvish warriors still pouring into the sqal. With the entranced now opened and accessible, the mounted lancers and archers filed in through the western gate; pushing the orcish militia back, deeper into the heart of their sqal.

With his blood-soaked scimitar in hand, Almardi charged in pursuit of the fleeing orcs alongside Namroden and his fellow countrymen. Any orcs still brave enough to stand against them were quickly hewn down and the elvish soldiers raced after the retreated ranks of Grishtan without the slightest deterrence from their course.The host of Gilan had been divided in half upon their entry into the squalid settlement; those who climbed atop the parapet to eliminate the orcish archers taking refuge there as well as the horsemen who were forced to wait whilst the main gate was opened from within, and the main forces of swordsmen and spearmen who'd pushed the orcish forces back, taking the sqal in the name of King Hassän and the people of Gilan. Almardi and his company did not see much action as they raced to catch up to the frontline that had already withdrawn deep into the heart of the outpost town.

The city was falling apart in the chaos of war that was engulfing the orcish sqal and they found themselves unable to withstand the superior strength in numbers of the elvish legions. When Almardi and his comrades reached the elvish frontline just outside the town centre, they came to find their kin clashing brutally against the remnants of the gathered orcish masses. An orc swordsman came at Almardi with a great goblin cleaver in hand as he swung on the elf; the blow was parried and in a split second the blur of Almardi's sword glinted in the torchlit streets of the sqal as he lopped the head off his opponent. The orc's decapitated head rolled off his shoulders and fell with a thud to the ground where it kicked up a tiny spray of blood and dust. Thrusting his blade through the chest of another nearby adversary, the orc dropped his weapon and clutched at his chest. Almardi pulled his own sword back out to allow the deceased warrior to collapse on the ground before him.

The forces of Gilan had numbered forty thousand strong against an initial force of 15,000 orcs prior to their engagement and now the numbers were significantly lower as the battle steadily drew to a close. All around, orcs let loose their battle cries to intermingle with the shrieks of death that emanated from both sides of the ranks within the walls of the sqal of Grishtan. They shouted to their fetid gods in prayer, pleading for victory and deliverance from the icy hand of death. The elves were already upon them however, and there was nothing their foul gods could do to save the orcs who so blindly worshipped the vile demons of that land. Forsaken by their gods, the orcs still attempted to flee, leaving their dead friends and relatives behind to burn away and smoulder in the wake of the elvish host as their city was swallowed whole by flames.

From outside the walls of the sqal Aush Wood archers rained down fire-arrows from above and they landed all throughout the sqal, setting the wretched buildings aflame wherever they embedded themselves. The black resinous material that the orcish bolts consisted of was high flammable and the elves used the foul shots to produce the flaming arrows they used against their enemies. The orcs fall was entirely their own doing and the elves used their own devices against them. Wondering to themselves how their gods could abandon them in their time of need, the orcs regrouped to make a final stand as their brethren had done in Sythin after seeing the futility in an escape. The few remaining orcish archers fired the last of their bolts into the midst of the approaching elf legions and some amongst their ranks fell even as they fell upon the remnants of Grishtan's orcish inhabitants.

Almardi and the forces of Gilan struck dead the weaker host of orcs without difficulty and the battle concluded. None amongst the orcish ranks had survived as far as the elves were aware and there were no signs of any life beyond that of their own forces within the sqal, as well as in the outlying wastelands. They gathered the dead orcs and piled their corpses in the town centre before setting them aflame, allowing the sqal to burn like a funeral pyre to the ground. Man, woman, and orcling foul burned together in the aftermath of the mass genocide and the elves looked upon the sight without emotion. To them, the orcs were a parasite of the earth and as such they were treated as the foul abominations that they were, wholly unworthy of the gift of life that they were given.

Almardi looked upon the sqal that burned not far away from where the host had erected their camp for the night with disdain; though there were children amongst the forces of orcs they'd found within that place, he felt no pity for them. *One day they will grow to become the very thing we hate most,* Almardi reasoned to himself before taking a sip from his wineskin. After the battle of Grishtan he personally felt that he'd earned it and, judging by the looks he received from the veterans, he was right in his assumption. He was one of the rest of them now, as were all those within the elvish ranks who could claim to have survived the encounter. Taking his attention away from the death and destruction all around, Almardi sought out his dearest friend, Namroden, to enjoy his company after the sight of so many of their kin dying all around them. It would be nice to reminisce with the fellow elf and keep their minds off the war that they fought; he was no longer so eager to fight after seeing war to be a much less of a playful game than he'd once imagined it to be.

CHAPTER FIVE
THE DEAD WOOD
Winter, 1E194

Ulrich looked up into the dark clouded skies that blanketed the woods that he and his fellow survivors of the fateful Nardic voyage prepared to traverse in their northward march through the Dead Wood. The voyage across the Sumatran Ocean had taken its toll on the Southern men; the wreckage of the ships had washed up on the shores along with the remaining survivors of the expedition. Gathering themselves and whatever supplies were salvageable, they departed from the coast and began their trek beneath the leafless boughs that made up the roof of the wretched forest they walked through. Creeping cautiously through the forsaken woodlands alongside his fellows, Ulrich kept an eye out for any signs of movement between the charred and withered trees and underbrush. They hadn't the slightest idea of what sort of foul creatures lurked in that place and so they were wary in their ventures in the southern reaches of its domain.

Wild wolves howled in the distance on the hunt for a meal and the men kept their weapons close at hand, clenched tightly to their chests in paranoid fear as they advanced. The men of the Nardic Tribes were a strong and courageous people, descended from vikings in the South, arrived in the Nardic Isles from far away lands across the Sumatran Ocean. During the Dragon Wars (1E23-47) dragons travelled from out of the South and settled in on the Nardic island of Elend before their Queen was killed by the Nardic tribesman, Hagaar Woolfsbarl, and his heroic band of men. This they did without the help of the elves of Gilan, who would have ignored their plight anyway, even had they asked for the assistance.

The men of the Nardic Tribes were a strong-willed people; a hardy folk who were built with powerful muscles gained from the toil of their daily labours. The men of the isles were quick to work and slow to tire, performing to the best of their ability in everything that they did. Their skin was tanned from long hours of working under the harsh light of the southern sun and their hair was dark like the night sky, complimented by eyes that were a pretty misty-grey. Attired in studded leather armour, they were armed with a variety of lethal weapons such as spears, axes, swords, and bows. Ulrich was no exception to the stereotypes of his people.

A woodsman by trade, under normal circumstances he reserved his hefty axe for the felling of trees. For the time being, however, he would suffice himself with the necks of his enemies in lieu of the pine trees of his homeland. The survivors of the Nardic voyage numbered sixteen thousand strong out of the 50,000 they'd started the expedition with. Nearly two-thirds of their entire host had been swallowed up by Urasmus, God of the Sea. It would prove to be a great loss to the elves, as well as their own forces, in their adventures in the mainland. As they began their journey through the Dead Wood, their navigators consulted the compasses they carried with them to find themselves in the darkness of the eternal night that lingered over the expanse of the orc country. Under the light of their torchbearers, the host disembarked on their travels and Ulrich marched silently alongside the remnants of their forces in formation as they marched North.

Somewhere not far from their position a wolf howled at the moon, shrouded in the smoggy sky though it was. The wolves had learned to sense the strength they gained from the moon in the long hours of the night through their countless generations that were born deprived of the light of the sun. Ulrich clung to his axe with slight unease at the sound of their howls. After surviving the wrath of the sea-god, there was little that the demons of the Desolation could throw at him to catch him off his guard. *As long as I can kill it, nothing can stand before me as long as I stand on solid ground,* Ulrich said to himself in an attempt to dispel his discomfort. The trees of the wood creaked and swayed eerily; from behind them a branch cracked and fell to the ground with a resonant crunch as it landed amongst the withered brambles that grew throughout the wretched forest. The air within that place was rank and stale and the atmosphere felt heavy with the presence of demonic energies at work.

Ulrich made sure to stay within the safety of the torchlight as he trekked along, even before they'd started to notice their men suddenly disappearing. Only a handful had gone missing when they'd finally noticed, but amongst the lost was Ulrich's friend Ralf. It was rumoured that none who entered the Dead Wood returned to the world of the living upon their entry, and it only grew more believable with each step that they took. The men passed through the wood uneasily, climbing up and over fallen limbs that blocked their path and pushing the dead and withered thorny undergrowth out of their way as the went along in the torchlit silence. Archers kept their bows at the ready, each with an arrow nocked at the ready for a wolf attack. The howls echoed in the depths of the night outside their perimeter of light and they were answered by resounding howls. They came from every direction, or so it seemed to the men as they continued in their journey to the sqal of Gregor.

Time drew on and after a while had passed the howls receded along with the darkness; the sky lightened to a graphite grey and the men took rest under the dim light of day in the southernmost reaches of the Gorgon Desolation. They unanimously decided that it would be much safer to rest during the daylight hours when the demonic hosts were less active and keep a rotating watch in the daylight whilst their forces slept and took rest. The day passed the by and Ulrich slept fitfully until woken from his nightmarish dreams by the cries and screams of his kinsmen. From the dark reaches of the forest, gargantuan spiders had been drawn to the torches of the the watch like moths and they snatched up the tribesmen as they slept. It was already dark again in the early afternoon when Ulrich was suddenly shocked out of his sleep. Taking up his axe from where it rested beneath his pillow, Ulrich stood his ground against the vile enemy that plagued his people. Though he could not see the creatures, the air was thick with the putrid odour that radiated from their bodies.

Men shrieked as they were snatched up like the fodder they were to the giant monstrosities and the few surviving horses they'd brought along on the voyage whine in fright. Ulrich joined some of his fellows in taking up a defensive perimeter around the last of their remaining ale-horses. Some had been laden with food, supplies, ale*, and other essential items they deemed necessary in their travels, though the majority had been lost at sea along with the seamen who'd brought them aboard. There was only one remaining ale horse, though the host had managed to find a few kegs of Nardic beer undamaged amongst the wreckage. Three men had been designated to be bearers of the beer and over the course of their travels they found the burden unfortunately easier to bear as the drew deeper into the heart of the woods. One of the horses bearing tobacco and medical supplies bolted in fear and a couple men ran after it even as a hulking arachnid beast snatched it up in its pincers.

---

*The Island of Dusseldorf was famous throughout the Nardic Isles for their ale and mustard, the second of the two was exclusive to the island and they maintained a monopoly on the cash crop.

The spiders ranged anywhere from eight to twelve feet tall and most spanned over fifteen feet in length. They leapt from the depths of the darkness and came crashing down amongst the men to snatch them up before jumping back out of the torchlight to devour their prey. There was no way of knowing who was next or when the next attack would come; it was as quick, sudden, and random as lightning. They injected the men with their venom and their victims quickly fell under its paralysing effects. Other symptom included skin and bone deterioration betwixt severe spasms of muscle pain as the toxin ate away at them. Along with the degradation of their physical selves, they experienced this suffering alongside extreme hallucinations in a sleep-induced state of paralysis. Even if the men managed to free their friends, the victims were still doomed to rot away in their arms into nothingness.

Arrows were let loose in every direction and archers even fired haphazardly into the ranks of their own countrymen in their overwhelming fear. The spiders continued to fall upon them like the deadly hunters they were and still the men fought back as futile as it seemed. The watch fires had been stomped out by the spiders in the initial onslaught, plunging the men into the darkness. A spider came crashing down from above just out of arm's reach of Ulrich, snatching up a man to his left only feet away. Being the brave Nardic soldier that he was, Ulrich swung his axe into one of the mighty legs of the creature in an attempt to free his comrade from its death-grip. The spider let out a hissing shriek and released the man; Ulrich rushed to his aid only to witness the husband of his sister, Till, as he was eaten away by the spider's venom. His brother-in-law melted away in agony in Ulrich's arms and he fought back the tears that choked him even as the spider lurched around, seeking vengeance for his wound.

Ulrich rose to his feet even as Till faded from existence and dealt of devastating blow to the spider even as it lunged at him. He hacked the left pincer of his adversary clean off with a one-armed stroke of his axe and glowing green blood spurted from its injury. It left a trail and lit up the spider as a target for nearby archers. Ulrich hit the deck as they fired a slew of arrows their direction without any regard for his safety. The spider shrieked as it was struck by dozens of the Nardic pine arrows and it crumpled dead upon the ground. In the midst of the darkness a couple of Ulrich's nearby fellows attempted to rekindle an extinguished watch fire and he raced towards the visible sparks of their struggles.

Rushing to their aid he brought his axe sweeping down in a fluid strike that caught itself in the spider's skull, splitting its face in half and filling the stagnant air with piercing cries of agony. The men covered their ears from the stabbing pain of its screams and a fellow comrade at arms thrust his spear through its wretched mouth even as the gigantic insect coughed up more of the glowing blood of his kind. Turning around just in time to witness a dark mass descend upon them, Ulrich spun round and his axe came crashing down in a mighty stroke upon the head of the new challenger. The beast knocked the Nardic man aside with a swipe of its leg and he flew several meters before snapping a tree trunk with the force of his impact in a flurry of rotted splinters of wood. Brushing himself off, the warrior stumbled to his feet even as gushes of glowing green blood-spatter indicated the triumph of his companions over the hulking beast that assailed them.

In a suddenly blinding flash of light, the perimeter fires were relit. The men who valiantly fought back the many waves of the arachnid assault were illuminated by the orange flames that encompassed their camp, within the surrounding darkness of those woods. The rekindled fires lit up the massive spiders who oppressed them for all to see; in the evened odds of a fair fight, the Nardic Tribesmen pushed their enemies back into the depths of the darkness from which they'd come. The southern warriors shouted out orders to one another and they fought with a renewed sense of hope and a better overall outlook on their chances of survival in the wood.

As more and more fires were lit there throughout the Nardic camp, the spiders began to flee from the blinding light in piercing shrieks of agony. Their eyes were burned by a light they'd never seen the likes of in that land of eternal darkness and it drove them berserk in their frenzied state of terror. Arrows were let loose upon them from every direction and the warriors of the Nardic host fell upon them furiously in the liberating radiance of the firelight. Axes, spears and swords mercilessly cut down the ranks of spiders and they were felled one by one until there were none left. By the end of the skirmish with the residents of the wood, the Nardic Tribesmen counted thirty two spider corpses amongst the fallen along with almost four thousand of their own lost in the effort.

Only a handful of spiders had escaped into the surrounding darkness, though the men cared not; they were safe for the time being. As tired as they were, the tribesmen packed up their things and prepared to move on. Ulrich poured himself a pint to awaken his senses and sipped on the rich dark ale of his country. There was not much of a supply left of the precious draught and he savoured every sip of it. He hadn't the time for breakfast and cutting their losses, the host pushed on without any further delay. Torchbearers amongst the host provided light for their fellows in the surrounding darkness of the land and archers provided an overwatch. It would prove to be a long and arduous trip through the Dead Wood, filled by encounters with wretched creatures and servants of evil.

When travelling in the Gorgon Desolation one had to come prepared for the worst and the same proved true only ten-fold under the lifeless withered canopy of the Dead Wood. The malevolent ruins of a once great forest were home to many intolerable creatures that hungered for unwary travellers. It was quite a rare occurrence however; not even the orcs dared to venture into the wretched wood in the southern reaches of their domain. They had once tried to kill the forest with fire, though it hadn't gone quite as planned. Even fire was unable to conquer the tainted southern woodlands from the evil that befouled them. It was a twisted wood, corrupted by the negative aura of divine wrath and insatiable rage whose roots ran deep. The Dead Wood manifested its bitter hate through the foul creatures that roamed those lands, swallowed whole by the hunger for retribution to satisfy their unquenchable thirst for blood.

The tangled strands of the cobwebs of their fallen adversaries hung from the blackened boughs of the Dead Wood, sizzling and shrivelling as the torchbearers of the Nardic host passed by them on their northern march upon the ground below. Though they'd been weakened by the casualties they suffered in the affray with the spiders, it was to be noted that there were no injured amongst their ranks; the venomous spiders had taken care of that. Stumbling along through the thorny brambles and undergrowth, they pushed forward, half-heartedly in their tiredness, through the wretched trees that covered the expanse of the Gorgon peninsula in the South. They would have to make some distance through the night before they could earn the right to rest at the morning's dim light. One of his fellows yawned beside him and Ulrich stifled one back as he fought against its contagious spread. All around the men's eyelids drooped and their faces sagged, haggardly marching along with bloodshot eyes ablaze in the torchlight.

From not far away a splintering crack resounded throughout the dense foliage and it was followed by echoing snaps and cracks as the surrounding trees gave way to some mighty beast or stampede of creatures. The men raised their arms at the onset of unrest within the wood and archers fired off their shots as a tree burst in an explosion of splintered wood chips and fragments. Out of the debris of the splintered trees, three gargantuan ogres emerged. They roared a challenge and rushed towards the host as all around the men flocked to defend themselves from the onslaught. Breaking upon the Nardic host with devastating force, the ogres swung the tree limbs they used as clubs and men were sent flying in all directions. Ulrich swung around to engage one of the hulking mammoths even as two more flanked them from behind. His axe bit into the leg of the ogre and it was as thick around as Ulrich's torso; the creature swatted him aside and he flew threw the air like a rag-doll.

Picking up a nearby combatant, the wounded ogre at his Nardic prey and made his way over to Ulrich. The torchbearers had begun setting the nearby trees ablaze and ran amok in the chaos. Even as the colossal beast ambled towards him, a second ogre came running forth to engage him. Whilst the two brawled over him, Ulrich got up and brushed himself off as they fought over the snack that he would be in their vile hands. Caught in the midst of a free-for-all between the ogres in their fight for food, Ulrich and his fellow kin of the Isles grouped together and fought their way out of the ogres grasp. A giant tree trunk came crashing down in their path as they retreated away from the battle, wielded by one of the ogres as a makeshift club.

In another swing he crushed two of Ulrich's fellows in a flurry of dust and debris. Ulrich and the remaining three men of his group had dodged out of the way just in time. One of the men armed with a bow fired an arrow into the chest of their opponent, only further enraging the ravenous beast. Ulrich and the archer fled from their position as the spearman in their company ran forward to meet the charging ogre. He dropped to the ground in a sliding tackle with the head of his speared aimed directly at the ogre's heart. The point of the Nardic spear thrust through it the hulking creature's chest, felling the large foe to the joyous cheer of the Nardic men gathered in the wood.

Still the Nardic men fought on, against all odds, seeking to escape the hungry jowls of the ogres who sought to turn them into a meal. In the heart of their host, two ogres had already been killed by their own kin; one of the dead being the ogre injured in battle earlier with Ulrich, to whom the Nardic man had dealt the injury himself. There were still two ogres remaining and some of the host of men were beginning to withdraw. Still a handful continued to engage the wretched beasts and Ulrich joined his fellows, providing support so that the injured could also escape being eaten alive. The men flung themselves against their burly enemy and hacked away at their massive muscular limbs as they were able with swords and axes. Spearmen prodded at the giant creatures and some amongst those who lingered assisted the wounded in the retreat North.

The ogres delivered devastating blows, crushing and smashing the men where they stood and flinging those who fled their wrath aside to break their fall on the trees of that forest. They were a relentless and terrifying force to be reckoned with, even in the face of defeat. Together with several of his countrymen, Ulrich led a charge and they clambered up the gargantuan colossus before them, bringing the ten meter tall giant to his knees even as they beheaded him. From where they were, the men could see some of their fellows not far off finishing the other remaining ogre. With the deaths of the ogres, the battle was concluded, and the Nardic forces rejoined their brethren on the northern march once again. It had been an eventful start to their day and the men hoped that the remainder of it would be peaceful after their encounter with not only spiders but also ogres. It was nearly enough to make the Nardic forces forget the voyage across the Sumatran Ocean, though even that was still fresh in their minds.

It was overwhelming to Ulrich and his fellows how many of their men they'd lost in the journey and how much further they had yet to go. None amongst the host had any hope of survival and few saw any chance of reaching the end of that foul forest with their lives. The men staggered through the woods and bramble and they left the scene of the ambush behind, allowing the fires they'd started to continue to burn and spread through the wood behind them. That place could burn to the ground and the ashes pissed on for all the men of the Nardic Tribes could care; that wretched forest had brought them nothing but misery and suffering from the start. Hacking their way through the thorny thickets of spiked brush, the undergrowth yielded to the swords and axes of the Nardic frontline. Archers and spearmen trailed behind in the freshly cleared wake of their comrades and the torchbearers provided light for all throughout the host.

CHAPTER SIX
THE GORGON DESOLATION
Winter, 1E196

Almardi ate an elvish honey roll filled with strawberry jam and washed it down with a sip from his wineskin, savouring the enchanted elvish wildberries of Gilan. The elvish host busied itself about in preparation for their departure; those out of Western Gilan had been humbled by the battle and no longer held the capacity for mirth they once had. Their glorious ideals of what war was had been shattered and the harsh reality of it all was steadily beginning to sink in. They would be setting out for another day's march eastward; Almardi sought out Namroden in the downtime, not having seen his friend amongst the fellows of their company. On the outskirts of camp he found the elf in the company of the Aush Wood elves. Together they were drinking in reverent silence with sombre looks upon their faces. Namroden ignored his friend and took another draught from his wineskin. The elf seemed as if he'd died on the inside and his face was entirely devoid of emotion. He didn't even acknowledge Almardi as approached from outside the circle of elves gathered around their camp fire.

"There you are friend; I've been looking for you!" Almardi exclaimed as he joined his companion around the fire, "Why do you distance yourself in the company of the Keepers? They are worried for you back at the camp, Namrien."

Namroden caught a strange look in his eye at the mention of Almardi's childhood nickname for him. The term of endearment brought the elf back to himself a little and he stirred where he sat.

"I know it's too much... what they ask of us, but we must continue on! If we don't stop this plague once and for all at its source, if we fall; what you see around you will be the future of our whole world. We can't let this disease spread, even if it means our death... I don't think we'll ever live to see Gilan again, but we can't let our deaths be in vain, or those of our fallen brothers. We have to stay strong Namrien." Namroden stirred from his trance-like state to stare upon his dearest friend without expression at the conclusion of his speech.

"You haven't eaten in weeks, not since the battle nearly two weeks ago. Please, take this for me friend" Almardi pressed a jam-filled honey roll into hi friend's hand and clasped Namroden's fingers around it before withdrawing his own.

After a moment's hesitation, Namroden brought the roll to his lips and took a bite of the honeyed bread before reaching for his wine flask to wash it down. Almardi was too quick for him, however, the nimble elf had already snatched it up before his friend even had the chance to extend his arm. Namroden looked up in miserable agony as he continued to chew the delicious pastry without the solace of wine to wash it down. He was visibly pained by the horrors of war that he bore witness to; the countless deaths of the recently departed had worn him down and killed his spirits, leaving him dead and empty on the inside. The company of his closest friend numbed the pain enough to allow Namroden to eat, though he was only a shell of who he had once been before the war.

Almardi drained what was left of Namroden's wine and the elf did not object, though he remained despondent and melancholy.

Namroden was younger than the majority of the elves amongst the ranks of Gilan's army by far and as such the war had taken a greater toll on the impressionable youth. He was mournful for his fallen kin, as were many amongst the host, though their deaths had drained the young elf of all hope and he could see no outcome other than their deaths. So it was that Almardi found him in the company of the Keepers, with whom he'd fallen in formation with during their travels in those lands, after the Battle of Grishtan. Even as they reacquainted themselves, the majority of the host had already begun to depart. The two made their way back to the Fourth Swordsman Company of Aereil and took up the day's march across the bleak barren lands of the Gorgon Desolation in rank with their comrades in arms. The host steadily made its way over the course of the passing weeks towards the sqal of Gorgor, where they hoped to find the Nardic host awaiting them upon the bloody barren ruins of a former orc metropolis.

Some of the elves were beginning to lose faith that aid would even arrive from the South. They believed in the rumours of the Dead Wood, that none who entered returned to the world of the living. None who stepped foot in those woods had returned to speak of it, and the Nardic fleet would prove no better than their finest scouts, or even the native orcs of that land themselves. The orcs they'd captured and interrogated in the past had spoke ill of those woods and dared not venture within the reaches of that forest themselves for fear of their lives. This only further strengthened their lack of faith in the Nardic reinforcements, though others believed the wood could be conquered and that the Southern woodsmen had the strength and skill to do it. Hope was becoming a limited commodity amongst the ranks of the Gilan host and the officers had quite the job of maintaining morale.

    Dissent was only growing the further they ventured into the orcish heartlands and Captain Vasil reigned on the low, seeing to it that the orders of Prince Rässan dutifully were carried out. None amongst the elvish legions truly followed the Prince's command; even his own folk out of the West had bore witness to the royal aristocrat abandoning his own men in desertion. He'd fled from the ranks of his own army before they'd even laid siege to the sqal of Grishtan, only to claim full credit once he'd regrouped with them at the heart of it all upon the battle's conclusion. On top of that, he had even been surrounded by an armed guard throughout the whole affair to ensure no harm came to him. Prince Rässan had ordered the day's march nearly half an hour before they'd set out for the day; that was how long it had taken for Captain Vasil to spread the word through camp.

    Almardi and Namroden fought their way eastwards alongside their kin as they were assailed by the dust storms and smoggy blanket that blanketed the heartlands of the Gorgon Desolation. The sky was a blurry red where the sun shone somewhere high up above the orcish pollution, though it provided them with no light on the ground below. It was the only source of light all around as far as they could see but for the distant pinpricks of light that were the sqals of Gorgor and Ishtan; they were like directional beacons to orcish nomads, as were Sythin and Grishtan before the elves had sacked and burned them to the ground. The elvish host travelled on both sides of the convoy that rode forth bearing torches to provide them with illumination on their travels, along with the supplies they carried aboard the horse-drawn wagons.

They trekked through the wastes in silence; although Gorgor and Ishtan were visible on the horizon, everyone amongst the host knew the sqals to be hundreds of leagues away. To the right nothing could be seen of Gregor's light or of the Dead Wood in the distance. The wretched forest of the South was far over the horizon beyond the sight of the elves, even if the lands weren't shrouded in the smoggy darkness that shrouded the orcish country from the light of the sun. Somewhere there, amidst the convoluted forest, the Nardic forces pushed their way through the cursed woodlands in their journey to join the elvish hosts on their campaign against the orcs. None amongst Gilan's ranks looked to to South, filled by the doubts that their allies had been devoured alive by the Dead Wood.

Hope had been exchanged for nagging uncertainty amongst the ranks of the elf host. It eventually gave way to a pessimism that would lead the masses to the brink of desertion. The orcish tribes already knew of the elven presence in their lands; the Battle of Grishtan had made that apparent to the legions of Gilan. Though they had no idea the extent to which the orcs had prepared themselves or even how much they knew of the invasive elvish force, the host of Gilan continued ceaselessly eastwards in their campaign against the orcish masses. Never before had a true assault been made upon the foul legions of the Gorgon Desolation, nor had the orc tribes been mustered to take part in full-scale militaristic warfare. Mostly, the orc tribes just fought amongst themselves or spread into the outlying lands in pursuit of undying riches and glory, drugs, or slaves to be sacrificed to the demon gods they worshipped.

Elvish scouts were sent forth in small companies to gather tidings of the Nardic host, as well as spy out the strength of their orcish foes. They would report their findings back to the Prince of

Aereil, however dark the news might be. The mounts of the scouts set out, spurring off into the wastes and leaving dust clouds in their wake. To those who remained behind, it seemed that the horsemen were like comets flying through the nothingness as the graphite-coloured plains met the grey sky, almost in a blur as the two shades of grey blurred into one. After the brief moment of rest, the elvish forces resumed their travels; they'd only made the stop so that the captains could sort out a scouting expedition East. The host continued onwards in their journey to Gorgor and marched across the desolate plains, disregarding their doubts, worries, and fears. They would march upon Gorgor whatever the cost, regardless the circumstances, and they would wage a righteous war upon its residents.

Almardi thought of his home in Aereil as he zoned out during the monotonous journey East. His house overlooked the seafront and he could recall the memories of staring across the Sumatran Ocean towards Auchtung, the nearest of the Nardic Isles, and wondering what laid across the horizon. He thought of the countless memories of watching the grandiose ships as they sailed the seas in their travels to the coast of Rome where they conducted trade with the merchants of the country. Their ships were beautifully wrought of wood with towering masts and majestic sails, embroidered with blue dragons intertwined amidst a silver border of Celtic bands around the edges of the sails. The elf had always fantasised finding himself aboard one of the great Nardic vessels, a sailor destined for some foreign unknown land abroad far beyond the horizon. He promised himself that if he did survive the war he would become a ship-master and travel the oceans; he would spend the rest of his life exploring the vastness of the world.

In the meanwhile, the time was nigh for war to ravage the barren plains and cleanse them of the filth that had taken up residency therein. The elves would free those lands from the orcs who defiled them and restore that wretched place to its former glory. It was their goal to smite down the debauched machines and devices that issued putrid smoke into the heavens, blacking out the sun and plunging their world into darkness. The smoky skies of the Gorgon Desolation had killed off what native life had once populated the rolling hills and forested plains. The toxic pollution of the orcs was responsible for driving out the native birds, plants, and animals out of those lands as well as pushing them to the brink of extinction. Carrion crows had taken up residence in their stead alongside the foul beasts and demons of the orcs; they feasted on the remains of the original inhabitants of that land, along with the corpses of those who futilely stood against the tyranny of the Gorgon legions.

CHAPTER SEVEN
THE DEAD WOOD
Summer, 1E195

The Nardic tribesmen trudged through the thorns and brambles that grew upon the forest floor, hacking and slashing at the undergrowth under the light of the torchbearers. The dense thickets of spiked brush gave way to the blades of the frontline warriors who cleared a path for their comrades. Ulrich trailed just behind them in the heart of the formation, a highly coveted and difficult position to maintain amongst the ranks of the infantrymen. He was jostled into the outer flank on both sides from time to time though he continued to fight for a place in the centre of the troop, away from the encroaching darkness. After some time, the remnants of the mighty Nardic host came across what once been a pathway through those woods in a time long since passed. Those were the days of old when the elves still inhabited that land before the orcs descended upon them from the North.

The men rejoiced at the change in their travels; the way was much less difficult and fewer brambles crowded the wood. The pathway was still visible and they followed it Northeast where it led them deeper into the heart of the withered forest. Had they known it they were heading directly for Umargathon, the heart of the Dead Wood and the ruined capitol of the fallen kingdom of the elves, Gorgorannon. Now the land was cursed and all that had once been fair and beautiful was dead and decayed; it was believed that Umargathon was the source of the evil energy present in those dead and withered woodlands. The host didn't halt for food, rest, or recovery; they pressed onwards as quickly as they could. Already their host was on the verge of defeat and they continued on with the growing fear of yet another attack.

They'd been ambushed recently by a pack of wolves. The dead had been left behind in their desperation and the wounded marched alongside their comrades in their haste to resume their journey. Death was the only outcome of lingering for too long in those woods and the Nardic men ceaselessly pushed forward with caution. Those who found themselves unable to keep up or carry on were left behind by their kin. There was no time to spare and danger lurked not far out of the firelight of their torches. Redistributing the remaining supplies amongst the few horses that had survived the journey thus far, the men loaded their beasts of burden with what was left of their meagre provisions.

The three remaining horses ambled along slowly under the overwhelming weight of the luggage they carried. The host kept their supply horses in the heart of the formation; it was the safest position in the event of an attack. Though they hadn't the time to give their fallen a proper wake or burial, the Nardic Tribesmen promised themselves they would roast the wood alive one day and give their friends a mighty funeral pyre. In the meantime they continued to pass through the forsaken forest in mournful silence and wary vigilance. Thorny black thickets of resinous roses lined their path on either side and the oily substance that coated the vegetation rubbed off on their boiled leather as the men passed through. None amongst their ranks knew how long they marched in the eternal night of that land; marching for days on end they steadily advanced upon the forsaken elf kingdom of old, nearing the forgotten burial grounds on the outskirts of Umargathon.

In the former land of Gorgorannon they traversed what had once been Amargaroth, the cemetery of the royal lineage of Umargathon. Tombstones, eaten away by moss and eroded with the passing of time, stuck out of the ground like broken teeth in rows and columns throughout the glade the spanned as quickly as they could. No trees grew in the clearing where the ancient aristocracy laid at rest. As they passed the graves of the forgotten the men felt a chilling breeze and shivers of unease ran down their spines. None too soon they reached the outskirts of the ruined city, dilapidated and fallen into disrepair.

The remains of the forsaken homes were rotten and decayed, covered in the putrid black resin that was all too common in the orc lands. Ulrich could taste the sickly oil in the air; he was beginning to suspect the substance to be the condensation from the pollution that was ever-present in the country. All that remained of Umargathon was the blackened foundations of the structures burnt down long ago in a time beyond the recollection of Man. The remnants of the Nardic host came upon the decrepit remains of the former metropolis of the eastern elves of Aerbon. They believed the lands they trekked to be the unholy burial grounds of an ancient demonic plague and many spoke of it being the source of all the evil in that wood.

As they entered the centre of the former metropolis the path transitioned from an overgrown dirt road to cobblestone streets drenched in coagulated blood from a war that took place centuries ago. They came upon the ruinous city and stared in awe. A malignant castle coated in the resinous tar of that land loomed tall amidst the surrounding trees. Ominous torches that burned an eerie green all throughout what was left of the outer battlements. The castle still stood defiantly in the heart of that dead forest. The air was heavy in that place and the men could feel the pollution that was thick in the air; some of the men even began to cough up the black oily substance, mixed in with a nasty green phlegm in their spit. Ulrich and his fellows were beginning to feel light-headed; this was only one of the many symptoms of the atmospheric pollution that was afflicting the tribesmen.

As much as they fought against it, the men could not deny their weary legs rest. For countless days on end beyond their reckoning, the Nardic men had been marching ceaselessly in their desperation to clear the foul would and put it as far behind them as they could before reaching the safety of the elvish legions. They could march no further, however; the air was thick with smog and it wore the men down and deprived them of oxygen. Their limbs grew heavier the further they travelled and finally after some time they stopped to take rest. Setting up camp under the gate entrance of the outer battlements, the Nardic forces set a watch and lit fires in the heart of their camp under the towering archway that cut through the perimeter wall of Castle Umargathon.

In their own language the men dubbed the fortress Schwarzeburg, the Castle Black. Making camp under the great archway of the outer wall, they kept sentries stationed on both sides of the entrance as well as the guardrooms on either side of the arched entry hall. With the opportunity to rest, many of the men took the opportunity to mourn the loss of their fallen friends. Ulrich was reminded of the death of his brother-in-law and he could not begin to imagine how he would break the news to his sister if he ever saw home again. As it was, he was beginning to lose faith that he would ever walk upon the soil of his hometown in Dusseldorf again. The weeks had turned to months and their numbers only continued to dwindle with each passing day under the leafless canopy of the Dead Wood.

Night drew in around them and they were enveloped by the surrounding darkness despite the fire's futile attempt to keep it at bay. The men were all wide awake as they laid under the entryway into the courtyard of what they knew to be the Schwarzeburg. Nothing stirred from the depths of the night outside the perimeter of their watch fires and the sentries were all on guard for even the slightest hint of a hostile presence. Fear kept their ranks wary and alert, though those who laid at rest fought off the thoughts of the night. They sought out the warm embrace of sleep that they so greatly desired to wash over them and refresh their weary spirits. The fires crackled and hissed and occasionally the watch mistook it for the snap of twigs giving way to the demonic creatures they believed to roam the outlying darkness around them.

Though they could neither see nor hear anything out of the ordinary in the blinding silence that smothered them, they could feel an evil presence lurking just out of sight, waiting. They watch sentries felt a prickling paranoia scratching at the nape of their necks and their brains ached under the overwhelming weight of the stress they carried on their shoulders. Ulrich laid on his back with his arms folded behind his head to suffice as a makeshift pillow. Eyes shut to fight off the surrounding reality of it all, he tried his best to ignore the doubt that was beginning to take hold over him and his kin. Sleep did not come as much as he fought for it and struggled against the gripping insomnia that dominated his over-active mind.

From somewhere outside the light of their watch fires, the muffled sound of scuffling feet as they dragged over the cobblestone roads of that place could be heard faintly by the some of the sentinels stationed nearby the mouth of the castle entrance. At first the watch attempted to ignore the noise, hoping it to be some far-off predator seeking out some of the native non-humanoid prey of that land elsewhere, away from them. Though they knew this to be no more than a hopeful nothing, the men attempted to stifle the fire so that it would not attract the attention of whatever it was that roamed the streets the outlying darkness. The sounds only seemed to grow louder like the steadily increasing gusts of winds at the onset of a storm. Before long the camp was engulfed in a demonic cackle of energy and the air was rife with the sizzling sounds of static.

A couple archers drew their arrows and a few of the guard stepped out of the protection of their camp's illumination to explore the darkness, searching for the source of the sound. Some of the men amongst those who laid at rest were already risen to their feet, shaking the wariness off as they joined the night watch in their discomfort. Damning the wood and his insomnia, Ulrich rolled on his side and pushed himself to his feet. His hair stood on edge, as did he, in his panicked state of alertness in the midst of the strange phenomenon that beset the Nardic host. A cry pierced the night and officers shouted orders to the sleeping masses.

"Aufstehen! Die gegner steht vor der tür!" a lieutenant cried out as he ran, shaking soldiers awake in his efforts to muster their defences against an inevitable enemy assault.

"Scheiß!" someone else shouted in response as a dark blur streaked across the camp, from one end of the archway to the other, snatching up any who were unfortunate enough to find themselves in its path of travel.

Screams came from the depths of the darkness where a patrol had just been sent to assess the situation. The archers fired off their arrows in the direction of the screams, assuming the scouts to be dead by the hand of whatever it was that assailed them. Dark swarmed and approached them from outside the castle entrance; distant shapes poured forth from the streets of the decaying town that surrounded them. The black masses closed in upon them and out of distant huddled blur they could make out humanoid shapes from the crowd. The initial onset of the undead legions began to make their way into the firelight, revealing their grotesque and rotten bodies to the terrified Nardic tribesmen. The zombified masses were terrible to behold and killing them proved much more difficult than the tribesmen had initially expected.

The rotten and decayed corpses of the former elves of Umargathon were even more powerful then they were in their waking life, in the times of their fallen kingdom long ago. They flung men aside without effort and dragged others to the ground to devour their souls. Ulrich swung his axe on one of the approaching wraiths and felt his axe bite into the sinewy muscles of the deteriorated corpse he'd engaged. The creature swung on him in response even as its arm was severed from the body. It screamed in agony and several of its fellows came rushing to the wounded zombie's aid. Some amongst their masses included the fallen amongst the Nardic host; at the sight of their defeated brothers, the majority of the survivors wailed and many gave up all hope of victory against the wood. The undead hordes that encroached upon their position at the mouth of the castle continued to pour in from the darkness outside and the remnants of the Nardic forces raced to the frontlines in efforts to quell the undead waves that assailed them.

CHAPTER EIGHT
GRISHTAN, GORGON DESOLATION
Autumn, 1E195

Orcish archers shouted out curses from their positions high atop the parapet that ran along the perimeter of their sqal; a ramshackle wooden plank wall, reinforced by whatever the orcs could salvage in preparation for the elvish assault. As it was, the elves were upon them and the forces of Gilan laid siege to their outpost. Bruh darted across the open streets between arrow volleys, taking cover as the elven arrows rained down death from above. The elvish host invaded their outer defences and Bruh looked over his shoulder as the west end of Grishtan went up in flames. There was chaos in the squalid streets as orcs retreated from the forces of Gilan; silver-haired archers picked off orcish deserters one by one with deadly accuracy and their swordsmen engaged those who stood their ground, slaughtering them by the dozens without effort.

Running through the streets, dodging orcs, elves, and arrows alike, Bear made his way northeast towards the stables where his warg mount was kept during his stay in the sqal. Rape and looting raged rampant in the anarchy of the collapse of their society even as the orcs raced to the frontline to respond to the call to arms. Those already on the frontlines were quickly realising the hopelessness of their resistance; they turned and fled from the superior might of Gilan's armies. The western half of the town was engulfed in chaos as the elves pushed deeper into the heart of Grishtan whilst their fires steadily devoured the orc settlement. Bear turned his back on the surrounding anarchy and fought his way to the northeast quarter of the sqal where his warg mount was currently held up in the dilapidated stables.

Taking cover under the thatched roofs and shabby structures that lined the streets of Grishtan on either side, Bruh struggled to navigate the convoluted mess in his desperation to escape. A scream went up amongst the orcish residents of the town as an explosion erupted a few streets away from Bear's position. Looking up over the rooftops that lined the street he found himself running down, Bruh caught a glimpse of Grishtan's guaka-guaka refinery even as the massive structure came crashing down. The giant furnace at the base of the towering chimney belched forth jets of fire and chain explosions erupted all throughout the massive construct as it fell to the might of the elves. Before its destruction, the refinery had been a great towering chimney that stood a respectable twenty meters tall with a factory-furnace serving as the base for the foundation of the device.

The wreckage was covered in a smoggy cloud of burning debris. Fuel that had previously fed the fires of the refinery's furnace birthed a raging inferno that quickly spread throughout the heart of the sqal. Though his warg mount was probably shaking with fear within the temporary safety of the orc stable, Bruh was sure the beast had found a way to escape its reins if it hadn't already. Even as the thought entered into his head, the orcish drug dealer spotted several wargs and other beasts running amok in the streets. They charged through the crowds, biting and snatching up any who crossed their path as they joined in the frenzied chaos of the orcs. Diverting from his current path, Bear clambered atop the roof of an orc structure. A pack of rabid wargs ploughed through the masses of Grishtan's residents even as they fled from the elves who were hot on their heels. The crowds of orc soldiers and deserters jumped out of the way as the demonic wolves rushed towards the elves to devour them in their frenzied bloodlust.

Bruh witnessed the whole ordeal from the rooftops above as he tried to make his way back around south before bearing west, behind the advancing elf host. From his elevated position, Bear could see the full extent to which the elves assailed them. The western half of the sqal was already beginning to smoulder as the flames died down with nothing left to burn, spreading east to devour what was left of the orcish settlement. The drug-peddler covered his mouth and nose with his left arm, clutching his right shoulder to keep his grip tight, as he charged squinting through the soot, ash, and smoke that lingered over the devastated streets. The filthy smog filled the air, blanketing the wreckage in a putrid cloud of darkness. The smoke stung his eyes and burned in his lungs with each breath he took as he ran across the rooftops towards the slums in the southwest quarter.

A splintering crack erupted and Bear felt himself fall through the ramshackle roof even as he landed on it, leaping across a small gap between two adjacent structures. He fell through the ceiling and crashed through the second floor before breaking his fall upon the debris on the ground below. Brushing himself off, the orc pushed himself to his feet and stumbled out of the building back into the streets. A volley of flaming arrows rained down from above and Bruh ducked into the safety the thatched roof once again before setting out on his journey once again. The orc ran back into the chaos of the streets and made his way through the charred ruins of the southwest slums. He headed north, running parallel to the elvish frontlines as they pushed eastward deeper into the sqal.

Dead orcs and elvish corpses littered the streets; Bear armed himself with a goblin cleaver dropped by one of his fallen brethren and made use of whatever he could scavenge from the dead to arm himself. An arrow whistled just over his head, fired by a lone silver-haired archer accompanied by a couple swordsmen. Bruh dodged out of the way of his second shot and snatched up an elvish bow from one of the nearby corpses, firing an orcish bolt in response from the fair bow he carried in his dirty grubby hands. The elvish archer caught the orc shot in his chest and crumpled to the ground as his companions charged towards Bruh in their wrath, and they were terrible to behold. Hands shaking the orc fumbled for another arrow even as the elves closed in on him.

Just in time he nocked the shot and drew the string back before firing again; he threw the bow before his shot had even landed, jumping to his feet from where he'd landed after leaping out of the way of the elf's arrow-fire. He rushed towards the other end of the street and watched even as his second shot caught one of the swordsmen in the shoulder. The elf had attempted to dodge the arrow and deflect it with his sword, though the attempt had resulted in a shaft protruding painfully from his left breast. The swordsman recovered himself and orc engaged his companion who'd already closed the remaining distance. He swung upon Bruh and the orc parried his blow with the goblin cleaver he carried. Using his free hand to stab the elf in his belly even as their swords clashed, Bear watched the elf sink to his knees in response to the low-blow the orc dealt him.

With one final swing from the cleaver he carried, Bruh dealt the killing blow that decapitated the elf-soldier's head from his body. Returning his attention to the final remain elf combatant, Bear flung the same knife he'd used to stab the other elf as a throwing knife, into the forehead of his only remaining adversary. The wounded elf's head jerked back from the force of the blade penetrating his skull and the swordsmen fell to the ground. With his enemies defeated, the drug dealer found himself once again running along streets unopposed as he made his way haphazardly through the smouldering wreckage of western Grishtan. Bruh sought out the safety of the West Gate, though even as he made for it amidst the flames and wreckage of the streets a company of elvish horsemen poured in. They came crashing through the ruined walls that only barely remained standing amidst the burnt wreckage and Bruh darted out of sight into an alley, falling back North away from the charging cavalry.

The orc desperately sought out an escape; surviving the elvish assault was the only thing he could comprehend as he witnessed the genocide of his people. He'd given up his warg for dead, he had no use or care for the ears in his purse, the guaka-guaka he carried, or even of his own fellow orcs. He could only think of himself and how he was going to get out of this whole mess before the elves stole his life away from him. Flames still burned and smoke lingered over what was left of the western half of the sqal as Bruh fled North. He encountered no opposition as he navigated the chaotic labyrinth of streets that made up the orc town, cutting through alleys as he was able. The fires that still burned blocked some roads and debris left others impassable. Bear knew the sqal well however, and he circumnavigated around the wreckage and made his way to what was left of the northern wall.

Covering his face with a rag, he kept the revolting smoke from choking him up; it was repugnant with the wretched smell of burning corpses paired with the harsh scent of burning wood. He reached the charred remains of the northern wall and clambered over a section that had splintered and given way, eaten away by the fire that blazed throughout the city. He dropped the whole of five feet to the ground after pulling himself up and over the ruined battlements. Picking himself up, Bear raced for the horizon before any elvish archers could pick him off from afar outside the sqal. Screams still pierced the air and the annihilation of his people weighed down on Bruh. He attempted to ignore the corpses of his dead kin that were scattered throughout the Northern plains, filled with arrows in their attempts to flee the massacre. There were orclings and women amongst them; he couldn't understand how the elves so easily slaughtered the innocent along with their warriors.

He kept his eyes focused on the Augen Mountains in the distance upon the horizon and ran as far as his legs would carry him for what seemed like weeks in the eternal night of that land. He ran for time beyond reckoning, at least several days on end without rest or stoppages. The sqal had burned out and over the passing days the fires died out and it was devoid of light on the southern horizon. After some time bear collapsed from exhaustion at the foot of the Augen mountains and he slept for an entire day. He could recall no dreams as he tossed and turned fitfully where he laid. When he awoke, the orc gathered his things and took an inventory of his supplies once he was ready for the day ahead. He stowed his man-skin purse, waterskin, and food supplies back into the pack and dug into his pockets for his pipe, clutching at his sack of tar.

Damn the Masters, I've lost my pipe! It must have fallen out of my pocket when I was scaling the wall! Bruh thought to himself as he frantically sought out means to smoke his dope.

Cursing himself as he desperately racked his brains for a solution to the predicament, the orc found himself on the verge of tears in his frustration. After a moment's thought, he took a small, stout, broad-bladed knife from his sleeve and dipped it in the gooey black tar. Once he had a fat glob of the resinous guaka guaka tar on the tip of his blade, the orc struck a match and held it under the blade. The tar began to hiss and sizzle as it bubbled and popped under the heat of the flame. A thin wispy black smoke began to trail from the oozy glob of tar and Bruh sucked it in even as it rose from the black bubbling wad. The tip of the blade started to blacken where the matched burned beneath it and the tar steadily oozed down the length of the knife.

    Frantically he sucked at the wispy smoke while the drug itself trickled away before his very eyes. The final drops of the substance dripped off the blade and fell upon the bare grey soil of the Gorgon wastes. Swearing aloud and screaming curses to the gods, Bruh flung the knife across the barren desolation where it clattered noisily across the wretched wastes. He sat for a while with his hands clasped behind his head, with his head between his knees, in his frustration. The orc hadn't the slightest inkling of a plan and no idea at all what he was to do after all that he'd witnessed. Desertion was a capitol offence throughout the orc country and the orc lands were steadily falling to the might of the elves. Sythin was fallen and with the loss of their sqal, so too was lost the premium guaka-guaka that grew out of those fertile farmlands. Grishtan was already a smouldering ruin and Gorgor was next in the elvish campaign; Bruh believed they even had the strength to oppose the Tuhk of Istul itself.

    The days passed by and Bruh made his way along east towards the distant light of Istul upon the horizon; it was the only visible light that he could see from his present position after the fall of Sythin and Grishtan. Around the Augen Mountains the torchlit town of Ishtan burned steadily upon the Lake Ishtan where the River Zûm ended and pooled outside the Northernmost sqal in the desolation, upon the border of the Northern Wastes. Over the passing days as Bear ambled along he began to feel the crippling effects of guaka-guaka withdrawal setting in. Without any tar to sate his cravings, the orc began to feel heavy and tired, weak, and frail. He even started to suffer debilitating pains throughout his body; his bones and muscles ached and his skin was ablaze. Icy cold pins stabbed the core of his bones and it felt as if his body was ready to shatter at a moment's notice whilst the bones themselves were like red-hoy metal coils that burned within him.

His heart was racing, beating as hard as it could to sustain him through his travels. It started out at a frantically fast pace and before long his heart had become a single vibrational hum, buzzing from within him. Time seemed to halt and the orc could feel the passing of seconds as if they were days; he began to experience intense hallucinations and lucid dreams in the withdrawal-induced state Bruh found himself in. He continued to push forward in his travels, desperately fighting off the pain and psychosis of the guaka-guaka detoxification. The effects of the guaka-guaka that plagued the drug-addicted orc only grew with each passing day and he felt himself dying in the wastes as he slowly made his way to the nearest sqal of Ishtan. It was his only hope of salvation.

One day as Bear found himself ambling along, parallel to the Augen Mountains on their easterly track, he thought he could just barely make out a gaggle of orcs gathered around some dark figure upon the ground. As he approached the distant group, Bruh identified the group for what they were; a gang of Pah'kan priests beating an injured orc where he lay upon the ground. The wounded orc was curled up in the foetal position and he attempted to ward off his aggressors blows even as they struck him. Bruh rushed towards the group as quickly as he was able in his sickly state, but before he could challenge their authority in the matter a firm hand gripped his shoulder, holding him back.

"Let it be lad," the words of his former friend and master, U'gra-hal, echoed in his head and he turned to stare into the face of his dead mentor even as the orc held Bear back. Looking closer, Bear could see that the victim of the Pah'kan assault was no less than his own father and the screams of his mother pierced the deathly silent darkness of the Gorgon night.

"What sort of devilry is this!?!" Bruh exclaimed, throwing his former master off him and charging into the midst of the orc priests who beat his father mercilessly. Even as he lunged and toppled a priest to the ground, the scene vanished before his very eyes in a wispy trail of smoke.

"You can't escape your fate." U'gra-hal's parting words lingered on the air, though he was nowhere to be seen. Bruh found himself alone, once again, in the wastes somewhere between Ishtan and Grishtan along the feet of the Augen Mountains. He was sure he'd imagined the whole affair, though he was beginning to question whether it was an illusion or merely the transition from life to death. Unsure of the remaining distance to Ishtan and how much time he had left in the world of the living, Bear resumed his journey onwards east with the knowledge that if he didn't keep on going he would most certainly die there.

CHAPTER NINE

"Bekämpfen sie zurück!" someone shouted from the frontlines as all around the undead masses closed in upon the position of the Nardic house, beneath the archway entrance into Schwarzeburg, the Black Castle of Gorgorannon.

Ulrich swung his axe into a towering elvish wraith who approached him from outside the fire's light. The fires that protected the remnants of the Nardic host from the surrounding darkness of the eternal Gorgon night still burned throughout the camp, providing them light to see the enemy who assailed them. Suddenly a cry went up from the rear and turning around, the host saw that a second host of the undead hordes of Umargathon encroached upon them from the castle courtyard behind their ranks, trapping them under the arched entrance. The zombie masses of that retched place trapped the men on both sides under the archway and they lashed out, seeking some means of an escape. Their previous encounters in their northward travels weighed heavily on the southern tribesmen.

The demonic creatures broke through their outer defences and before long the undead masses were upon them, stumbling openly and unopposed through the heart of the Nardic camp. The tribesmen slowly stopped in their efforts and yielded to the icy chills that shivered down their spines. Some dropped their weapons as they stood in place, frozen in fear. Others broke free of the curse and gave in to their terror, fleeing into the depths of the outlying darkness, only to be snatched up and devoured by the undead wraiths of that wood. Amongst the ranks of the risen dead hosts of elvish warriors from a forgotten time, some of the Nardic men recognised the familiar faces of their fallen companions, lost to the evil of the wood.

At the sight of their own slain brethren rising up against them, the remnants of the Nardic men gave up all hope as the sheer terror of it all swallowed them whole. The bloated and half-eaten corpses of the men they'd lost at sea hobbled along as they were able before dragging their living kin to the ground to devour. It was a bloody gory mess, the zombies thoughtlessly tore out their victim's intestines, ignoring the screams of the men they ate alive. Ulrich snapped out of his shock as the fallen corpses of his neighbours, Wilhelm and Sonk, ambled along towards him. Tears welled in his eyes as he realised they must have been members of the patrol that had initially discovered the undead threat. He'd seen them within the camp that night, before they'd gone to sleep, and that was how he knew. It was the only way they could have joined the listless ranks of the undead within the short span of time since he'd last seen them.

"Töten die toten*!" a shriek went up in the midst of the camp and one by one the men were woken from their reverie.

The bold shout from a fellow tribesman had shaken the shackles of fear that gripped the men of the Isles; it was enough to motivate them for one last offensive strike against their undead oppressors. Ulrich joined his fellows in the joint offensive assault as they fought to break free of the demonic entrapment. He brought his axe crashing down upon the necks of his neighbours, severing both of their heads as their ambled towards him. The corpses returned to peaceful death and Ulrich returned his attention to the fight at hand. Nardic forces broke upon the undead wall that barred them in the elegant entry hall of Castle Umargathon's outer battlements.

*Kill the dead, literal translation.

The living valiantly fought their way out of the undead mosh pit and broke free of the wall of death, into the outlying streets of the ruined elf city. Ulrich charged through the crowds of zombies alongside his fellows and those who survived the push regrouped before fleeing North away from that foul place. The demonic assault had severely depleted the remnants of the Nardic host, leaving them with less than four thousand men still in fighting condition. Their supply horses were all lost and they barely had enough provisions left to carry them to the edge of the wood. The survivors of the undead ambush fled together into the darkness of the night with no torches to guide them; elvish wraiths chased them down like rabid wolves on the hunt.

Stragglers were tackled to the ground, screaming in agony as they were eaten alive by the demonic creatures of the dark. Others ran, crashing through the growth of that wretched forest, stumbling through the brambles into the open arms of death's embrace. Those who survived the chase continued to throw themselves through the wood as they flew from the terrible hunters that followed, close behind, in pursuit of their Nardic prey. Crashing through the wood in an attempt to escape the nameless horrors of that nightmare realm behind them, the Nardic remnants fought their way through the dark for days beyond count without stopping, even after their vile foes ceased pursuit. After some time had passed them by, the men stumbled wearily until their bodies one-by-one collapsed from the immense exhaustion they suffered.

Finally the weariness took its toll upon Ulrich and his legs gave out beneath him even as he stumbled through the northern reaches of the black forest. He fell, overcome by his extreme sleep deprivation and physical exertion. A warm tingling sensation spread from the base of his skull, dripping down his spinal cord where

Ulrich laid, curled up in the foetal position. His body began to shut down under the stress he'd put it through and he gave into to the buzzing darkness as his eyelids grew heavier. He couldn't keep track of how long he slept, though to the Southerner it had only been but a passing second. When the survivors of the undead assault awakened they found that none of their kin had been spirited away, though they knew not how long they'd slept in that timeless land of darkness.

After quickly devouring what was left of their food provisions in what barely sufficed for a frugal breakfast at best, the final remnants of the Nardic host resumed their Northern march. Before setting out they rekindled their few remaining torches so as to illuminate the path on their travels in the Dead Wood and protect them for the evils of the Gorgon night. Men looked over their shoulders in fear and kept alert for any signs of trouble, straining their eyes in the paranoia that gripped each of them. Shadows darted in and out of the corners of their eyes and the fire danced eerily in that spooky forest of old. Nothing could be seen and the snapping of dead leaf and bough under their heels was the only sound to be heard all around in the muffled silence of that forsaken wood. This improved their spirits somewhat as the men ambled along on their journey; they had beaten the wood and escaped its wrath.

Some amongst their ranks even claimed they could see the wood's end not too far away; already the trees were beginning to thin out, or so it appeared. Had they known it, they were little over two-thirds of the way through the forests of former Gorgorannon. They were ignorant to this fact however, and the knowledge wouldn't strengthen their resolve or boost their morale anyhow. Walking onwards, the men continued to make their way through the withered undergrowth of the wretched woodlands, impervious to the sting of thorny brambles in the numbed and wearied state. Following the path religiously, they warily ambled along; to divert from the path meant certain death and so they followed it in a state of constant vigilance.

The men feared what foul things might be lurking in the depths of the wood, creeping and crawling along in the darkness. Pale bulbous eyes hung like lamps in the darkness around them, stalking the host and attracted by the light of their torches. A wolf howled in the distance, sending shivers down Ulrich's spine. He swore a silent curse to himself and gripped the haft of his axe firmly in his white-knuckled hand. Throughout the host, the tribes clung tightly to their shields and weapons, clutching them for dear life. They prayed silently to their gods for deliverance out of that evil wood and for protection in their travels. Ulrich muttered curses to Hasst under his breath, damning the damnable Nardic God of Death. All around Ulrich strained his ears in an attempt to drown out the prayers of his fellows.

Though the Nardic men held to their beliefs, it did little for Ulrich as he attempted to listen for any sounds of an ambush. The men droned on as they stumbled along, praying for the destruction of their enemies and safe passage through the Gorgon lands. Even as they pressed on in their journey more wolves began to howl, resonantly answering one another from every direction. Had the Nardic tribesmen been fluent in their language, they would know that the wolves were mustering their packs on the hunt for living prey. Archers nocked their arrows and the host extinguished their fires as they quickened their pace. The wolves descended upon them even as the men plunged themselves into darkness and they fled with what remaining strength they had. Arrows flew in every direction and hulking wolves yelped in pain as they toppled, crashing through the trees, as the Nardic arrows pierced their hide.

The wolves stood as tall as a man on four legs and spanned

ten feet tall when standing on two. They were like massive horses cross-bred with wolves and the hulking leviathans were great in stature and terrifying in their appearance. With claws like daggers and teeth like glass shards they came at the Nardic men and ferociously broke upon their ranks. The wargs swallowed the men up and shredded their flesh as easily as a grinder did herbs and the remnants of the Nardic host fled before their might. Those wolves were a breed that was not natural in the world of the living; they came from the very depths of *Hölle** itself. The God of Death himself had sent his wretched hounds of Hell after them, and Ulrich ran in fear for his soul. He begged Hasst for forgiveness of his blasphemy, believing this to be the divine retribution of the Gods for his blasphemy.

Ulrich instinctively flung his arm forward as a great warg lunged at him; his axe caught the beast in mid-air as it open its gaping jowls in a ravenous bloodlust. His axe crunched into the wolf's chest and it came toppling down on top of Ulrich. All around his fellows ran, ignoring him in his struggle as he fought to push the massive carcass off and regain his footing. The wargs continued to assail his kin even as they fled North and he hopelessly called out for assistance. A couple tribesmen diverted from their course to rush to his aid and they rolled the dead hound of hell off him, helping the weary Ulrich to his feet. He thanked them and staggered a ways before rejoining them in their retreat. The wargs trailed close behind and picked off stragglers as they were able, though the majority of the pack focused their attention further ahead.

---

*Hölle was believed to be the realm of Hasst, the God of Death. It was said that he kept hounds of darkness to guard the border of his realm; they were kept to prevent travel between the worlds of the living and the dead.

Even as he left the wolf-corpse behind Ulrich witnessed its body evaporating in a smoky mist that rose from its dying carcass like a soul leaving the body. Ulrich shivered at the thought of demonic hounds of hell sent by the God of Death, though in the terror of that deathly forest Ulrich truly believed anything was possible. In a state of sheer and utter terror Ulrich charged forth into the night, trailing a ways behind the bulk of their people alongside the men who'd helped him to his feet. Together the trio raced behind the creams of death that pierced the night all around them. Sounds of resistance intermingled with the death cries; arrows whistled and the sound of whimpering wargs as they laid dying also filled the air and Ulrich took joy in it. Hundreds of demon wargs crashed through the woods on the hunt for the Nardic tribesmen, and they numbered far too few to match the terrible foes in combat.

Demonic wraiths joined them and rode upon the backs of the wargs that came pouring in to join the vile hunters in their pursuit. Ulrich dodged out of the way as a wraith-rider snatched one of his companions, dragging the screaming man into the depths of the darkness to devour his soul. Hounds and reapers chased the men down and they cowered before their unholy might. Ulrich managed to catch up to the rearguard of the host, though in reality they were no more than stragglers in the midst of a full-scale retreat. The wolves and their riders hunted the men down like rabbits; those who found themselves unfortunate enough to be tackled to the ground or snatched up the the wraiths died gruesome deaths. Ulrich hacked and slashed his way through the brambles that obscured his path and swung his axe aimlessly in the sheer terror that engulfed him. They seemed to grab at the Southerner like the cold dead hands of death and he fought as hard as he could against the twisted growth.

Time seemed eternal and the men saw no hope of escape; they ran four what seemed like years. Their bodies knew no hunger, pain, or weariness as they instinctively continued to run. Escape was all that they knew, and the men fought for it with every last fibre of their being. Finally, after some time the trees truly did begin to thin out and the men actually could see the wood's end as they pushed themselves to their limits. The frontline had already cleared the forest and ran joyously across the southern plains of the Gorgon Desolation. Ulrich threw his axe at a wolf-rider even as the creature swung in his saddle to grab the Nardic warrior and his axe bit into the muscle and tissue of the demonic manifestation. He hadn't broken his pace throughout the exchange and Ulrich hopped over the wraith even as it evaporated back into darkness. Breaking free of the treeline, Ulrich lunged for the ground as a warg leapt upon him. The beast tackled him to the ground, disintegrating even as it dragged him down. The Dead Wood's curse had no power beyond the borders of its domain, or so it seemed to the Nardic man as he picked himself up once again.

With their victory against the Dead Wood the men rejoiced for a moment before they fell back into despair. They mourned the loss of their friends and country men, the supply horses, their food and ale, but most importantly for their families. Each man present knew in his heart that none amongst them would ever see their homeland of Dusseldorf again in their waking lives. The survivors of the plight enjoyed their brief relief from the accursed demonic assaults that constantly plagued them, resting on the barren fields of the orc lands for some time before resuming their travels. The men had no supplies to make camp and so they simply laid with arms folded behind their heads as they slept on their backs upon the bare grey soil of the desolate Gorgon plains.

Ulrich felt his stomach grumbling and he tried to recall exactly how long it had been since the last time he'd truly eaten. It was no use; he couldn't even keep track of the countless weeks they'd spent traversing the sickly forest behind them. Ulrich gladly welcomed the warm embrace of sleep and he let it seep through his body whilst a rotating watch kept guard over the remnants of their people. When he awoke the tribesmen were talking amongst themselves of the course of their travels. To their right, the Iron Teeth Mountains loomed not far away on the horizon, not far behind behind the tiny pinprick of light that was Gregor. Though the mountains were visible on the eastern horizon, they were still a decent ways away from the sqal of Gregor. The Nardic men weren't even sure if they were fit enough to wage war against the orcs of that land after the casualties they'd already suffered up to that moment, though they prepared for their eastern march towards the sqal nonetheless.

CHAPTER TEN
ISTUL, GORGON DESOLATION
Summer, 1E196

The cramped and crowded streets of the Market District were teeming with orcs and the city was bustling with activity like the inside of an ant mound. It was just another day of life in the malignant Gorgon capitol. Orcs walked to and fro between the many shops, stalls, and vendors that littered those streets, ignoring the buskers and beggars where they sat on the sides of the road dejectedly. Merchants bought, sold, and traded their wares openly with the orc masses who filled those cramped and squalid streets. The masses made their way through the streets between the many military checkpoints scattered throughout Istul. The city was divided into four districts, each divided by ringed walls under the constant watch of orcish guards.

The Tuhk stood malignantly tall in the heart of the circular city, stretching above the blanket of black smoke that covered those hands as it reached for the heavens above. Serving as the base of the Tuhk's citadel, the Church of the Masters was the innermost district. Its courtyards stretched to the foot of the 75-meter tall battlements that surrounded the holy gardens of the Pah'kan Priesthood. Outside the Church District were the barracks, armouries, and arms factories that made up the Military District of the Tuhk; fifty-meter walls spanned their perimeter, followed by the Marketplace under the protection of a 30 meter parapet. The final outermost district was known as the Slums of Istul, comprised of ramshackle living quarters. The buildings of its residents were a convoluted mess of towering skyscrapers that swayed as they stood, haphazardly stacked atop one another in an effort to save space.

The city that surrounded the monstrous Tuhk of Istul was liken to a favela, or shanty town, and it was a sprawling mess under constant construction. Housing complexes were no more that buildings stacked atop one another until they were too unsafe to add on to, leaning towers with highrise walkways to connect them in a futile attempt at improving their stability. Occasionally the towering structures of the orcs would collapse under their own weight. The dilapidated constructs were not structurally sound and the houses they piled atop one another would sometimes come raining down in an avalanche. The debris would come crashing into the neighbouring highrises in a domino-effect of destruction; this phenomenon was commonplace in the orc capitol and it was no more uncommon to the residents of Istul than a mild thunderstorm was in the midst of heavy rains. Although the casualties were also countless, it barely made an impact on their day-to-day lives and generally went unnoticed except in extreme circumstances.

G'hnak weaved his way in and out of the bustling crowds of orcs who filled the busy streets of the Market District. The orcish masses flowed like a river and the young orc struggled to fight the currents that dragged him off his course. G'hnak was 14 years old, one of the many sons of a minor Slumlord, and he made his living as a smuggler. It was an exaggerated job title for the petty thief that he was; the young orcling was an albino native of Istul, having spent the entirety of his life within its walled safety. He stood five feet tall and his build was relatively average given his age. His pale eyes scanned the crowds for any patrols or guards who might spot him out; the luminescent bulbous eyes of his kind were well-adapted to the darkness of the Gorgon night,. Those orcs whose families had lived under the darkness of the heartlands for generations had grown accustomed to their surroundings and adapted to the change, better suiting their needs.

G'hnak made his way west towards the Southwest entrance into the Military District, making his way through the crowds and cutting into alleys as he was able. Taking a stairway up to the rooftops above, G'hnak followed a sky-rise walkway directly southwest a ways before turning right at a ninety degree angle to span the remaining distance along the length of the intersecting highrise walk. He ran openly hundreds of feet above the ground and the towering structures surrounding him passed the orc by as he closed the distance between himself and his destination. The orcish guards and soldiers of the Tuhk didn't patrol the highrise walkways or smugglers paths, simply for the fact that there were far too many for their manpower, though they occasionally took the routes themselves to cut the length of their travels. This did not prove the case as G'hnak ran unopposed down that rooftop highway in the sky.

He slowed his pace before leaping from that walkway, hundreds of feet in the sky, as he lunged for a cable that ran from a beam up above all the way down to the ground below. The beam was a cast-iron pipe that provided sewage for the surrounding apartment block of towers around him, it ran between two buildings and held the cable firm as G'hnak slid down the length of it. His leather gloves hissed and sizzled as the cable wore away at them in his descent and the ground rushed forth to meet him. Once his feet made firm contact with the solid ground beneath them, the young orc was off running once again. He reached the high street that ran from the mouth of the Military District entrance directly southwest where it forked in a two-way intersection nearly a mile away. It was a road filled with premium food stalls and stores.

Vendors waved their bundles of man and elf flesh for sale to the masses; there was no foul warg meat, carrion, or putrid vegetation amongst the wares of the upper-class food sellers. They only sold the finest human and elf meat, though man-flesh was rare in the Gorgon Desolation. Their only supply came from the goblin slavers in the North; the fell creatures of the Northern Wastes were locked in a bitter war with the peoples of the West. Occasionally the goblins that took residence in the ruins of the Necromancers found success in capturing the men and elves who fought back the Northern legions, though the men were a prized delicacy where their meat was sold in Istul. G'hnak found his mark with little difficulty; an unattended stall in the heart of some rather chaotic traffic where the vendor himself was chasing down passerby in an attempt to sell his stock.

Approaching the absent merchant's stall, G'hnak helped himself to several bundles of man-flesh before turning and fleeing from the scene of his crime. The infuriated butcher shouted after the orcling calling out accusations after the young thief even as he chased him. Alerted to the criminal offence that had just taken place, guards were snapped from their impassive sentry duty to take part in a full-on pursuit of the suspect in question. G'hnak didn't look over his shoulder once as he frantically pushed his way through the bustling crowds. The vendor had realised far too late what G'hnak had done and the shouts of the city watch receded in the distance as he successfully evaded their wrath.

Had they caught him, G'hnak would be facing a Pah'kan tribunal in the courtyard of the Church, where he would be convicted of theft. The punishment for theft was decapitation and the Priesthood was merciless when it came to the conviction of slum dwellers. G'hnak ran with all of his might, clutching the stolen meat tight to his chest with the hands he sought so desperately to protect from the swift justice of Pah'kan blades. He dodged in and out of alleys and smugglers routes that cut through the rooftops in his attempt to throw off any pursuers. He found a ladder leading to a highrise walk and ascended high up above the city streets. Reaching the top, he found himself on a platform between two rope bridges going in opposite directions.

    The bridge behind him stretched due west whilst ahead its opposite followed an easterly path. He followed it east towards the Southeast Gate, back into the Slums; the only home he'd ever known. Making his descent, G'hnak scrambled across the roof of a five-floor apartment complex and leapt. He cleared the gap between it and an adjoining open-walled smoke-house* even as the edges of the housing complex began to crumble beneath him. He broke his fall with a barrel roll, tumbling in a crash of noise as tables and chairs yielded to his mass. The gathered smokers were aroused in an uproar of shouts as G'hnak continued on his way even as guards raced to apprehend him. He sprinted past the bewildered guaka-guaka connoisseurs and leapt to the safety of single- and two-floor shops before making his way back to ground level. He blended into the flow of traffic and hid his prize beneath his ragged clothes. The shouts of the guards were drowned out as he put distance between them in his travels to the Southeast Checkpoint.

*In the orc lands, smoke-houses were generally open-walled structures if they were multi-story or single-floor open-roofed longhouses in the sqals outside Istul. The orcs would go there to smoke tar and socialise; orcish smoke-houses were similar in function to the bars of Western men. Most smoke houses usually carried a good selection of various blends.

Making his way into an abandoned cul-de-sac in the back alleys, G'hnak slid down the ladder that led from an open mouth into the sewers beneath the city streets. Navigating through the underground labyrinth, G'hnak made his way back to the familiar surroundings of outer Slum District. Keeping an eye out for the raiders and marauders who would surely rob and slaughter the young orc for the goods he carried, G'hnak cautiously crept through the sprawling ghetto that was the Slum District of Istul. He sought out a *gûk*, a blackmarket dealer of stolen wares, to sell his score in exchange for ears. Though he could feast for weeks like a wealthy orc lord with what he carried, G'hnak knew it was much more profitable to sell the goods, even if only for a fraction of what they were worth.

Dilapidated shacks and provisional housing crowded the hectic streets of the slums and orcs gathered around camp fires even as they slept in the road. The slums were poverty-stricken and over populated; disease was rampant amongst the slum dwellers. G'hnak ignored the moans of the sickly and homeless masses of peasantry and made his way to the gûk whom he normally conducted his business with, in the heart of the Northeast Quarter of the sprawling urban orcish ghetto. His father laid claim to a minor territory outside the South Gate; his clan of bandits made a living through robbing lone travellers who entered the city without protection. The young orc thief made his way as quickly as he could, skirting out of the attention of the slum dwellers in his efforts to remain unnoticed.

As he cut through an abandoned alley, he turned the corner to find two orcs up ahead, leaning menacingly against the wall of a building in the distance. G'hnak skidded to a halt though it was already too late; he'd already caught their sinister stare. He could feel their unfriendly eyes boring into his very soul as he cautiously walked along through that forlorn alleyway. Turning onto another back-road as soon as the opportunity presented itself, G'hnak quickened his pace. He raced down the intersecting alleyway only to stumble upon a great big raider wielding a bent lead pipe for use as a makeshift club. Behind him the malicious orc pair from before blocked off any chance of escape while bandits and raiders came crawling down the walls of the surrounding orcish highrises by the dozens.

Turning around, G'hnak attempt to flee, though much to his displeasure he found his way barred by the pair of orcs from before. He dived and slid beneath them before jumping back to a running sprint, bolting down the alley and clutching to his stolen goods for dear life. During his slide-tackle manoeuvre the orc had managed to sprain his ankle and he winced as he continued to run, ignoring the pain to the best of his ability given the circumstances. The slum bandits chased after him, brandishing their provisional weapons as they hunted the orcling thief down for his expensive loot. Slum dwellers were generally unable to afford true arms and armour, though they often used debris and the bones of their enemies to craft deadly weapons in their own right.

In order to make a living, the majority of the slum's residents stole, smuggled, or killed; those were the only means of getting by in the sprawling ghetto outside Istul's walls. The slums were encircled by a fifteen meter wall, crudely constructed out of whatever materials they could scavenge, compared to the towering stone battlements of the inner-city. Theft and trade were the only ways to provide the means for a better life within that ghetto; left to their own devices the slum's residents would have starved to death long ago. They had no resources, no products, vendors, shops, factories or jobs; just a sprawling mess of housing and the populace who inhabited them. The slum dwellers were tribal cannibals who fought amongst themselves for food, glory, and other useful commodities.

G'hnak sought to protect his own valuable commodities as he fled for his life from raiders armed with shivs, clubs, and other makeshift weapons as they were able to salvage from the slum-debris. More and more slum dwellers joined into the chase as G'hnak ran, crashing through the tight convoluted streets. In his haste, the young orc found himself barely making some of the various twists and turns between the dilapidated alleys. They were like halls that intersected the crude monstrosities that were their highrise housing complexes, and the cut-throughs were sometimes easy to miss even in the best of times. Suddenly the scraps of tin plating that made up the second floor wall of a building ahead burst forth in an explosive avalanche as the surrounding structure began to come crashing down; an orc had leapt through the wall to lunge at G'hnak even as he fled.

Dodging his assailant, G'hnak turned into another alleyway and ran North as quickly as he could before the structural integrity of the surrounding constructions gave way. Even as he sought to escape the impeding demolition of the neighbourhood, the buildings were already beginning to collapse and crash into one another. Wreckage blocked some of the streets and smoke was already beginning to fill the air as the foundations of their towering skyscrapers caved in upon themselves, bringing their constructs crashing down. G'hnak ran for his life, no longer worried about the raiders who gave up the chase at the realisation of their present danger. Fires and smoke filled the streets and G'hnak ran through it all, coughing up phlegm and choking as the smoke and dust filled his lungs. He pushed himself beyond his exhaustion; his legs were ready to buckle beneath him and his lungs were on the verge of bursting. Still he ran on, straining himself past his limits in the midst of the destruction that surrounded him. The deafening roar of it all engulfed him and his ears rang from the sheer volume of the noise. Breaking free of the soot and debris that clouded the air, G'hnak gasped for breath as he escaped the devastation behind him to the South.

CHAPTER ELEVEN

Ambling along in a wretched state through the wastes, Bear fought off the debilitating effects of his drug addiction. It had been weeks since Bruh last smoked the sickly tar, though he managed to plough through the vast expanse of nothingness nonetheless. He had no idea how long it had been since the Fall of Grishtan and he was beginning to lose hope that he would make it in those wastelands. One day he saw the distant light of Ishtan on the horizon and he couldn't believe his eyes, at least not until he was standing outside its battlements and passing under the entrance. He found himself passing through the haphazard mess of streets and highways wearily on his trek to the marketplace. He stumbled and tripped before the vendor even as he reached for his purse.

Ears fell about on the bare streets and orclings and petty thieves alike raced to snatch up his monies. Bear warded their blows as they beat him whilst he sought to recover himself; the merchant fought them back as well though he tried his best to remain impassive in the affair, lest they rob him too. Crawling away from the scavengers who scrambled to profit at his expense, Bruh drag himself to the feet of a nearby pipe vendor and handed the bewildered merchant a handful of ears. He snatched the pipe out of the merchant's hand even as the orc offered it. Packing the bowl with all that was left of his Sythic tar, Bruh lit his new pipe and inhaled the first hit over several deep drags. The tar bubbled and sizzled as a red cherry steadily spread across the black glob whilst Bear puffed away until it cached.

Tapping the ashes out, he packed the pipe again with some of his spare supply. It was a lower quality resin, grown out of Gorgor and synthesised in the local refinery. Getting high was the only thought present in his mind. His surroundings faded out as he continued to blaze the bubbling resin pack, refilling the bowl as needed. Once he was recovered, Bear brushed himself off before rising to his feet to buy supplies. He hadn't gone unrecognised after the commotion however, and he quickly found himself the target of the Thru'ahkuk Huang. A thief suddenly struck him from behind, knocking him to the ground where he was assailed by a gang of the petty robbers.

They knew Bruh for being the famous dope peddler that he was, seeing him in his weakened state the fledging members couldn't help but cash in on kicking him when he was down. The Thieves Guild of Ishtan waged and endless war upon the merchants and Bruh's death would prove highly profitable to the thief or thieves who took him down. Swooping in like vultures they beat him mercilessly; he was stabbed several times by a shiv and even broke a rib or two in the thrashing he received. Merchants and vendors raced to Bear's aid and fought off his assailants as they called out for help. Ishtan's warriors heard the cries and, after seeing a handful of orcs dragging the half-dead body of Bear away from the scene of the crime, decided to take up arms against the Thru'ahkuk Huang.

A small contingent of merchant fighters joined the ranks of Ishtan's soldiers as they set themselves loose upon the thieves and filth of their sqal. Meanwhile, the nearby merchants dragged Bruh away to safety whilst the city guard fought back the legions of Thru'ahkuk Huang, who were taking to the streets in an act of open hostility. There was chaos in the high street that ran through the sqal as the soldiers of Ishtan were met with resistance by the thieves of that city. Thieves fired arrows openly upon the ranks of charging orcs and the warriors fell to the foul shots. Those who survived broke upon the fleeing archers and hacked them down as they ran. Arrows pelted the small group of merchants who carried Bruh away and they dodged the deadly bolts even as a company of soldiers raced to support them. Coughing up blood, Bruh faded in and out of consciousness whilst merchants and warriors escorted him to safety. The last thing he remembered before everything went black was a platoon of orcish warriors racing by in the opposite direction as they made for the heart of the chaos amidst the insurrection...

Over the passing days, orcish shamans tended to Bear's injuries within the safety of a warehouse the merchants had converted into a temporary hideout. The sqal had been torn apart by a civil war that violently raged between the Thieves Guild, merchants, and warriors of Ishtan. After the incident in the streets, the Thru'ahkuk Huang had sent out their finest bounty hunters to seek out the infamous dope peddler and bring back his head as a trophy. There was a lavish reward for his head, offered up from the vast fortunes of their acquired wealth as an underground network of thieves, and there were few who could resist the promised prize. Ishtan's residents rose up against the warriors who protected and oppressed them in a bid for wealth beyond their wildest dreams.

It was for this reason that the merchants of Ishtan spirited Bruh away and sought to protect him whilst the healers did what they could. Once he was recovered and well again, Bear told his nearby comrades the news of Grishtan in the West. They were gobsmacked by the news of the fall of the two biggest sqals; they made up the Slaver's Highway and their destruction would prove a fatal blow to the orcish empire. With the fall of Sythin their guaka-guaka production would be crippled; along with the loss of their primary slave route, the orcish legions had been greatly weakened by the elves of Gilan.

At his bidding, the gathered merchants attempted to account for the two weeks that Bear had been incapacitated. Whilst he'd been stowed away in a cramped storeroom with shamans, healers, and a handful of merchants, the Thieves Guild had extended their dominance throughout the sqal. The soldiers of Ishtan were at their mercy and the orcish masses themselves had risen up in the hopes of promised riches. The whole city was engulfed in chaos in the midst of a full-blown manhunt for Bear's head. After the Thru'ahkuk Huang assault, the Pah'kan Council of Ishtan declared a war upon the Thieves Guild in the name of the Masters, requesting reinforcements from Istul in the wake of a holy war that threatened to devour their sqal.

There was a price upon Bruh's head, along with anyone caught harbouring or assisting him. Thieves systematically raided the homes of Ishtan's residents and tore the sqal apart in their search for the drug dealer, though none could find him as hard as they tried. Soldiers futilely fought back the flashmob waves of Thru'ahkuk Huang assaults as the orcish thugs fought for control of the outpost. Anarchy reigned in the streets and chaos spread like wildfire as orcs killed each other indiscriminately in the mass disorder that engulfed them. The Merchant's Guild had already begun the preparations for transporting Ishtan's guaka-guaka reserves to the capitol in the midst of the insurrection. Where the Thru'ahkuk Huang had grown too powerful within the sqal, they sent a convoy to deliver their stores of the widely sought after tar; it would be safe in the great Storeroom within the Tuhk of the Masters in Istul. The merchants of Ishtan were afraid that the Thru'ahkuk Huang would steal their stockpiles of the drug in the heat of the chaos. They had grown powerful where the underground network of thieves had been allowed to reign unopposed for some time; now they were an unstoppable force that threatened to swallow the city whole.

"Well, if all that's left is *guap** then we might as well follow the tar to the capitol." Bruh firmly stated in response to all that he was told.

"What!?! The elves match upon the Tuhk and you would have us walk into the eye of the storm? This is the beginning of the end and there is nothing that can be done to quell the evil that rises against us!" one of the five merchants present replied; a fat second-hand sword vendor whose wares were of poor quality at an extortionate price.

"Our people have damned themselves! Though we might escape with our lives, what would be the point if we spend the remainder of them in miserable poverty?" Bruh answered.

---

*A poorer quality tar that was comprised of the resin from recycle pipe filters. Used filters were recycled in the major refineries and the resin was extracted for use as a cheap substitute for addicts.

"What exactly are you suggesting Bruh?" a rival guaka-guaka peddler questioned, openly suspicious of his competitor. It didn't help that the rival dealer was a goblin* either, which only further fuelled his dislike of the orc before him.

"We are faced with the extinction of our race; the elves are going to march upon Istul and it will fall before them. Why then should we not profit from our own destruction? Let us storm the Tuhk with the element of surprise and steal their stores of premium tar for ourselves!" Bear exclaimed in the company of his fellow conspirators. At his exclamation they all eagerly drew in close around him, even the goblin dealer who'd previously been wary of the orc.

"What of the Masters?" H'gruak, the fat sword vendor, spoke up shakily.

"Nevermind the Masters; what of Ishtan? The Thru'ahkuk Huang have taken the sqal for themselves and it's only a matter of time before we're found out!" U'gro-sha'kal, an armourer, shot him down before Bruh even had a chance to reply.

---

*The goblins had never forgiven the orcs for their enslavement in the times of Myth before their liberation during the Gurka-zurgh'aught, or the Goblin Uprising in the Common Tongue. Goblins were wary of the orcs and maintained an intense distrust of their provisional alliance, along with a burning resentment towards the Masters.

"Where were the Masters at Sythin or Grishtan? As for our current predicament, I didn't realise we had any options outside of escaping the confines of this sqal that imprisons us or awaiting our impending deaths at the hands of the Thru'ahkuk Huang." Bear replied coolly.

So it was that the five merchants convened with Bruh in the safety of a merchant's warehouse. The storage facility belonged to D'hak-tal, a small Ishtan-based arms dealer. He owned three warehouses throughout the sqal along with two stores within the inner-city. The depot where they took refuge was situated in the eastern industrial hal of Ishtan where the smithies and refineries were predominantly based. Together the gathered traders spoke amongst themselves of what was to be done prior to their departure as well as upon their arrival in Istul. When they were finally satisfied with their plans the gang prepared to depart.

Arming themselves with the wares of the merchant's storehouse, they equipped themselves appropriately for the dangers they would face outside. D'hak-tal and the goblin, V'rznk, armed themselves with crude crossbows whilst Bruh and U'gra-sha'kal took up goblin cleavers. H'gruak chose a great warhammer for himself to match his stature and the other merchant present, an orc by the name of L'hu, took up a barbed spear and spiked rectangular shield. Together, they departed from the safety of their warehouse hideout and charged forth into the open warfare that was tearing the sqal apart. The clash of steel and cries of death echoed in the streets and the sqal was plunged into disorder in the midst of the fighting. The bulk of the battle raged on in the eastern industrial districts as well as the marketplace in the south.

The thunderous noise of death and destruction boomed all around, polluting the silence in a cacophony of sound. Though Bear was not yet fully recovered, he ran alongside his companions nonetheless, brandishing his goblin cleaver as they raced through the streets. They darted in and out of arrow fire from both sides and dodged the combatants as they navigated the sprawling mess that was the sqal of Ishtan. Upon bursting out of the safety of their provisional refuge, the gang sought cover from the arrow volleys that seeming came from all all directions. The party ducked into the collapsed remains of a three-floor apartment complex and took shelter from the arrows in the debris. Bear clambered up the caved-in ceiling of the first floor and followed his companions as they made their way to the rooftops above.

Though they were relatively close to the ground, the gang took advantage of their elevated position and sought the least populated path they could on a north-easterly course towards Ishtan's farmlands. It consisted predominantly of guaka-guaka grow houses and a few farms that grew the sickly vegetation that served as a substitute for meat in those lands. The population of Ishtan's northeastern farmlands was relatively low-density in comparison to the other districts of the sqal. Although it was out of their way, the party would safely make their way to Istul via the North Gate, a much safer route than travelling directly East through the sqal's warring masses. The orc L'hu caught an arrow in the large shield he carried and another bolt of the same volley brought D'hak-tal crashing down to the ground below.

None of the present company had time to mourn the loss of their companion and they ran on without D'hak-tal's company, leaving his corpse in the streets where it lay as they continued to make their way across the rooftops above. Arrows continued to pelt them and bounce harmlessly off the shingled rooftops they spanned.

Soldiers and thieves fought in the streets below and they fled North in their attempt to avoid the conflict entirely. Two thieves sought to prevent that however, climbing the buildings up ahead to bar their way. Bruh lunged at them and swung his cleaver in mid-air, slicing their throats before breaking his fall with a roll. He landed badly on his ankle and toppled off the side of the roof, falling two floors to the ground below. The others continued to run and they called out to him as he ran alongside them from the streets.

He had a bad limp and it was good that they were reaching the outskirts of the action; he dodged out of the attention of combatants by cutting through the back alleys as he made for a rendezvous point to regroup with his fellows. The other merchants made the descent to ground level and they gave Bear some brief medical treatment before returning to their quest. A crude splint and a longsword that served as a crutch would have to make due for the wounded drug-peddler as he ambled along beside them. He attempted to keep up with them, though after some time they diverted from their course to the stables, where they sought out warg mounts to take them to Istul. Bear wasn't nearly as fit to travel as he'd thought, but there was no time for rest or recovery in the midst of Ishtan's civil uprising.

Fleeing into a nearby alley that ran west, they followed the path through the residential neighbourhoods of the North. A handful of thieves cut their party off further ahead and more joined them from behind. Before they knew it, a dozen mercenaries of the Thru'ahkuk Huang were upon their band and Bear was quickly spotted out amongst them. The thieves shouted out to any allies in the area that they'd spotted Bruh and called out for assistance. Others ran forward and engaged the gang of merchant fighters, though they were hacked down by goblin cleavers or shot dead by V'rznk's crossbow. Three dead thieves laid before them and more were beginning to pour in from behind. Bear decapitated another thief even as the orc challenged him and joined his companions as they cut through a back road onto the Northern Highway that led to the gate not far way.

Thieves, assassins, and mercenaries chased them from not far behind and Bruh ambling along as he desperately sought to keep up with his companions. H'gruak cast aside his great warhammer and scooped Bruh in his arms; though he was rather large for an orc, Bear was like a child in the large sword vendor's arms. Together the merchants ran with all due haste towards the stables, even as the legions of the Thru'ahkuk Huang amassed not far behind, closing in upon them. L'hu cried out and Bruh saw from where he was cradled in H'gruak's massive arms as an arrow pierced the trader's unprotected back. He flung up his arms as he crumpled to the ground, a shaft protruding from the nape of his neck.

H'gruak barrelled through the stable entrance, splitting the door as he crashed through, and he threw Bear in the saddle of a warg before slapping its flank and setting it loose. Looking over his shoulder, Bruh saw H'gruak mount his own warg, followed by V'rznk and U'gra-sha'kal. Together, the four warg riders charged through the streets and flew through the North Gate out into the wastes. From there they took an easterly course, out into the depths of the Gorgon night towards the distant light of Istul upon the horizon, away from the chaos that engulfed Ishtan behind them. With the clamorous sounds of rioting and insurrection shrinking back, the pack of traders made their way East to the capitol.

CHAPTER TWELVE
GREGOR, GORGON DESOLATION
Winter, 1E195

With the woods behind them, the survivors of the Nardic host set out with a fresh outlook on the war and a renewed sense of hope. It had been a year since they'd set out on that accursed voyage, though still men stood amidst their ranks. Ulrich marched in tow alongside the fellow remnants of the Nardic expedition, keeping an eye out for anything unusual whilst he remained prepared for the worst. They made their way West across the desolate southern plains towards Gregor where they would ransack the rural orc settlement and raze it to the ground. Though his fellow tribesmen believed they were the superior few who managed to successfully thwart the evil of the Dead Wood, Ulrich was not so bold. He held to his wariness, believing that the foul forest behind them was only the introduction to greater evils within the heartlands of that wretched orc country.

A prickling sensation began to occur at the nape of Ulrich's neck as if something were watching him from afar and he took heed of his growing suspicion. Though he looked around as far as he was able and even strained his eyes upon the listless plains of darkness upon the horizon in every direction, he couldn't catch any signs or presence of life in that place. He couldn't shake the feeling that beset him and it only grew worse with each step he took. *Maybe it is no more than fear or even anticipation of the upcoming battle,* the tribesman reasoned with himself. When the feeling had finally become unbearable he stopped and spun around, only to collide with the bewildered companion who marched behind him. They fell upon each other, causing a commotion with the Nardic ranks.

"*Verpiss dich!* What has come over you!?!" Varg exclaimed as he attempted to regain his footing after crashing into Ulrich.

"It's nothing, my mistake." Ulrich mumbled as he brushed himself off.

Varg had fallen on top of him and a couple others had stumbled over the pair and it had caused a stoppage throughout the host. All eyes were on Ulrich and the embarrassment only added to his headache. He walked with his eyes towards the ground for the remainder of the day and was withdrawn for the duration of the day's march. Over the passing days, they drew closer to the sqal, and Ulrich's unease let up. They weren't far from the settlement of Gregor; already they were beginning to reach the outlying farmlands. The tired and weary survivors of the Nardic host stumbled across a vast expanse of brackish thorny growth, coated in a black grime.

Round mud huts dotted the fields of black resinous growth that the Nardic host traversed on their easterly march and they encountered more than a few orcs in their travels. The archers made little work of the orcish farmers and they allowed none to escape their wrath, lest the fleeing orcs alert their kin to the approaching threat. Torches dotted the farmlands, providing some illumination throughout the outlying area surrounding Gregor. The tribesmen made sure to steer clear from the fire's light, keeping to the shadows instead for fear of being seen. Cautiously creeping through the repugnant fields of vegetation, the Nardic men stealthily made their way through the outer reaches of Gregor, picking off the workers in the fields who tended to and harvested the wretched crops. There were sentries amongst the vegetation as well and the men were careful to eliminate them without drawing attention to themselves or causing a disturbance.

As they neared the outer battlements of the sqal, the Nardic host halted and took rest. There were some surviving officers amongst their ranks who took charge as leaders and plotted their course of action in the impeding assault. Consulting their maps provided by the elves, they planned out their assault and the positioning of their troops prior to engagement as well as upon entry. All together they barely made up a brigade, though of their original force they were but the leftover scraps of a mighty army. It was for this reason that they plotted a tactical assault against the rural orcish settlement. Their forces were equally matched and so the Nardic men would take them by surprise.

The leaders returned to their rag-tag companies and gave them their orders; Ulrich fell into formation and joined his companions as the host broke up into smaller ten-man squads. Together they would each make their way into the outskirts of the farming town and weave their way through the thick fields of sickly vegetation before mounting their assault. Each squad was acting independently from the main host whilst they simultaneously made their way into the heart of the town from all sides. Ulrich followed his squadmates to their designated position and waited for the rest of the host to fall into place before proceeding. The Nardic host encircled Gregor outside the perimeter of the sqal's watch fires and awaited the signal to strike. Anxiously anticipating the assault, Ulrich was stirred from his thoughtful state by the command to advance.

Alongside his squadmates Ulrich advanced upon the sqal, sticking to the darkness and extinguishing torches as they were able. Quickly making their way to the dilapidated remains of the outer battlements, Ulrich and his companions stacked up against the ruins of Gregor's perimeter wall. Some parts of the wall were missing entirely or rotten and the makeshift fence provided no safety against an invasive assault whatsoever. All around the tribesmen fell against the dilapidated remains of the outer wall whilst the archer companies led the advance. The outskirts of the sqal ahead of them were made up of a series of convoluted streets and back roads that cut and intersected one another haphazardly throughout the decrepit remains of the southernmost orc outpost. It was built out of the wretched wood of the trees gathered from the Dead Wood long ago and torches lined the streets, providing its residents with light to see in the eternal darkness of the Gorgon night.

Ulrich and his fellows trailed closely behind and advancing archer company and they stealthily pushed forward. Following the back alley path they made their way into the heart of the sqal; archers took out any orcs they came across stealthily whilst the infantry continued their silent invasion of the sqal unnoticed and unhindered. From somewhere in the west, on the other end of the sqal, an alarm sounded shrilly, announcing the unwelcome guests to the orcish inhabitants. Though Ulrich and his companions were relieved that the attention of the orcs was centred around the western half of the sqal, it was only a matter of time before the orcs came to the realisation that they were surrounded on all sides. The tribesmen openly raced through the streets, hacking down orcs as they bewilderedly responded to the frantic call to arms.

Ulrich flung his hatchet and watched as it took an orc down even as he took to the streets brandishing a great broad-bladed cleaver. Taking up the massive two-handed great sword for himself, Ulrich took the weapon and charged into battle to freely engage orcs as he spotted them. Swinging the two-handed orcish machete, he decapitated and disembowelled his adversaries without difficulty. The clamorous sounds of fighting were on the rise throughout the sqal and although it was late in the Gorgon lands to its natives, they were quickly awakening to respond to the hostile presence within their domain. An archer fired off at a nearby orc as the wretched scum blew into a horn with his last dying breath. The arrow cut him off too late as his kin rushed to the call and more joined in to oppose Nardic assault upon hearing the alarm.

Hacking his way through the fleeing crowds of orc peasants as they took to the streets in fear, Ulrich fought back the warriors who were steadily rising up to defend their homeland from the encroaching ranks of Nardic tribesmen. The orcs were like barbaric warriors and their strength was far greater than that of the southern men, already weakened and wearied by their travels through the Dead Wood. Men screamed in agony as they were beaten and brutalised by the primitive orcs; clubs smashed their skulls and splattered blood and gore all throughout the sqal. Bodies were steadily piling up in the streets and still the Nardic forces made their advance. Before long Ulrich's squad was forced to abandon their position as more and more orc warriors began to pour in from all around.

Varg, the squad leader, called for a retreat and their friends in the archer company who accompanied them provided covering fire whilst they fell back in search of a better route. Without slowing or deterring from the retreat, Ulrich cut down a hulking orc with a single swing of the giant blade he now carried in lieu of his traditional Nardic axe. The orc was chopped in half at the waist and his torso and legs toppled separately to the ground as Ulrich ran past without hesitation. In another sweeping blow, Ulrich mowed down another five orcs even as they charged towards him. The blade of the cleaver he carried was nearly a foot thick and five long, it required the use of both hands, though it was manageable as a single-handed weapon for the hulking orcs of the Desolation.

Making their way back around to Gregor's main street that cut from East to West, Ulrich's squad joined into the greater battalion of tribesmen who made the advance upon the eastern frontline. They made their way West alongside the majority of the surviving eastern tribesmen and sought to join their fellows in the heart of the sqal. Together, the unified masses fought their way through the orcish natives who assailed them from all sides in their attempt to regroup with the other battalions in the town centre. The orcs desperately sought to stem the tide of Nardic forces as they flooded the streets and took to killing the sqal's inhabitants indiscriminately. Ulrich continued to hack and slash his way through the dense crowds of orcs in the midst of the turmoil. He found that he was desensitised to all of the death and destruction that surrounded him after all that he bore witness to within the reaches of the Dead Wood.

"*Kommen sie mit!* This way!" Varg shouted, waving to Ulrich and the other survivors of his squad. They followed their leader through an alley away from the bulk of the fighting where they joined a parallel offensive strike in a flanking manoeuvre with another battalion of Nardic troops. Together they assailed the orcish masses gathered in the main street from the side whilst their counterparts continued the assault head-on. Varg led the attack against the orcs with the dual axes he wielded and Ulrich assisted him with his gigantic cleaver. Their fellow squadmates were strangers to the pair; Varg and Ulrich were the last of the tribesmen originally deployed from Baiern. The tribesmen who formed the greater part of their ranks were from Sehnshult, the capitol, or the southern woodlands. All of their friends and neighbours sent to war were dead; they were all that was left of their hometown in the orc lands.

They pushed forward and fighting their way through the orcish masses, the eastern forces of the Nardic host fell upon the town centre. Ulrich took up defending their position from the surrounding orcs alongside his fellow tribesmen whilst they awaited the surrounding Nardic reinforcements to join them. Fires were beginning to spread in the west and it was discovered that the western assault had been unsuccessful, as the tribesmen who joined them from the north were reporting. The orcs in the western half of Gregor turned their attention the the southern frontline upon the victory over the western Nardic forces. Meanwhile the northern and eastern Nardic battalions were steadily taking the heart of the sqal while more of their forces convened upon the city centre, fighting their way through the sqal's residents who crowded those wretched streets.

Suddenly a cry went up amidst the Nardic forces gathered in the heart of Gregor; Varg and Ulrich turned their attention away from the battle at hand to gape in shock as a massive orc swung his spiked club into a group of tribesmen. They were flung helplessly through the air where they crashed lifelessly to the ground. Archers fired their arrows at the mammoth but there was no stopping him. He was like an ogre compared to his fellow orcs, standing tall at eight feet with a muscular body that only matched his stature to the dismay of the Nardic men. Arrows protruded from every inch of his thick skin and still he walked amongst their ranks, swinging his gargantuan club and felling tribesmen by the dozens.

From the corner of his eye Ulrich spotted Varg even as he charged towards the hulking orc; his squad leader swung one of his axes into an opposing orc even as he launched the other in the direction of the towering orc ahead. The orc caught the axe in mid-air with his free hand and used the weapon to parry Ulrich's blow even as he swung the great goblin cleaver, using Varg's unsuccessful attack as a distraction to mount his own. They had failed on both attempts however, and the orc countered Ulrich with a deadly swing of his mace. Sent flying through the chaotic masses of men and orc alike, Ulrich felt several bodies break his fall beneath him. The attack had left him coughing and breathless and as he rolled off the pile of orcs and men who also sought to regain their footing, he could feel the ground quake beneath the might of the great orc beast that stood against them.

His cleaver was lost in the crowds of warring orcs and men. Weaponless, Ulrich fell back a ways and sought out a weapon amongst the dead, settling for an orcish crossbow with a repeating magazine. Firing off a few shots into the masses, he picked off a handful of orcs as he was able, though he quickly replaced it for a jagged Gorgon short-sword and found a nearby Nardic round shield amongst the loot of the dead. Adequately armed once again, he regrouped with Varg and his fellow squadmates who had also retreated in the midst of the giant orc that beset them. The remnants of the southern battalion of tribesmen began to join into the affray, though they'd been severely depleted after fighting off the bulk of the orcs of western Gregor.

With the aid of their southern reinforcements, the Nardic men swiftly killed the brutish orc giant, though not without difficulty. Numerous dead littered the battlefield in the wake of his course of destruction and after his death the orcs fell back to retreat and regroup a ways. The tribesmen took control of the south and east ends of the town centre whilst the orcs held steadfast throughout the northwest. Warriors from both sides ran across the high street that served as the no-man's-land between their forces, only to be pelted by arrows and slaughtered in the streets. The fighting died down and silence followed over the course of the passing days in the midst of the stalemate...

Gregor's peasants and farmers had long since fled the sqal to seek out refuge in Gorgor whilst the remaining orc soldiers triumphantly awaited their reinforcements from the North. Spirits were low within the Nardic camp where they remained holed up in the southeast of the town centre. Isolated sounds of fighting echoed broke out every so often; death cries and the clang of steel upon steel, or arrows whistling through the stagnant air. The streets were filled with the countless corpses of the fallen and arrows pelted any who dared cross the no-man's-land amidst Gregor's occupancy. Ulrich readied himself as the tribesmen mustered their forces for a renewed assault upon the orcs.

Nardic archers fired off a volley, providing cover for the first wave to make the advance across the intersecting main streets that divided the sqal into four quarters. Though they only held the sqal's northwest quarter, the orcs were still a force to be reckoned with. Several of the tribesmen were felled by orcish bolts as they ran, charging across the no-man's-land. Those who survived broke upon the orcish ranks alongside their kin, even as the Nardic archers let loose another volley to signal the second wave. Varg led Ulrich and their squadmates and together with the men of the second assault, they sprinted across the street, dodging friendly arrows and orc bolts alike for fear of their lives.

The first two waves of Nardic warriors had provided quite the challenge for Gregor's residents, forcing the main force of orcs to fall back and regroup further outside the heart of the sqal. Turning around just in time, Ulrich witnessed as a fellow behind him was pierced with a dull *thud* by the orcish bolt aimed at his head. Ulrich spotted out the responsible orcish archer and flung his jagged short-sword at the orc; the unfortunate archer toppled to the ground clutching at the sword that jutted grotesquely from his chest. Once again weaponless, Ulrich grabbed the wrist of an opponent even as the orc swung on him, head-bashing the orc and stealing its weapon for his own. Now wielding a hatchet, his armament of choice, he chased the orcs who now fled the scene of the battle in the face of their imminent defeat.

A third volley from the archers amongst the Nardic host signalled the third and final wave; the tribesmen washed over the orcs with the force of a dam bursting as they eradicated what was left of the orcish resistance. Archers picked off the fleeing orcs while the Nardic infantry chased them out of their town as one united force. When the battle was finally concluded the tribesmen collected the corpses of the fallen and piled them in the heart of the sqal. They set the mass grave aflame, indiscriminately burning friends and foes alike in the funeral pyre, though they kept it contained within the town centre. Once the fires had begun to die down, the tribesmen prepared a camp on the outskirts of the sqal. The designated night watch maintained a defensive perimeter throughout the ruinous settlement whilst the remnants of the Nardic host took rest.

CHAPTER THIRTEEN

The Slumlord was dead. A rival had sent an assassin in the night and now G'hnak's father was dead by the hand of a member of the Murghat-Khet, the orcish word for maggot-spawn as well as the name of the slum-based assassin's guild. They were the lowest rung of society within the capitol; bottom-feeders who often killed for little more than scraps to eat. His five older brothers fought amongst themselves for control of the clan and anarchy reigned within the leaderless gang. Amidst the chaos of his clan's turmoil, G'hnak continued to take on smuggling jobs as well as sell stolen wares to members of the Slum's underground blackmarket network.

Seeing the futility of slum-life in Istul, he sought to break free of his imprisonment within that wretched ghetto and become great in his own right. If he stayed in that place he was doomed to the same life of failure as his fellow slum dwellers; he'd spent the entirety of his miserable existence trapped in the vile clutches of poverty with no means of an escape. Over the years he'd been saving the money he made through his craft, though the cost of surviving was high in the Slums and payouts were slim. Life outside the walled safety of the capitol was no better with raiders, slavers, marauders, and elves roaming the wastes to provide trouble for lone travellers as they found them. Sqals and other orc settlements were few and far between and food was ever sparse in the Gorgon Desolation.

In comparison, Istul was like a glorious safe haven to the orcs of that land. Although the majority of its residents were poverty stricken, overall living conditions were much better there than outside the walled safety of the Tuhk. There was food and supplies in abundance within the inner city and they were safe from attack within the confines of those walls. Orcish society was predominantly ruled by a caste system and this was no different in the capitol; the peasant slum dwellers lived in a chaotic state of destitution. Anarchy reigned in the sprawling ghetto and Slumlords fought for dominance in the endless civil war that engulfed the outlying Slum District.

The residents of Istul's slums were far too poor to afford a life inside the capitol and so they built their own houses and other such structures around the outermost wall of the Tuhk. In order to protect themselves from the dangers of the Gorgon wastes they constructed a crude wall that encompassed the whole of their derelict shanty town, thus creating the Slum District of Istul. Over the generations, slum dwellers forged their own paths, shortcuts, and secret passages throughout the city. These became known as smuggler's routes and they were an underground network of interconnected highways that provided quick and direct paths throughout the Tuhk, free from the scrutiny of military checkpoints or patrols. Occasionally, some of the bolder amongst the slum dwellers would take to the secret routes and sneak into the inner city where they would steal and plunder goods in the Market District to sell back in the Slums.

Others sought the weapons and armour of the Military District, a highly coveted and expensive commodity amongst the poverty stricken masses. Generally stolen goods were sold to blackmarket slum vendors where the profit margin was slimmer, though payouts were consistent and guaranteed. Sometimes they were sold out on the streets to the highest bidder for much greater rewards, however the risk of being robbed or cheated was significantly higher as well. This was the main means of making a living in the slums outside the orcish capitol, though smuggling jobs were also a lucrative business opportunity for the slumling orcs. G'hnak would occasionally take up smuggling jobs, which usually consisted of transporting slum dwellers bearing identification papers, forged at a great expense, to relocate them into their new lives within the inner city.

Before they could assume their new identities however, they first had to bypass the several checkpoints that divided the city and sneak their way to whatever district their papers registered them as a resident of. The punishment for any caught committing or assisting in such an act was death, as was the punishment for the majority of crimes in the orc country. Though their papers registered them as a resident, they could not forge the visa stamps that were changed daily, and so they required the assistance of smugglers to aid them in their cause. Where the Thru'ahkuk Huang provided forged papers at a steep price, they made it nearly impossibly for the slum dwellers to afford their own and so as a result smugglers were rarely paid much for their services.

An arrangement had actually been made some days ago with G'hnak for the aforementioned service. He'd already been paid the fee, five human ears, and the job was set to take place that day; the very day of his father's death. Though he did not especially love or even care for his father, the death still had an affect on him regardless. His home was upturned in the chaos of the clan war that threatened to tear his family apart. G'hnak was not well-acquainted to his brothers; indeed, he barely knew the majority of his family at all. The clan was divided and his life had been flipped upside down over the course of a single night amidst the strife of the inner-clan turmoil. As a member of the clan, G'hnak was obligated to choose a side, however, instead he chose to abandon his family and his legacy to further his own life as he saw fit.

"Have you got your papers?" he asked his contact gruffly. The only thought on his mind was of how he would escape the Slum-life himself.

"Yes, yes, they're right here!" the slumling orc fumbled for his false documents, procuring them from the inside pocket of his ragged coat.

Looking over the paperwork to make sure all was in order, G'hnak returned the identification papers to their owner, an Outsider who introduced himself to the smuggler as Bhug. He said that he'd come from the Northern Wastes, where the peoples of the West waged a bitter war against the unspeakable terrors of that land, as well as the orcs who inhabited the southernmost reaches of the frigid wasteland. He'd been part of a slaver company based outside of the ruins of an old Necromancer fortress, up until they'd been ransacked by the high elves of Aenor. Being the only remaining survivor, he'd fled South back into the Gorgon lands. G'hnak was uninterested in his tale, however; he had his own worries without turning his ear to the news of foreign lands.

"I can see you're anxious to get going, is now really the best time, in the middle of the day*?" Bhug asked skeptically from where he stood uncomfortably tense in the crowded streets of the Slums; it was noon in the West End of the Slums, the exact time and place where G'hnak had arranged the meet to take place.

---

*Though the Sun failed to penetrate the eternal darkness of the Gorgon Desolation, the orcs bodies grew naturally in tune with the passage of time. They had no need for timekeeping devices as they were mentally in sync with the passage of time.

G'hnak explained the ways of the city to his unfamiliar companion; it was better to commit a crime in broad daylight (or so to speak) when the streets were at their busiest. When the streets were busier there were fewer guards to spot suspicious activity amongst the populace. Comparatively, in the inactive hours of the night when the streets were dead, patrols were on high alert for the slightest of infractions. It was for this reason that they set out on their adventure at noon in the packed streets of the cramped and squalid capitol, when there was too much noise and activity for them to attract any unwanted attention. Bhug was fully satisfied by the smuggler's response and upon hearing G'hnak's logic out, the pair set off on their quest.

Bhug stuck close to his smuggler guide and together they navigated the hectic streets of the northwest slums. It was a little easier to breathe upwind of the putrid smog that belched forth from Istul's factories, though the air was not much better than South of the Tuhk. The pair made their way through the tight spaces between dilapidated and ramshackle highrises that barely sufficed as alleyways, towards the 30-meter wall that encompassed the whole of the Market District. The inner wall loomed high above the rooftops of the slum dwellings that comprised the city's outskirts. Though they were several blocks north of the road they'd need to take to pass through the Northwest Gate, G'hnak knew his way through the streets. Their destination was a little over an hundred metres to the left of the Market Entrance, via a smugglers route that led through the wall itself.

They reached the base of the wall without difficulty and within minutes they were climbing great rockface, using a series of hand- and foot-holds carved by their ancestors in a time long since forgotten. G'hnak took the lead, assisting his companion through the cracked opening where their ascending path ended, roughly twenty metres from the ground. The crack was just barely large enough for an orc to squeeze through, though it led straight through the wall into an unoccupied storage facility on the other side, within the Market District. Crawling on their bellies, they clambered out of the crude tunnel and into the musty darkness of the abandoned warehouse where it led them. The building was condemned and on the verge of collapse, supported solely by the battlements to which it was adjoined. It served no purpose beyond functioning as a hideout and refuge for the slum dwellers and smugglers who used the secret passage that intersected the outer wall of the Market District.

This was not quite the end of G'hnak's adventure, however, as his escort was destined for military life far beyond the wall they'd only just spanned. Five human ears was more than enough to compensate the smuggler for his services, though the destination was deep in the Tuhk and far from his comfort zone. The streets of the marketplace were riddled with military checkpoints as well as patrols; if they were so much as asked for their papers they were both as good as dead. G'hnak couldn't afford his own forged documents and his counterpart's passport was useless without the current visa stamps. Once Bhug was within the safety of the Military District he could claim his passport was freshly issued and thus empty, though until he was within its walls both slumling orcs were susceptible to the harsh death penalty applicable by Pah'kan law.

Making their way back out onto the streets from Smuggler's Point, as the hideout was called, they joined into the daily flow and hustle of traffic without arousing attention to themselves whatsoever. Trailing a little ways behind G'hnak to detract from them being mistaken for travelling together, Bhug followed the veteran smuggler through the haphazard labyrinth of roads that made up the Market District unfalteringly in the midst of Istul's bustling crowds. They took to the highrise walkways as they were able along with smuggler's routes and the like; anything they could do to avoid catching the eye of the orcish patrols. Though it wasn't G'hnak's first smuggling job, he wasn't well accustomed to the northern marketplace. He'd never had the need to travel to the barracks before for any reason, not even to steal soldier's arms from the Military District's decadent armouries.

G'hnak was no more bold than his job title required him to be, however, in the wake of his father's death he'd come realise his immediate need for money. With his clan's instability there was no protection for him or his kin from the neighbouring rival clans and marauding gangs. His only chance at a better life was escaping the Slums and to do that he would need ears, ears he could only gain through odd jobs such as his current undertaking. He turned his attention back to the task at hand, guiding his contracted accomplice to the inner wall of the orcish market. The wall stood over one hundred and fifty feet tall and encompassed the whole of Istul's Military District, easily seen from their present location as they made their way towards it.

After several hours of traversing the convoluted network of back alleys and highways of the unfamiliar northern marketplace, G'hnak finally brought them to the base of the inner wall. Though he had never ventured so deep into the Tuhk, G'hnak found the smuggler's route into the barracks with relative ease. It was simply a matter of following the trail of hidden markings and secret symbols of the precursor smugglers. The route was a mere stairway that ran in the space between the wall and an adjacent highrise. It led up a ways to a rooftop plateau where a handful of footholds in the wall brought them to a upturned ledge that just barely stuck out enough to hold them. The small crag served as a porch; there was a crack where it jutted out of the wall and they slipped under it, sliding down into the passage it led on to.

The pair found themselves running along an abandoned passageway within the battlements surrounding the Military District. Istul's labour force was constantly at work within the Tuhk's multiple ringed battlements; delving new tunnels, guardrooms, and stores whilst maintaining the pre-existing passages as needed. Mostly, the orcish labourers of that city spent their time piling new buildings atop the original structures. They worked tirelessly until their constructions were too tall and unstable to support themselves, only to repair the damage caused when the colossal towers finally came crashing down. This generally left the working masses scattered throughout the Tuhk, stretched thin by the monumental amount of work required of them.

As it was, this fact played to G'hnak and his counterpart's advantage as they navigated the abandoned passageway they'd stumbled upon. The passage was old and forgotten in its derelict state, without any torchlight to illuminate their path whatsoever. On one side the tunnel had caved in, leaving the path blocked behind them. They jogged along in the opposite direction, their only option as they swiftly and silently traversed the dark hall, passing by long-since forsaken storerooms and empty chambers. After some time the hall ended suddenly not too far ahead.

It was as if one day the workers had suddenly decided to give up in their endeavour and never returned to finish the job. There was an arched hall to their right that served as the landing of a winding flight of stairs that seemed to spiral down into the depths of the Void itself. Taking to the stairs, the pair descended several floors without coming across any adjoining halls or even the slightest sign of a transition between levels. At the bottom of the staircase its mouth opened up into a crude cave. The round chamber was roughly seven feet in every direction and it had equilateral dimensions. In the centre of the cave there was a makeshift dumbwaiter large enough for one orc at a time to descend.

"Oh no, not at all! There has to be another way!" Bhug stammered, eyeing the ramshackle contraption with obvious discomfort.

"You didn't have to waste your ears hiring me if you'd rather go through the front door." G'hnak replied, motioning for his companion to mount to crude elevator.

"Wait, you're not coming!?!" Bhug exclaimed.

"This is the end of our journey together. At the bottom of this shaft your freedom awaits you." G'hnak replied.

"How do I know this isn't some sort of trick?" the orc rebutted, a hint of suspicion in his tone.

"If I was going to betray you I wouldn't have gone to this great an effort; your only options are to trust me, kill me, or follow me back to the Slums." G'hnak replied, patiently awaiting his final payment.

After a moment's thought, Bhug paid his guide and obediently mounted the platform. Pulling the rope lever, G'hnak lowered the dumbwaiter and watched as Bhug descended to the bottom of the shaft. A bell clinked, signalling the elevator had reached its destination, and G'hnak brought the dumbwaiter back up, returning it to the chamber ready for its next use. Upon completion of his contract, the smuggler departed from that place to return to his home in the Slums.

CHAPTER FOURTEEN
ISTUL, GORGON DESOLATION
Summer, 1E197

A lone foreigner traversed the tight and twisted streets of Istul's outer slums on a journey of his own. The orc was a dark-skinned Outsider and the indigenous folk of that sprawling ghetto knew he was not one to be messed with. Brandishing a blood-stained and battle-worn goblin cleaver, it was clear to all who gazed upon him that the orc was a wary traveller, well-accustomed to the Gorgon way of life. He knew the way he walked and traversed the tricky roads without difficulty. Slum dwellers cast dice in the streets before him and looked up as he passed them by; nearby a squabble broke out between a handful of orcs over some petty argument. No one paid the foreigner any mind as he navigated the abominable maze of shabby housing that made up the Slums of Istul.

Those wretched streets were a chaotic mess of zig-zagging roads filled with tents and other such provisional structures. Countless corpses littered the streets of the neighbourhoods and homeless orcs slept amongst the dead, using the dead bodies as well as other rubbish to keep themselves warm. Others slept around makeshift fires they burned openly, piling on whatever trash they could salvage in an attempt to keep them alight. Even in the midst of its blatant poverty, the Slums were still bustling with activity. The orcish masses traversed Istul's impoverished streets with a blind eye towards their city's inhospitable living conditions, as did the Outsider as he made his way along.

The thirty metre wall of the Tuhk's outermost battlements surrounding the market loomed in the distance high above the rooftops of the slum structures. Making his way northeast from where he was in the outlying neighbourhoods of the South Gate, the traveller weaved his way through the shabby tents and dilapidated shacks that filled those ramshackle roads. Avoiding the confrontational gangs of bandits and raiders that were rife in that place, he stuck with the flow of traffic as he navigated the sprawling mess of streets and roads. He took his time rather than cut through back alleys and side roads as rushing in the orcs lands generally proved less advantageous than the risks involved with cutting the time.

Dark and shady characters filled the bustling streets of the slums. Sketchy thieves and drug addicts lingered in the background waiting for a chance to swoop down upon the dropped spoils of a petty orc squabble. Few could be trusted in so depraved a place; so it was that the mysterious Outsider kept to himself and spoke to no one in his travels. Eventually he slipped away from the ebb and flow of slum-traffic and took to the sheltered pass of an alley running adjacent to the road he walked. It was a rundown path, rubbish littered the road and the walls on either side were in a moulding state of decay. He followed the path to the foot of a rusted iron stairwell and made the ascent to a flat single-floor rooftop adjoined to a L-shaped highrise, forming a square base. There was a ladder that ran the length of the surrounding skyscraper, leading up to a platform several storeys up above.

Upon climbing the ladder and reaching the platform at the top, the Outsider found a zip-line and flew down its length to the rooftop on the other end. The smuggler's route led him through snaking rooftop alleys and highways, though the latter consisted of no more than wooden planks connecting the gaps between the roofs of the towering slum structures. He followed the winding and steadily ascending highrise path that led him northwards, high up above the streets that ran through the rougher East End of Istul's outer slums. Travelling the rooftop highways and passages that cut through the buildings themselves, the orc made his way to the Northeast Quarter. He made his descent down a shaft in the heart of one of the highrises; a great fireman's pole ran the length of the skyscraper, serving as the primary structural support beam as well as the exit from what the smugglers referred to as the Slum Highway.

Making his way of of the building, he found himself in a small alcove surrounded by housing complexes on all sides. The only exit was through the alley that cut straight through the buildings. He took the path and found an enclosed courtyard on the other side and dozens of doors opened up from the surrounding walls. Several sickly guaka-guaka plants grew in the courtyard, withering away in their pots due to the inhospitable atmosphere of the malignant Tuhk of Istul. The enclosed allotment was roughly twenty square feet and it was entirely devoid of activity but for a single orc who lingered in that place, leaning against the wall opposite the Outsider and staring directly at him.

The mysterious orc was almost invisible where he hid in the shadows, just outside of the dim torchlight of that wretched courtyard. He propped his back against the wall with his arms folded across his chest and legs crossed as he leaned relaxedly in place, watching the Outsider impassively without interest. Raising his hooded head to stare directly into the newcomer's eyes, the stranger got up from his spot and cautiously approached the foreigner. The two met in the centre of the courtyard before a brief exchange of words was made.

"So you are the one they call G'hnak? You're not easy to find." the foreigner spoke gruffly.

"Neither are the majority of those who live long in this abominable place." was the stranger's rebuttal, "Now how can I be of service master?"

"I have need of a Smuggler. Your job will be to guide myself along with a companion to the designated location. The contact will disclose any imperative information relating to the contracted assignment upon your meeting." the mysterious Outsider cut directly to the chase, leaving G'hnak with no options but to accept or reject the arrangement.

"When and where is the meeting set to take place and what's the payout?" he asked in as cold and business-like a tone as he could manage.

"High noon tomorrow in the Market District near the Southeast Gate. Once you've accepted the terms and conditions of the contract you will be paid twenty human ears and an additional thirty upon completion." throughout the whole affair the Outsider remained blunt and matter-of-fact, which only added fuel to G'hnak's growing wariness of the mysterious stranger.

"The meeting is tomorrow, *within* the marketplace!?!" G'hnak exclaimed.

"Considering the payout, this is really a rather reasonable job. If you should choose to decline, do it now, as time is of the essence and I could better spend this time seeking the orc for the job." the Outsider pulled a drawstring purse fashioned out of man-skin leather and juggled the purse in one hand, allowing the ears to bounce around haplessly within.

G'hnak looked once more into the stranger's face before turning his attention to the bouncing pouch in the palm of his hand. Striking up the deal and taking the payment for his own, he agreed and they departed to go their separate ways. G'hnak was wary of the stranger; something seemed off about him and he wasn't very forthcoming with details of the job at all. The contract was highly suspicious to the seasoned smuggler and he eagerly took it up with caution. It was a lucrative business opportunity, though it was equally matched by the many risks and dangers of the great unknown...

* * *

"*Murghat*! This tar is no better than a stinking pile of dung!" Bear exclaimed, hurling his pipe at the wall of the shabby hut he took refuge within. The clay pipe shattered into a million pieces upon its impact against the dilapidated wall of the tiny room. A puddle of black rancid resin oozed from the remains of the wretched pipe and pooled on the bare earthen floor.

"What did you expect? They keep all of the quality stuff locked away in the great stores of this Tuhk. You'll find naught but disappointing guap out here in the Slums unless you cam settle for what you've got." his heavyset companion, H'gruak replied sullenly.

They'd been making due for weeks. The cheap resin barely sufficed as a temporary fix for the hardened addicts of the drug, though as H'gruak had pointed out, it was their only option in that place. Though it kept their insatiable addiction at bay, the stuff was of poor quality and it showed. The cheap tar was no more than the extracted oil from recycled pipe filters, cut with filler-ingredients such as coagulated blood, faeces, and mud. Coughing and wheezing, they began to cough up phlegm. Upon taking a closer look at their spittle, they found that it was intermingled with blood. This was entirely due to their consumption of the wretched tar they smoked, which only made them sicker with each hit they took.

"When are U'gra-sha'kal and that accursed hobgoblin expected back anyhow?" Bruh continued to moan.

"I don't see what good their return will do for you, considering the fact that you've shattered your only smoking pipe." the fat sword vendor sneered.

"Shut up you fat oaf, before you find yourself without lungs to smoke with!" Bruh snapped back before resuming his miserable sulking in the corner.

The day passed them by as the pair sat there, listlessly awaiting the return of their comrades, over the course of what seemed like an eternity. After some time the door suddenly swung open outwards, nearly coming off its hinges in the process, as U'gra-sha'kal and V'rznk entered the shabby residence. The hour was late when they'd finally returned and Bear franticly scrambled to his feet upon their arrival. V'rznk tossed Bruh the tiny pouch he so dearly craved; delightedly extracted the tar contained within the sack before recalling his prior conversation with H'gruak. The sword vendor watched the whole thing play out from where he sat in his corner and presently chuckled at Bear's sudden realisation.

"You! Hand it over!" Bruh pointed menacingly at the rotund merchant.

"I haven't the slightest idea what you're talking about." he replied mischievously.

"What are you playing at H'gruak? What have you stolen from him?" U'gra-sha'kal was clearly not in the mood for the pair's antics.

"Dare you accuse me of theft?" the sword vendor irritably snapped back.

"What exactly is going on?" the goblin, V'rznk, inquired.

"This doesn't concern you." Bear retorted.

"We haven't got time for this, hand him you own." U'gra-sha'kal said with authority, seeing the shards of Bruh's broken pipe strewn across the dusty floor of that dilapidated hut.

Reluctantly, H'gruak handed his pipe to the smug orc who then proceeded to blatantly parade his victory, puffing hard on the pipe and blowing massive sickly clouds in the sword vendor's face. V'rznk rebuked them for their pettiness whilst U'gra-sha'kal attempted to restore order. They spoke amongst themselves of the Plan; U'gra-sha'kal, V'rznk, and H'gruak had each been sent in preparation for the heist and each had accomplished what was required of them. V'rznk had also been given the task of buying up some decent tar from within Istul's Market District which explained his late arrival along with U'gra-sha'kal, who'd had to traverse the Tuhk from end to end and back. During all of this, Bruh was left to himself within the confines of their provisional headquarters in the South Gate district of the outer Slums; he was too famous for his own good and would have attracted far too much attention had he accompanied them. Now that they were all returned and everything was ready for the heist, they had nothing left to do but sleep and await the events of the following day as it unfolded...

CHAPTER FIFTEEN
GORGOR, GORGON DESOLATION
Summer, 1E197

Looking upon the horizon in the distance, Egorin could vaguely see a convoy approaching the elvish host's encampment from afar. The elves of Gilan had mustered all their remaining forces in preparation for their final battle against the orcs of the East. Their scouts had already returned, having been sent South after their victory against the orcs of the sqal they currently took refuge within. The Nardic host had been discovered just a ways north of Gregor after having conquered the sqal, though not without casualties. From the scout's report, they numbered less than 2,500 strong and their commanders were all dead.

Upon hearing the grim news, elvish messengers were sent West, back to Gilan, to seek whatever reinforcements hadn't yet received the call to arms. Now all of their able-bodied warriors were gathered in that sqal awaiting the arrival of the distant Nardic tribesmen. The convoy of remaining Southerners steadily approached, though the procession was slow in their worn and wearied state. The Dead Wood had taken its toll heavily on the Men of the Isles. There was no hope of any further aid from the Nardic Tribes; the expedition had cost them far too many lives and besides, it would take longer to reach the elvish forces than they could afford to wait. Indeed, any further support in the elvish campaign would have to come from their own people.

As the approaching caravan drew nearer, Egorin found that he could spot out the individual ranks of tribesmen. Their host consisted of no more than a handful of spearman and archer companies and only a battalion or two of axemen. The Nardic men were accompanied by a convoy of elvish wagons and a light cavalry to safely transport their wounded as they marched alongside the caravan on their way to Gorgor. They were roughly a league away, though Egorin's keen elvish eyes could still spot them in the dark depths of the eternal night that lingered over that land. He spent his little remaining free-time leading up to their arrival pondering how the southern tribesmen tended to their dead.

Will they send their people to collect the fallen, or did these soldiers simply bury their dead themselves? In some cultures they burn their dead in reverent funeral pyres... Egorin's thoughts trailed off and he lost track of time until he was finally brought back to the present, even as the Nardic convoy filed into the sqal.

The Nardic reinforcements arrived around noon and they were immediately greeted with murmurs of discontent. With less than twenty-five hundred remaining warriors in fighting condition, they were more of a liability than a blessing. Where they'd previously expected an army of 50,000 men, the elves saw before them the disappointing remnants of a once mighty force. The Nardic men joyously embraced their elvish companions and they were met with cold apathy. Few amongst the elvish ranks found themselves able to maintain faith in their fellow countrymen. The majority had given up what little hope they'd managed to keep hold of whilst the captains and commanders of Gilan's armed forces continued to carry out the orders of their king without hesitation.

Captain Vasil and Prince Rässan's falling out some days ago didn't help the situation at all; rather, it had done quite the opposite. The entire ordeal had arisen from a simple disagreement that quickly got out of hand. Prince Rassan had proposed marching on without the aid of the Nardic men, arguing that they hadn't the time or resources to spare to await help that might not arrive. The Captain's reply was that they hadn't the manpower to assail the Tuhk as they were. A courier had been sent some weeks ago West with all due haste to request supplies and still they awaited the King's response. Prince Rässan impatiently waited until one day he could take no more, having reached his boiling point...

"Who are you to defy the orders of a prince!" Prince Rässan screamed in the face of the decorated and renowned Captain Vasil of the First Swordsman Company of Graenor. He stood calm and impassive before his irate liege, though he did not submissively accept the rebuke. A crowd of elvish soldiers had gathered around as the two proceeded to cause a scene in the heart of the elf camp.

"I am the Captain of this army, appointed by your father no less!" Vasil shot back, taking a grim pleasure in the Prince's reaction.

"To reject the rule of your liege is treason against your country!" Prince Rässan exclaimed in a final desperate bid to undermine the Captain's authority and take back the support of his people for himself.

"You would have us to march needlessly to our deaths in your reckless imprudence. You're no general; you're a nobleman, so why don't you just sit back and take the credit for our efforts like your kind always does." the Prince went red in the face at the Captain's bold speech and the gathered crowd was silent in the midst of their rapidly-escalating heated confrontation.

"Enough!" Prince Rässan shrieked, "I will not tolerate this blatant insubordination and neither shall my father when he hears of it!"

Upon making his decision that he would not stand the insulting remarks and outright defiance of his inferior, Prince Rässan ordered the forces of Gilan to disembark at once or face the capitol offence of high treason. Much to his dismay, he found that his only followers were those of his own forces and there were few amongst them at that. Those who remained by his side only did so out of fear, though at the sight of the mass rejection of his rule a few of them even joined the ranks of Captain Vasil's loyal legions. In his stubbornness Prince Rässan refused to swallow his pride and humble himself before his subjects. Instead, he and his kinsmen departed from that place on a hopeless northward march that would only end in their failure.

The fact that they'd become deserters was only made worse by the arrival of the Nardic remnants. They had traded their Prince for a couple brigades of tribesmen and a handful of battalions sent from the West as a final reinforcement for the elvish host in their campaign. The reward for their wait had been worth it as well as necessary, though they paid the price in troop morale. With the loss of their Prince, the "deserters" were hapless and miserable as they went about their duties within the camp. It had been four days since the royalist had abandoned them and the Nardic tribesmen arrived in the midst of it all, totally unaware of the elvish politics at play within the camp.

Amongst the reinforcements of West Gilan, siege engines had also been sent along with the additional troops. Horses pulled the supplied ballistae and catapults along, in tow with the wagon convoy, as Giessen's reserves marched into town. They brought with them the additional supplies that the elvish host would need on their journey to Istul. The tribesmen brought nothing with them; instead, they took from the elvish supplies, drinking their wine and eating their food as the men had none of their own. None prevented the worn and weary men from replenishing themselves, though there was an air of discontent that lingered over the camp. The Nardic warriors felt the uncomfortable tension and some amongst them resented it, though none spoke out.

We've left family, friends, and our very homes behind, witnessed the countless deaths of dear friends and loved ones, fought through the depths of Hölle itself and survived, and still these elves have the audacity to treat us as beggars even as we join them as allies in their campaign. Ulrich tried to keep a hold of his temper whilst he waited in line for a meal at the elvish supply wagons. Once he'd received his portions of elvish berries, bread, and wine Ulrich made his way towards the outskirts of camp, away from the main congregation of elves. He came upon elvish sentries gathered around an outer watch fire and joined them in their solitude. There were a handful of Aush Wood archers present, though two golden-haired swordsmen also found solace in their company.

"*Wie geht's?* Do you speak the Common Tongue?" Ulrich sat down beside the lone elves in his attempt to make small talk.

"No." the first elf replied absent-mindedly.

"Pay him no mind *freund*; this war has made him bitter. My name is Almardi and this is Namroden." the second elf reproached his friend for his rudeness and greeted the Nardic man. He continued to sulk however, and even attempted to drown out the babble of his unwanted companions.

The natives of Western Gilan, as Ulrich came to discover were bilingual, having been taught the Common Tongue in school at an early age in those aristocratic cities. A fair number of the eastern elves also spoke the universal language whilst none amongst the Aush Woods contingent spoke anything other than the native tongue of their people, in the rare occasions where they spoke at all. Together with Almardi, the pair exchanged news of their travels in the elvish campaign, as well as stories of their homeland. Ulrich told Almardi of his wife, Aeryn, and his two sons. Almardi spoke of his home in Aereil and watching the magnificent Nardic ships that sailed the southern waters.

He reminisced on staring after the ships, desiring nothing more than to pilot his own as the captain of such a beauty. They told each other their hopes, dreams, hobbies, and interests; the pair came to find that their people weren't so different as they'd once thought. Never before had either of them travelled outside the border of their home and never had they met a foreigner. Almardi had lived a peaceful life in Aereil where his house overlooked the Sumatran

Ocean in the South. Ulrich told the elf of his experience on the great Nardic warship in the voyage to the Dead Wood, giving him the positive highlights of the expedition whilst leaving out the rest. It was his only experience aboard a ship and he didn't want to kill the young elf's passion for the sea.

Together they conversed around the watch fire for awhile and after some time Namroden came around as well, occasionally interjecting and contributing to the conversation. Before long he was laughing and joking with the pair, as if they were back in the comfort of their respective homelands. They lost track of time in their merriment and suddenly came to find the host preparing for sleep. The night watch was being assigned and all around men and elves were withdrawing to the sqal centre to sleep in the erected tents and pavilions. Ulrich wished the pair of elves a good night and bid them farewell; Almardi and Namroden had both been selected for the first rotation of sentry duty. The Nardic man made his way back to the area of camp where his own fellows were held up and found Varg along with a handful of his squadmates, still awake and speaking amongst themselves in their native tongue.

"*Grüß dich!*" Varg called out to his approaching comrade. Ulrich tiredly waved in their general direction and attempted to make his way to the tents, turning in for a quiet night's sleep. That is quite the opposite of what happened, however, as Varg got up and wrapped an arm around his friend's shoulder, dragging him along in a friendly way to the small circle of tribesmen. They asked him of his adventures within the camp and his thoughts on the elf army. Seeing that rest was out of the question, Ulrich gave in to his companions and spoke with them for a while, seeking to satisfy their unquenchable curiosity and ease their own restlessness.

He told them of his encounter on the outskirts of camp and gave a brief summary of his conversation with the elves, giving the assembled tribesmen the elvish perspective of their arrival. After hearing all that Ulrich had to say, Varg and his fellows were a little more sympathetic towards the elves, though they were still affronted by the elvish reception upon their arrival. They did not feel welcome and gratitude for their undertaking was seemingly scarce amongst the elves of that camp. Indeed, they felt a resonant resentment emanating from within the ranks of Gilan's host towards their people. Ulrich's opinion was that as the Nardic tribesmen proved their usefulness the elves, they would become more accepting and appreciative of the southern aid.

With nothing left to say, the men readied themselves for bed. Each man wrapped himself snugly in his blankets before nodding off under the watchful vigilance of elvish sentries. It was probably the first decent sleep any of the tribesmen had experienced since they'd embarked upon the accursed expedition. Their bellies were full and their insatiable thirst was quenched by the enchanted wildberry wine of the elves; none amongst them could ever recall a better night's sleep than the one they experienced there in that camp under the wine's intoxicating effects. They slept comfortably without fear there under the watchful eyes of the elves and the night quickly passed them by. In the morning, Captain Vasil sent a handful of messengers throughout the ranks of their mighty army, issuing the orders to disembark on the final leg of their campaign. Gruffly shaken awake, Ulrich stumbled to his feet grumbling oaths in his native language as did the majority of his fellow countrymen. The men prepared themselves for the impending departure, though not without some moaning...

"But we've only just arrived!" one of the tribesmen could be heard arguing with a commanding elvish officer.

"And now we're departing. Gather your things soldier; we haven't the time to spare." was the elf's impassive response. Obediently following the elf's orders, the tribesmen continued to pack their gear in preparation for their day's march. They did this without any further gripes or remarks. Once they were ready, Captain Vasil approached the Nardic contingent and properly introduced himself to their forces before addressing them prior to the departure.

"I apologise for my lacking presence upon your arrival; I was caught in the pressing matter of deciding what is to be done with your forces. In my absence, I have concluded that a full integration into our army is the only suitable option for your people. We are of the understanding that you lack in leadership and so you will be divvied up amongst our companies as you are needed and serve under our own elvish officers. I have also taken into account your weariness and if you are unopposed, I would offer that you ride along in our wagons whilst you recover your strength on the journey to Istul." throughout his speech, Captain Vasil spoke entirely in the Nardic language, fluently and without error.

This feat alone earned him a great deal of respect upon his introduction to the tribesmen, alongside his personal explanation and apology for his absence until just before their departure. He explained to them the elvish sentiments towards their people and the reasoning behind it, as well as the recent events within the elf host and the news of their travels since their departure from Gilan. This information calmed some of the men's feelings towards the elves and helped others to understand the feelings they had previously misinterpreted as animosity. Once the Nardic tribesmen had been assigned to pre-existing elvish companies within Gilan's ranks, they clambered aboard their horse-drawn wagons as the host embarked upon the day's march.

CHAPTER SIXTEEN
ISTUL, GORGON DESOLATION
Summer, 1E197

G'hnak licked his cracked dry lips eagerly in anticipation of his employer, with whom would he would be meeting at any moment now. This job he'd been hired for was his golden ticket out of the Slums; it would provide him with more than enough ears to start a new life anywhere he saw fit. His mysterious associate had been rather vague about the details concerning his assignment however, and he was hoping that his contact would clear things up for him. The smuggler had gone against his own good judgement and accepted the contracted job, knowing that an opportunity such as this only presented itself once in a lifetime. So it was that G'hnak found himself waiting outside the Southeast Gate within the hectic squalor of Istul's marketplace.

It hadn't taken him long to calculate the risks as opposed to the payout in the event that he survived the whole affair. He was just as likely to die tomorrow in the Slums as he was in the middle of the job; the only difference was simply a matter of the survivor's reward. If he chose to reject the contract his only reward was another day of life in the sprawling ghetto, compared to a fresh start in a new life, entirely paid off by a single job, if he accepted the assignment. The job was dodgy and he knew he was risking his life by undertaking it, though G'hnak also knew that the reward was worth his life and so he waited. After some time he found the contact, accompanied by the mysterious Outsider who had hired him in the first place. He was noticeably larger than the orc who was responsible for employing the young albino smuggler.

The employer's companion had a dark grey hue to his skin. It was somewhere between the shades of graphite and charcoal, signifying that he was a native to the Tuhk and that his life had taken him far from home. G'hnak also took note that the pair of orcs had passed through the military checkpoint, taking the Southeast Gate into the Market District rather than the unguarded smuggler's routes. The only explanation was that it was a merchant who had hired him, which only raised more questions than it provided answers. G'hnak's employer weaved through the crowd alongside his thicker set grey-skinned companion and together they made their way over to him. The trio met up in the hectic squalor of the bustling downtown street and turned off it to convene in the semi-privacy of an intersecting alleyway.

"So you are our Smuggler?" the Outsider's grey companion spoke up rather gruffly, roughly breaking the ice.

"As soon as I know what I'm smuggling." G'hnak retorted.

"Not here." the Outsider replied curtly, with seemingly feigned reluctance.

"Then where!?!" G'hnak exclaimed testily.

"Lead us to the Barracks." the grey orc answered.

This seems like a great big pile of murghat-khet to me... G'hnak thought to himself as he took the lead, not before muttering a choice selection of curses under his breath as he embarked upon the quest with his fellow companions. Together they followed the busy roads that zig-zagged haphazardly in conjunction with the countless intersecting streets, alleys, and highways as they made their way West. Led by G'hnak, they reached the Southern Highway, though they made an ascent via a neatly placed ladder to a Smuggler's Highway several hundred feet up above the streets. They traversed the crude rope-and-plank bridges that constituted for the smuggler's route and steadily closed the distance between themselves and the Southwest Inner Gate that led on to the Barracks. Continuing to take the rooftop express routes, they passed the guarded entrance and ran parallel to the Northern Highway, hundreds of feet beneath them.

As a smuggler, G'hnak made it his personal duty to scout out, discover, and memorise the many paths, roads, and shortcuts that Istul had to offer. It only took him a single run to memorise a path and he knew his way to the smuggler's route he sought. He found the same patch of wall as he'd navigated on a past job into the Barracks, though he himself had never stepped foot upon the Military District's war-torn grounds. Upon making their way through the abandoned passageways that constituted the smuggler's route they took, the trio descended one at a time down the crude dumbwaiter that led to the Barracks on the other side of the Tuhk's towering battlements. At first glance, the Military District appeared to be no more than a war-ravaged gladiatorial battlefield, dotted with barracks, smithies, and armouries.

Natural selection was the way of life within those walls; only the fittest survived in the harsh kill-or-be-killed environment of the militaristic inner city. There were many rival orc factions within the army that Istul housed in its barracks and they fought amongst one another for supremacy. Their training exercises were somewhat liken to a cross between war games and actual battle. Large-scale clan warfare weeded out the weak and those who survived were amongst the fighting elite who would protect that city from attack. Life as a soldier in the capitol was rough, though it was rewarding to those who survived the deadly daily struggle.

As it was, the trio presently emerged from a crack in the wall that the elevator shaft they'd descended in turns led on to. They found themselves standing on the northernmost outskirts of the Military District. G'hnak looked around anxiously to make sure that none had spotted them as they entered the ravaged lands that made up the unholy arena and breathed a sigh of relief. The air was rife with the sounds of eternal battle. Arrows whistled as they flew haphazardly in every direction and putrid steel clanged as the orcish soldiers and warriors of the Tuhk mercilessly hewed one another down or parried the deadly blows of their rivals on the field of battle. The clans took up residence in miniature sqals that dotted the desolate war-torn fields of the Barracks and rival factions fought for control and dominance of the sqals in a never-ending civil war.

Suddenly a series of crashing booms erupted from far away in the South. The thunderous clamour of Istul's divided military had died immediately upon the first explosive burst of noise and seconds later the cries of Shak'hal* could be heard as they poured out from within the Tuhk to investigate the disturbance. They rallied the warriors of the Tuhk and the whole of the barracks was deployed South in the midst of whatever was starting to unfold.

"Quickly, in the heat of the chaos!" the grey orc whispered hoarsely.

They raced through the battle-torn environment under the dim illumination of the Tuhk's light in the skies above. High up in the heavens above, the chimneys of that wretched citadel spouted blurry red flames, intermingling with the dark black clouds that blanketed those lands. The shrouded flames provided a dim light to the war-torn fields of the Military District. Sticking closely to the shadows, the trio of orcs raced towards the inner wall that encompassed the Gardens of the Church of the Masters. The northernmost section of the ring wall housed a great archway that spanned nearly an hundred feet from the ground and it ran ten feet wide. There was no gate and the entrance was unbarred an unguarded. Generally the entrance was guarded Shak'hal sentries, though due to the mysterious disturbance they were nowhere to be seen.

---

*Where Sikhan bone spites take up the bones of fallen warriors, Shak'hal are greater demonic entities capable of manifesting muscle tissue, flesh, and armour out of their energies. They were the captains and commanders of the Masters legions and they united the orcs under one unified mass out of sheer terror in times of emergency.

While the demonic overlords and their orcish underlings ventured South into the outlying city to investigate the source of the explosive disruption, G'hnak led his fellow companions through the arched entrance into the Gardens of Istul. The rancid gardens were no more than a barren expanse of land covered in fields of the most premium guaka-guaka in the whole of the Desolation. Those wretched fields stretched from the Church, serving as the base of the Tuhk, all the way to the circular wall that surrounded the unholy citadel. Upon making their entry into the Gardens, the dark-skinned Outsider stopped in his tracks and his fellows halted at the gesture.

"This is where we part ways. I'll be here waiting upon your completion of the job." he patted G'hnak on the shoulder and sent him on his way with the grey stranger.

"What in the name of the Masters are you planning exactly!" G'hnak angrily hissed between clenched teeth. He was shaking in terror and he was boiling over with unchecked wrath.

"You're not being paid to ask questions; the hardest part of the job is behind you now; keep your eyes ahead and don't dwell to much on the present." his employer replied, shoving him as their charcoal companion led the smuggler in tow.

Together they made their way without the black Outsider to the extravagant entrance of the Church of the Masters. They found two Pah'kan robes in a side entrance around the rear of the Church as they stealthily made their way around. Donning the garments, they entered the citadel as Priests, impersonating the roles as best they could. Only the highest ranking orcish soldiers found a place within the ranks of the Master's Watch, though the Tuhk was constantly teeming with Sikhas and their Shak'hal overlords. No one suspected the pair as they made their way along through the back halls and passages that ran like a labyrinth behind the sanctuary room where the priests daily gathered in worship of the Masters.

*　　*　　*

H'gruak and V'rznk ran out from their hiding place nearby the Northeast Entrance into the barracks, just as they'd planned. A chain of four strategically plotted explosions had brought the southern skyscrapers of Istul's marketplace crashing down. The entire southern half of the Market District was utterly devastated. In the midst of the wreckage survivors later came to find that the outer wall of the Market District was in a ruinous state, where nearby highrises collapsed all around and brought entire sections of the wall down in the destruction. The military had been deployed to investigate the cause of the disturbance and in the heat of the moment they used the momentary distraction to infiltrate the Barracks. There they would rendezvous with their fellow comrade, U'gra-sha'kal, as they'd arranged beforehand.

"How do you reckon Bruh is getting along? It's a shame about the Market District; it would have been nice to invest in some property." H'gruak laughed heartily as they jogged through the abandoned archway that served as the entrance into the Barracks.

"What's the point when the elves are going to burn this all to the ground anyhow?" V'rznk didn't have to patience to humour his fat companion as they traversed the desolate fields that housed Istul's military.

They skirted around the mini-sqals and made their way to the North Gate that led into the Gardens of the Church. There were no soldiers around as they'd all been deployed South in the Market District to combat the chaos of the destruction. As they ran the echo of their feet slapping across the barren plains was all that could be heard within the inner arena that served as the Barracks, totally silent and devoid of life in the state of crisis. Upon reaching the North Gate they passed under the high arch and came through the other side to convene with their fellow comrade whist they awaited Bear's return...

"Do you know which way it is from here?" Bear asked impatiently.

"No; I've never stepped foot inside the Tuhk before today, and hopefully never again, granted I survive this whole mess." G'hnak replied heatedly.

"What use are you then?" Bruh snapped back.

"I'd be of more use if I knew why you brought me to this accursed living hell!" G'hnak retorted with a rising hint of anger in his tone.

Bear hushed the smuggler and took the lead in his stead. They made their way through the maze of passages and after some time they came across the lift they'd been seeking. The elevator pad was a round platform that was raised nearly ten feet above the floor of the room. A winding staircase led them to the top, where they pulled the lever that would activate the crude elevator. Gears grated and ground against one another as the contraption steadily began to rise, creaking and rumbling as they made their ascent. Ropes pulled at the platform and they fought to stand their ground as it swung helplessly in its ascent.

They rose several floors before a roaming patrol stopped the lift to board it alongside the pair. The two parties struggled to stand in an awkward silence together for a while as the platform continued to rise. They had greeted the sentry and received muffled grunts in return; the guards kept their eyes downcast throughout the entirety of the ascent. After some time it dawned upon the false priests that the guards were actually afraid of them! Bruh took advantage of this fact to interrogate the patrol and instil terror in their hearts.

"You lot! Whereabouts are you off to so silent? Off committing blasphemies?!?" he shouted over the constant screech and rumble of the lift as it made its climb.

"What? No! No, never! We never go against the Masters, all praise be to them! We serves them, protects them!" one of the soldiers trembled with fear at the thought of the consequence of Bear's accusations as a Pah'kan priest.

"Then you won't object to proving your allegiance, no?" Bear grinned mischievously in his delight.

"Yes of course!" the pair of sentries blurted out simultaneously.

Bruh successfully managed to convince the pair of guards to lead them to the great storeroom, and so they followed their fellows to the vast wares. It was a great storage facility within the heart of the Tuhk, containing all of the capitol's premium tar reserves. None would dare question their party as the guards escorted them to the tar reserves. To question the authority of their guides was to question the pair of priests themselves, which was one in the same as questioning the authority of the Masters themselves. So it was that G'hnak and Bear made their way together to the stores, led along by the pair of guards they'd commandeered into their service.

CHAPTER SEVENTEEN

"So this is what you've hired and brought me all this way to my death for; to steal the tar reserves of the Masters from right under their very noses?!?" G'hnak exclaimed incredulously, barely believing all that he bore witness to.

"Relax. It's not so bad. Here, have a smoke." Bruh replied with a cackling laugh as he packed his pipe with some pure uncut Sythic Tar.

Lighting the bowl and filling his lungs with the first toke, Bear passed the smoking device to his companion, the smuggler. G'hnak snatched the pipe even as it was offered and he sucked heavily on the pungent smoke before exhaling a grand cloud of it in the vast room they found themselves within. The storeroom was magnificent. It was like a bank for the tar they sought after; vials of the black resinous drug filled the shelves that made up the walls of that room. Presently, G'hnak turned his attention to the corpses of their escort, laid out like a pair of marionettes with their strings cut upon the floor of that circular chamber. Bear had killed the first soldier with a dagger hidden in his boot and G'hnak followed suit, taking advantage of the distraction to slay the other guard even as he drew his weapon against the notorious drug dealer.

"How can you be so nonchalant, you bastard! We're going to die in here!" Bruh continued to ignore the irate smuggler's shouts as he merrily puffed away at his pipe, blissfully ignorant of the world around him.

The tar in that room was extremely potent stuff, refined in highly concentrated dosages so that it could be cut and diluted in order to increase the volume and profit margins. Afterwards, it was sold to distributors where it was further adulterated before they passed it on to the merchants and vendors throughout the capitol. Though his tolerance was significantly greater than that of a hardcore user, the Tar of the Masters was powerful stuff, and already Bruh could feel it taking hold of him in a deathlike grip. His brain started to buzz and tingle, steadily growing heavier as his eyes began to droop. His heart was beating so fast that it had become a single vibrational hum resonating from deep within his chest. His fingertips were beginning to go numb and he could no longer had any feeling in his feet.

Suddenly everything seemed to glow with an energy that glowed beneath the surface of everything, as if colour was no more than a naturally radiant light that enveloped the objects they covered. Bruh lost track of his surroundings and the flames that danced in the torches upon the wall stretched and expanded to cover the walls and it dripped like water from a leaking ceiling. Spreading across the floor, the room was ablaze with devilish flames the hisses and cackled all around him, rising in pitch until all he could hear was the piercing shriek of Death itself. Suddenly he opened his eyes to find that his hands were gripping his face and the piercing shriek was his own voice. It was as if his lungs were being compressed and the cry was his soul leaving his body, the sound liken to a whistling tea kettle, and he felt his heart on the verge of imploding.

"Damn you, you bastard! You've doomed us both to our deaths!" G'hnak shouted over Bear's shriek. The distant muffled sounds of guards shouting could be heard from far off beyond the iron door of the great storeroom.

Suddenly his heart burst and Bruh tore the flesh off from his face even as his cry ended. Bear felt himself shoot out of his body, beyond the fabric of reality into a realm of nonentity. Out of the nothingness the sentient skull of an ancient colossal beast appeared, with horns and burning black flesh set aflame like a bowl-pack of guaka-guaka. From the depths of its eyes there burned an eternal hatred deeper than the depths of the Void itself. Bruh could feel its energy and thoughts telepathically; they spoke to him in many voices and he knew that it was the Masters judging him for his sins. Deeming him unworthy the skull devoured him whole even as a jet of hell-fire spewed from its open mouth to wash over the orc. Bear screamed in agony as its jaws closed around him to swallow his soul and he felt himself disintegrate into nothingness, digested by the monstrous beast though it had no body. Out of the nothingness the skull of the beast appeared once again and so he fell into the eternal cycle of being devoured by the skull of the Masters, doomed to an eternity of death as punishment for the life he chose to live...

Frantic in the midst of a full-blow anxiety attack, G'hnak tried hard to calm himself under the amphetaminous effects of guaka-guaka intoxication. Bruh had only just lost consciousness; he was ailing with seizures and his mouth foamed whilst his body floundered there like a fish out of water. Before falling into a fit, he'd been screaming and tearing at his face. The muffled shouts of guards outside and the growing patter of feet rushing toward them could easily be heard from outside the walls of that room. G'hnak gathered his wits about him and stripped naked. Realising he only had but one option, he replaced his Pah'kan robes for the attire of one of the fallen soldiers of the Tuhk. He dressed one of the deceased sentries in his former garments and disguised himself as a fellow patrol in preparation for what was next to come, thinking up a cover story as quick as he could given the circumstance.

"What happened here?" an orcish sentry questioned G'hnak, standing over the bodies of what appeared at first glance to be the corpses of two Pah'kan priests.

"This one ordered me to escort the pair of them to the Storeroom," G'hnak began, pointing at Bruh's dead body, "and I hadn't realised they were imposters until he began to loot the stores. That's when they killed my comrade and the first one fell into seizing. I took the distraction to kill the other and then you got here."

"That was quick wit and cunning on your part soldier; the Masters have seen your loyalty and it shall be rewarded. What is your name, brave hero?" one of the Pah'kan priests present spoke up.

"G'hnak... G'hnak Bruh'khakka*." he faltered.

There was a slew of soldiers and Pah'ka within the room, conducting an official investigation led by the Priesthood, due to the nature of the crime and so his nervousness was easily excusable. They granted G'hnak his leave upon concluding their interrogation and he was granted the title of captaincy within the ranks of the Istul's vast army. Meanwhile, news of the incident was spreading and two more suspects were arrested in the Military District to be charged as fellow conspirators to the crime. Originally, a patrol had stumbled across three suspicious characters hanging around the outer wall of the Gardens, though two of the fitter suspects had initially managed to flee. Taking the fatter of the three to the Priests to be interrogated, the soldiers managed to capture another in the outer Military District where the apprehended merchant was tackled to the ground by a handful of warriors. Only one had managed to escape, fleeing North away from the bulk of the Tuhk's military forces as he sought to escape the city.

Along with his promotion, G'hnak was granted the honour of killing the perpetrators, whom he knew to be companions of the former drug dealer, Bear. He feared for the worst, that of the two captured one was the Outsider whom had been responsible for his employment. Surely the orc would rat him out to save his own neck, or even just to gain the satisfaction of bringing him down alongside them. G'hnak cursed his misfortunate luck and tried his hardest not to let his terror show, lest he give himself away. Following the priests who led him along, he made his way to the unholy courtyard surrounding the Church that served as the base of the malignant Tuhk.

*Translates to "Bear-Killer."

"You stand before the Mouth of the Masters accused of high treason, the destruction of this city, blasphemy, heresy, theft, conspiracy, murder, assassination and impersonation of Pah'kan priests, not to mention illegal immigration to restricted areas beyond your caste." The Pah'khan* spoke condescendingly to the criminals who knelt before him.

"It wasn't us; we were misled by another!" they cried, begging pathetically for forgiveness, though their efforts were futile.

"Your comrade is dead by the hand of the Masters himself! As for the one who escaped... He shall meet his fate yet. None who oppose the Masters escape their wrath, as you will soon see for yourselves; let the will of the Masters be done!" the Pah'khan cried in response.

G'hnak followed the orders of the High Priest, beheading both H'gruak and V'rznk simultaneously with a single stroke from a mighty Gorgon cleaver. The blade of the mighty cleaver spanned six feet and it was longer than the young smuggler-turned-soldier was tall, though he swung it with surprising strength. Their heads rolled off their shoulders and their bodies dropped; blood poured from their headless bodies and pooled around the corpses. G'hnak breathed a sigh of relief; the Outsider might have escaped, but he'd never met the two dead strangers before him and so his identity as a soldier of the Tuhk was safe and secure.

---

*The highest ranking priest of the Pah'kan order; referred to as "The Mouth of the Masters".

Over the passing months, orcish labourers worked at repairing the mass destruction done to the southern half of the Market District. The entire area had been levelled as a result of the explosions. It had been a part of Bear's plan to hire four bombers to plant and detonate explosives at the base of four key structural points throughout the Southern Market. The countless deaths resulted in an economic boom throughout the capitol. Slum dwellers surged into the Market District, collecting the ears of the dead whilst they rebuilt the former metropolis out of the debris they were able to salvage from the wreckage. Orcs were a resourceful folk, capable of building something out of nothing so to speak, and before long the Tuhk was restored back to its former glory. They reconstructed the outer walls of the Market District, inadvertently sealing the smuggler's route of old that once cut through the wall. They would further fortify their Tuhk upon the discovery of elves in their domain...

One day a convoy of slavers entered the Tuhk, returning from a wasteland expedition bearing a small contingent of elves with them. It had been some time since Istul last received a slaver's shipment from the outlying sqals, though this one had only just departed a day ago. The captain of the caravan came bearing strange news indeed, for within his shipment was the corpse of elvish royalty, no less than the Prince of Gilan himself. The presence of elves so deep in their land was disturbing enough without the fact that their slaver caravans were disappearing or that there had been no word from the outlying sqals in some time. The elves being a royal contingent from the capitol serving under the prince didn't comfort them at all. In fact, it only confused the orc masses and made their fear and paranoia worse.

The slaver captain led his convoy along, bearing their precious cargo to the very heart of the Tuhk itself, and they passes through the streets and checkpoints unopposed. The soldiers allowed him through the checkpoints without question, though their faces gave away their immense curiosity. He led the caravan along all the way to the Gardens of the Masters where he was greeted by the Pah'khan and his small inner circle along with the chief warlords of the Military District. Together they convened and the slaver captain told his tale. After their brief interrogation, they came to find that the slavers had stumbled across the elf party and they were already deceased upon their arrival.

The elves were dead of seemingly natural causes which only further perplexed the slavers. They somehow traversed the whole of the Gorgon lands unopposed, or victorious in their campaign. There was no light present in the outlying lands, which was strange; *for what reason would the beacons of the outlying sqals be extinguished?* The leaders of the capitol spoke amongst themselves and decided that the city must be further fortified against the might of the elves. Where their population had severely declined after the terrorist attacks of the infamous Bear and his band of merchant mercenaries, the inhabitants of the Slums had withdrawn into the safety of the Market District to take up residence therein.

Bombs were planted beneath the streets of the abandoned Slums as a last ditch defence in the event of an elvish invasion. Their outlying sqals were assumed to be fallen and they didn't know what to expect from the elves. Scouts were sent into the icy reaches of Northern Wastes to seek out their kin from the North along with aid from the vampires and other creatures of the night that took up residence in that northern tundra, though the Western presence in those lands left them otherwise engaged. The elves of Aenor fought a long and bitter war against the residents of those lands with the aid of the wolfmen, and so the Northerners had little to spare for their allies in the South.

CHAPTER EIGHTEEN

The hosts of Gilan marched alongside the convoy of wagons bearing their Nardic allies, wounded, and supplies. The men recovered from their treacherous journey over the passing months as they made their way to Istul. Over time, they took to walking on their own feet alongside the wagons in formation with the elves, and they gained the respect of the elves of the course of their journey. Where at first the elves had viewed them as no more than leeches, they now saw the battle-hardened warriors as they truly were. The Gorgon Desolation had taken its toll on Man and Elf alike, and they were equally united against their devil-worshipping adversaries. Some of the tribesmen spoke amongst themselves of their thoughts on the elvish campaign, though there were no such conversations within Gilan's ranks. Indeed, the elvish soldiers marched in a highly disciplined silence, focusing all of their attention upon the horizon or their footfalls.

Though they were close to the final destination of their long and arduous campaign, the days seemed eternal. To the Men of the Isles it seemed that they made no progress in their daily marches. The bleak red glare of Istul continued to burn like a tiny distant blur upon the horizon and it never grew in size regardless how much headway the host seemed to make in their northerly trek. Endless days and sleepless nights plagued their joint forces and the beleaguered warriors pushed onwards with all their might. Their haggard faces sagged low, worn down by the drawn out war to which they marched against the orcs. Their travels had visibly scarred the survivors of that wretched demon-land; elves who had once been cheery were now drained of mirth and the men had steadily given up any remaining hope of ever returning home.

Few amongst their legions could see far in the eternal darkness of the Gorgon night, though the eyes of the native orcs who were raised in those sunless lands were accustomed to it. This fact held all the more true amongst their joint forces where the wastelands were completely devoid of the light of the outlying sqal-beacons in the midst of the elvish conquest. All that could be seen throughout those black smoggy lands was the faint glow of the spirit-fire that emanated from the elves and their caravans. The Nardic Men had stared upon the elves in wonderment upon their first meeting, though they'd quickly grown accustomed to the strange oddity of the difference in their skin pigmentation over the course of their travels together. The days were long and they seemed to make no progress with the passage of time, however the elves of Gilan paid time no mind.

Days turned to weeks which quickly became months in those timeless lands. The supplies continued to dwindle and still the Tuhk seemed no nearer than when they'd first began the great undertaking. Compared to the seemingly introverted elves of Gilan, the Nardic tribesmen were a rather chatty bunch, conversing amongst themselves as they monotonously marched away. Time appeared to have no effect upon the elves, however, the Men of the Isles felt it. Three years had come and passed since they'd set out on that fated expedition and countless hundreds upon hundreds of leagues had been travelled by their forces in that time. Those who found themselves lucky enough to be counted amongst the survivors of that harsh journey certainly looked the part.

Ulrich had been assigned to what was left of the Fourth Swordsman Company of Aereil, along with a handful of his fellows. Others had been distributed throughout the ranks of the elvish host as needed, filling in the vacancies of key roles within their army. For the most part that consisted of strengthening the frontline. So it was that Ulrich found a friend within his conscripted post; Almardi, a fellow soldier of Aereil's deployed reserves. Together they spoke between themselves of their homes with occasional input from Almardi's dearest friend, Namroden. The trio had warmed up to one another over the course of their travels and Ulrich even introduced them to his only remaining acquaintance, Varg.

"*Wie geht's?*" Almardi greeted Ulrich's kin in their native Nardic tongue.

"*Sie sprechen sehr gut.*" the tribesman replied as he fell in line alongside them in their northerly march.

"*Ich verstehe nicht*,*" the elf replied, much to the confusion of Ulrich's companion, further explaining that Ulrich had only recently started teaching the elf his language.

"I was only stating that you speak the Nardic language well for *ein ausländer.*" Varg replied before properly introducing himself to the pair of elves.

*I do not understand.

Together they walked and talked beneath the dark sooty skies of the orcish wastelands on their journey to the capitol and they grew close over the course of their travels. Before long they were laughing and chatting amongst themselves as old friends would, and they even had their own inside jokes. They spoke of their homelands and told tales of their experiences; though their cultures and lives were vastly different, the group shared many common interests. There was much to talk about between them and so they spent long hours exploring the vast multitudes of topics as they traversed the bleak and barren landscape of the Gorgon Desolation. Throughout their travels the group had felt something nagging away at them for a while, like the feeling of having forgotten something, though it was many months before any of them became aware of it...

"Don't you find it rather strange that we haven't come across any opposition? Not since we arrived in Gorgor have we seen so much as a single living thing apart from ourselves." Almardi took note, suddenly interjecting the conversation of his companions.

"Surely no word has reached the capitol of our presence in these lands; they would set all of their forces upon us and crush what little is left of our armies!" Varg exclaimed in response, greatly perturbed by the observation.

"And besides, none escaped our might in any of the orc sqals; not even the deserters out of Gregor who fled seeking reinforcements to defend their town against the Nardic advance." Namroden sided with the tribesman over his childhood friend, for once taking the role of the hopeful idealist.

"Yet we haven't seen any slaver caravans or even a tar merchant in months! How can it be that we find these wastelands entirely uninhabited in the most densely populated region of the country?" Almardi rebutted, momentarily stumping his companions.

"If they have discovered us then their most likely course of action will be to muster their forces in Istul to await our inevitable arrival." Ulrich spoke up.

"Unfortunately, there's no easy way of reading the enemy's mind. The only means to find the answer we seek is to wait and see while hoping for the best." Namroden's pessimistic outlook had great improved since he'd taken up the company of his newfound Nardic friends.

"It's a shame that Prince of yours up and left; we could have used the extra scouts..." Ulrich mumbled in response.

"That's it!" Almardi burst forth with the same conviction as a scientist on the verge of a breakthrough.

"*Scheiß! Gottimhimmel;* what's come over you!?!" Varg nearly jumped out of his own skin as the surrounding troops all around them took up a defensive formation in response to the elf's sudden exclamation.

"No, no; it's nothing!" Almardi called out to the presently halted host in an effort to calm the paranoid alertness he'd only just caused within their ranks before he continued in his explanation.

"Think for a moment of Prince Rässan's troop; we've been travelling for months without the slightest sign of them! What possible explanation is there, but that they've been intercepted and captured by the orcs? They know of our presence and they are preparing for our arrival!" even as Almardi finished his sentence the elf captain of their company approached him with eyes full of rebuke.

"What has come over you that you felt the urge to incite such a scene?" Captain Sendil of Aereil's Fourth Swordsman Company reprimanded the young elf as he began his investigation into the matter.

"What news do you have of Prince Rässan?" he replied to his superior unapologetically.

"Have you partaken in the tar of the orcs? There are no tidings from him or his people. They deserted us to seek their untimely demise in the wastes that we presently traversed before your outcry." Sendil replied, not in the mood to humour his subordinate's own investigation.

"Exactly!" Almardi triumphantly exclaimed before elaborating on his thoughts, "Would we not have passed them by already, if they were truly dead in the wastes? Is it not strange that we've yet to stumble upon any signs of life in our travels to their stronghold?"

Captain Sendil took in the elf's words and chewed on them thoughtfully for a moment before coming to a decision. Without a word he dismissed himself and sought out Captain Vasil to discuss with him the findings of his inquiry. Together the elf captains convened amongst themselves and the host was halted indefinitely, much to their confusion. Word of Almardi's disruption was quickly spreading through the host and rumours were already starting to arise before Captain Vasil called his troops to order. Acknowledging the recent turn of events, he addressed Almardi's outburst firstly in order to deter any further unfounded assumptions from taking form and spreading throughout their ranks. Rather than disregard it, however, the elf captain only confirmed Almardi's hypothesis, much to the discontent of their gathered forces.

Upon hearing their commander out, the elf host resumed their travels without so much as a gripe or a moan on both the part of the men and elves. Being the bearer of bad news, Captain Vasil had taken the opportunity to remind his men of their triumphs and the extent of their prowess in those lands rather than dwell on the facts that would only go on to demotivate and drain them of their morale. His speech hadn't quite had as much of an effect as he'd hope, though the experienced captain was nowhere near naive enough to believe that he could boost their spirits in the face of all that opposed them. Captain Vasil knew that the only way he could return their peace of mind was through winning the war and so that was exactly what he planned to do. He promised his men that he would return as many of them whole and healthy to their homes as he was able, though he also warned them that the majority of those gathered would never see their homeland again. It was the sacrifice of those who would give up their lives in that desolate country that would allow their friends and family to continue to live happily without the fear of what threatened them in the orc lands. Captain Vasil emphasised the fact in his speech and it was solely responsible for their continued trek North. Regardless of what awaited their forces within the Tuhk of Istul, the combined host of men and elves would make their way to the stronghold and free their world from the evil demons and devices of the orcs.

CHAPTER NINETEEN
ISTUL, GORGON DESOLATION
Spring, 198

G'hnak shifted his weight, leaning uneasily on his jagged broad-bladed sword. He remained in a thoughtful silence, keeping watch over the labourers as they repaired the damage done to the Tuhk by Bruh and his band of merchant mercenaries. Leaning upon the Gorgon-forged blade, the young smuggler-turned-soldier reflected upon the recently passed events once again. Somehow he'd managed to convince the Tuhk's guard that he was also a fellow member of their ranks. As it was, they decided to promote him to the rank of captain, giving him command of his own company of an hundred orcish warriors.

The whole of Istul's military forces came together in the time of crisis to oversee the city's reconstruction. They kept watch over the labourers who worked away at repairing the damage done by the former drug dealer, Bear, whose wretched scheme to steal the tar reserves left the southern half of the outer city in a ruinous state. It was their duty to oversee the reconstruction as well as stabilise the influx of slum dwellers who clamorously made their way into the city. With the help of Istul's military, the residents of the Slums migrated into the inner reaches of the Tuhk in an orderly fashion. Where the southern marketplace had basically been razed to the ground, the population of the capitol had drastically decreased which created a booming demand for workers. The slum dwellers took the opportunity and rushed in through the broken walls surrounding the Market District, erecting their own homes amidst the wreckage of the prime real estate.

Though the slum dwellers were finding an improvement in their overall quality of life, the city's destruction came with more misfortune than just the deaths of nearly half the city's populace. The Pah'ka came forth from the Tuhk declaring that the sudden destruction was a message from the Masters. There hadn't been any incoming shipments of slaves for some time. The Masters were getting impatient and the Market's devastation was only the beginning, or so they said. It was decreed that a monthly tribute was to be made, though G'hnak knew it to be no more than a ploy. He had been indirectly responsible for the mass destruction and although he couldn't prove it without incriminating himself, he knew they were simply justifying population control; the killing of Slum Dwellers to control the inner city's population in the midst of the massive influx. So it was that G'hnak played the silent observer to the blatant corruption before him. Before long it would be driven completely out of his mind, however, upon the arrival of a strange shipment of elvish slaves one day...

A clamour arose in the distance and G'hnak ordered his crew to ready themselves in response. There was an uproar of activity in the outer reaches of the Slums and it steadily made its way towards G'hnak from where his company was positioned nearby the remains of the Southeast Market Gate. Though his plan had failed and he was dead, G'hnak couldn't help but admire Bruh's handiwork. The drug dealer had strategically plotted the bomb locations perfects, causing the complete destruction of the area in a domino effect that resulted in masking all evidence of the very bombings themselves. Interrupting him from his reverie, a caravan of slavers suddenly approached his checkpoint from the slums in their travels to the heart of the Tuhk itself.

"What devilry is this?!?" G'hnak couldn't believe his eyes as the slaver captain approached him.

"I come bearing tidings for all to hear in our travels to the Pah'khan, though I don't know what they mean." the slaver boldly announced, "We came across this elvish party midway in our travels to Gorgor, but get this: *they were already dead!*"

"*Murghat-khet!* Your eyes must be brown your so full of it!" G'hnak snapped back.

"No, really!" the slaver quickly replied, "There haven't been any shipments of elves in years; who is there to rob? And besides, we've got the King of the elves himself, and you can see that for yourself!"

G'hnak was dumbfounded as he stared upon the corpse of an elf, obviously of high royalty. He wore a crowned helm upon his head and his guard was attired in a way that G'hnak had never before seen on any of the other elf slaves brought into that city. Their armour was beautifully wrought, engraved with a pattern of flowering vines and forged more intricately than any other elvish armour G'hnak had ever stared upon in his entire life. *Surely they are of noble birth*, he reasoned, *though their leader is most certainly royalty.* Bearing this in mind, he made his decision.

"I have no idea how you came across these elves, though I'm certain you haven't the slightest clue yourself. You don't need my permission to take this news to the priests; we both know its your duty." he let the slaver through and they parted company.

It was ill news indeed, however, and G'hnak felt a sinking feeling in his belly as all life drained from him where he stood. *So the rumours are true; the brughkt-prah have come to destroy us,* he took a toke of some tar in his pipe with a hint of bittersweet nostalgia. Though he'd played Bruh, G'hnak now saw that Bruh had played everyone in the bigger picture. Seeing an opportunity to pull off a grand heist in the midst of the annihilation of his people, that bastard hadn't even thought to warn anyone where he'd been so caught up in his selfish endeavour. The sudden realisation hit G'hnak with the force of a train and he fought with all of his might to hold it in, lest he incriminate himself in the whole affair.

"Wait! Halt! Stop in the name of the Masters; I'm going with you!" he shouted as he ran to catch up with the slaver who'd already travelled some ways down the road.

The slavers took him into their company without question and together they made their way to the Gardens of the Masters in the heart of the Tuhk. There they found the Pah'khan roaming the gardens on his own, lost in thought. They approached him and interrupted the orc from his reflective state, shocking the orc priest out of his silence. He beheld their cargo and exclaimed at the sight of the elvish nobleman. The priest questioned the slaver deeply of all that he knew pertaining to his cargo. G'hnak listened attentively to the slaver's account of his findings and upon his conclusion interjected quickly before the Pah'khan even had a chance to respond.

"It's true! These elves must have been part of a scouting party, though I don't believe it to be their king. Maybe a prince, but this is nothing compared to what marches upon us! I am Captain G'hnak Bruh'kulka, and I believe that Bear saw a lucrative opportunity in the midst of the extermination of our people. There has been a rise of homeless orcs in the Slums claiming to be survivors of an elvish assault upon the sqals and I believe them. Bruh had no other reason to steal the tar reserves; he was a successful dealer in the wastelands. There's no other explanation as to why there would be a squad of dead elves, and *royalty* no less, upon our doorstep!" he burst forth with the information, wording it so as not to give himself away in the heat of the moment.

"In the name of the Masters!" the priest cried out, "If what you say is true, this is an omen of the end of our people! Gather the Tuhk's forces and muster them in the defence of our city. You, G'hnak Bruh'kulka; spread the word to all of those fit to fight! We must focus our efforts on restoring the fortifications of this Tuhk before our enemy falls upon us with all of their might!"

* * *

"The brughkt-prah* would never awaken the woods of death; it would swallow them whole and they'd never be seen again. Nothing comes out of those woods that goes in!" an orc in G'hnak's company by the name of Rah'shaq spoke up, arguing with a handful of his squadmates as word spread through the Tuhk like wildfire.

"Not if they used their witchcraft and devilry against the wood; they've summoned its wrath and they're taking their vengeance upon us!" Sh'auk quickly rebutted.

"What does it matter anyhow? All of the outlying sqals have fallen and soon they'll be upon us. What chance do we stand where our brethren have all failed?" a third orc wailed.

"So what? You would have us give ourselves up to the brughkt-prah to be slaughtered like sheep? To those of you whose plan it is to fight to your last dying breath; show this blasphemous scum what we have in store for the elves who march upon us!" Captain G'hnak Bruh'kulka shouted as his company of warriors closed ranks around the traitor, tearing him apart limb from limb just as their superior commanded.

---

*The orcish term for elves, literally translates "bright people" due to their radiant skin.

The blasphemer screamed and cried out as orcs piled on top of him. An orc stood on his back with one foot to hold him down as the oppressor pulled at his victim's arm, severing it in a flurry of blood spatter. Another of G'hnak's company did the same to the other arm whilst another orc picked the traitor up, wrapping his arms around the armless torso of the screaming orc as two more soldiers tore his legs from under him. The orc that held him dropped the limbless torso before catching his head and snapping his neck, ending the war criminal's cries. Upon his death, G'hnak shouted out an order to his men and they dispersed to return to their duties of keeping watch over the city's reconstruction.

Over the passing months leading up to what the orcs believed to be an elvish invasion, they quickly restored the Tuhk to its former glory. Upon completion of the restoration they went on to further militarise their city, just in case the elves did lay siege upon their glorious stronghold as the priests forewarned. Ballistae lined the rooftops of the Market District and they filled the sewage network beneath the streets of the former Slums with explosives. This was as a last resort in the event that the elves took the outer city, though many feared it was their only chance of survival. The brughkt-prah were a terrible foe and the orcs of Istul were taught to fear them at an early age.

The Pah'kan priests that taught school in the capitol ingrained into their students the teachings of the Masters along with their divine commandments. It was taught that only through partaking in the consumption of guaka-guaka could one achieve true enlightenment and inner peace, as well as through the weekly sacrifice of slaves and the unworthy. Believing that the brughkt-prah were descendants of the fire-demon in the sky, otherwise known as the Sun in the rest of the world, they were told by their priests that the elves took on the form of angels to blind them to the teachings of their true gods, the Masters. In reality, the Pah'kan priests told their young charges, the elves were truly demons; *no good things walked under the light of the fire-demon.* That fact alone was reason enough for the orcs of those lands to worship their foul gods and the drugs they created.

In the process of guaka-guaka refinement the skies grew smoggy from the pollutants released, though the orcs believed this to be the work of their Masters. They believed that the pollution was in actuality the protection of the divine deities they worshipped, keeping them safe from the fiery demon-god of the elves who lived in the sky. Only the orcs of the Desolation's outer reaches travelled abroad under the light of day, though it was mostly slavers seeking out elves to deliver to the capitol. The albino orcs of the heartlands suffered debilitating blindness and their skin burned under the daytime sun. So it was that few amongst Istul's populace had ever travelled outside the walls that protected them from the harshness of the Gorgon wastelands. Indeed, the only experience the majority of Istul's inhabitants had with the elves was simply staring upon the captured sacrificial slaves in their deliverance to the Tuhk. They were paraded through the streets in crude caged wagons for all to stare and gawk upon as they were brought before the Masters to be given as tribute in the highest reaches of that wretched tower fortress.

CHAPTER TWENTY

Looking out from where he stood upon the outer battlements surrounding the Market District, G'hnak oversaw the war preparations of the Slums. The whole of the Tuhk's population had come together in the midst of what rumours foretold to be the end of their civilisation. Behind him, he could see the towering monolith that was the Tuhk of the Istul deep in the heart of that wretched city. The antechamber of the Masters burned radiant in the heavens above, glowing a blurry red where flames angrily spewed from the chimneys that jutted out of the unholy citadel, high above the dark blanket of smog that covered those lands. Ahead of him the streets of the Slums were teeming with orcs as they ran to and fro the bomb wagons that were scattered throughout the sprawling ghetto.

The residents of the Tuhk unloaded the wagons, taking their cargo down into the sewage network beneath the city streets where they filled the underground labyrinth of interconnected tunnels with enough explosives to decimate the entire Slum District. Others worked away at prepping the outermost wall against an elvish assault, driving spikes into the ramshackle battlements surrounding the Slums so as to prevent the elvish horses from charging through. They even coiled barbed wire around the spikes to dissuade their elvish adversaries from scaling the walls using them as hand- and foot-holds. Even from where he stood upon the parapet of the Market District G'hnak could see the preparations of war fully underway. Ballistae and trebuchets lined the ringed 30 metre tall ringed wall that spanned the outer reaches of the Market District, ready to fire upon whatever invasive force found itself misfortunate enough to lay siege to their city.

All around the wrath of the Masters manifested itself visibly throughout the orcish capitol. The flames that spewed forth from the Tuhk's multitude of chimneys burned brighter and hotter than was normal and the city's residents could feel the distinct presence of an otherworldly being. Taking another hit of tar to clear his head, G'hnak found that consumption of guaka-guaka only made the static noise in his head worse. To the orc it was almost as if he could hear the whispering thoughts of another inside his own head, though they were frenzied and angry. He couldn't make any sense of it in the slightest and pondering it only made his head hurt worse. With a pounding head he turned to depart from his position atop the battlements back down to the ground below just as a quarrel started to kick off nearby.

"What concern is this war of yours to us? It was *your* people who angered the brughkt-prah; this is *your* war, not ours." a goblin archer sneered at the orcish captain whose authority he challenged, much to the amusement of his rowdy crew.

"*You* mountain-folk are scum; once we're finished with this war of ours see if we don't burn you out of the filthy holes you call homes." the orc captain snarled in response, picking the goblin up by his genitalia, "You've got some balls for a grunt... Let's fix that."

The orc ripped his hand back as he flung the goblin from the parapet, tearing his genitals off in the process. Holding the mangled cock and balls of the mutineer in his tightly clenched fist, the orc captain roared a challenge for all to hear upon those battlements.

"This is what happens when you fuck with me!" he shouted into the surrounding crowd of goblins and orcs alike.

"The brughkt-prah will burn this monument of waste to the ground and you'll witness your own gods abandon you before the elves run their blades through your bellies!" a goblin spat in the face of the dominating orc captain and his response was to throw the goblin cock in the face of the new contender.

A handful of the goblin's bolder comrades joined him upon witnessing the offensive act and together they rushed the captain. The hulking warrior swung his massive mace, flinging two of the five goblin aggressors off the wall to join their dead friend below. With a second swing from his powerful weapon, the orc captain flung another goblin and he landed with a crunch at the feet of the outer ring of spectators. Orcs laughed and jeered in unison at the mutineers as the beastly officer mauled his enemies without mercy. Out of the two remaining goblins one laid down his arms and gave up the fight, but the captain wouldn't hear of it. Kicking the pathetic coward in his chest, the orc captain stomped the surrendered goblin's skull and crushed it beneath his heavy iron-shod boot. He ended the conflict by ripping the tongue from his final opponents mouth, even as the goblin opened it to let loose his piercing death-cry.

Turning away from the scene before it grew any bigger, G'hnak returned to the streets below. Upon reaching ground-level, he sought out his company amongst the bustling crowds as the city's residents busied themselves about the war preparations. Goblins had started to arrive from the Iron Teeth Mountains in the East upon hearing the Tuhk's call to arms, though they were not unanimous in their support of the orcish cause. Indeed, the sole reason for their presence all boiled down to the goblin chieftains. They ordered their subjects to join the orcs after seeing that it was mutually beneficial to their survival.

It was imperative to the orcs of the Tuhk to seek out whatever aid was available from the outlying lands and so they didn't have much room to be picky in their recruitment. Though the goblins brought dissent and counter-productivity with them amongst the legions of Istul's orcs, they were a much-needed ally and a necessary evil. So it was that G'hnak found himself wandering through the streets, attempting to avoid confrontation at all costs. Where he was a captain himself, it attracted unfriendly stares and muttering wherever he went amongst the goblin forces. The orcs were already a brutal warmongering race under normal circumstances and the addition of their rowdy goblin neighbours only pushed them to the extreme.

It already took little to provoke a fight between two orcs; a simple misunderstanding could quickly escalate into a full-blown duel. With the addition of the goblins there was chaos and disorder within their ranks. Goblins were quick to challenge the authority of their orcish superiors and the orcs barely had the tolerance to deal with them in the best of times. Civil disorder spread quicker than spilt milk in the sprawling convoluted mess that served as their capitol. G'hnak sought out some peace and tranquillity in that place where there was seemingly none.

He found some of his crew overseeing the bomb distribution throughout the Slums. Others went about unloading the wagons and it was just as he'd previously observed from upon the battlements, high up above the haphazard streets he presently navigated. It was rather noisy work and the orcs all shouted to one another as they toiled away, which only made G'hnak's pounding headache all the worse. Though the constant clamour didn't help his headache, it wasn't the noise that caused it. He was riddled with stress and the volume of his thoughts left him feeling as if his skull was about to burst at the seams.

Where the goblins had already answered the Masters call to arms, somewhere to the North Istul's messengers were flying upon the backs of their great wargs with all due haste. They bore the very same message as they'd delivered to the goblins, though they took it to the orcs and vampires of the Northern Wastes. Following the River Gorgon upon its eastern bank as they made their northerly trek, the messengers would cross it near its mouth. There it was iced over just enough for them to cross without their mounts, and from that point they would make the journey by foot to the former stronghold of the Necromancers in Alvaria. Others had also been sent West towards the only remaining sqal of Ishtan, though no message had been received in response and the neighbouring city's beacon died out some weeks after the messengers were sent.

These were the thoughts that plagued G'hnak's mind and left him unable to clear his head. The elves marched upon them, drawing nearer every day, and still they busied themselves about preparing for their arrival. Most of the orcish population put their faith in the Masters or their demonic overlords, the Shak'hal. G'hnak was not so naive as his kin however. It would have taken something truly terrible to behold to send the wealthiest of the country's drug dealers on such a fool's errand as Bear undertook. The young smuggler knew in his heart that it was the end of days and also that it was nearly upon them.

He cursed his lot in life, sullenly staring upon the captain's gear in which he was attired with eyes full of resentment. Wanting nothing more than to escape his people's untimely demise, G'hnak swore aloud in frustration as thought of all the horrible things he would have liked to do to Bruh, had he the chance. The drug dealer had already met his fate as it was and so G'hnak struggled to accept that fact. He would never find closure or relief in his desire for vengeance, except at the hands of the elves who would release him from the shackles of his life. Issuing an order to his troop upon their completion of unloading the bomb wagon, G'hnak and his company escorted the wagon back into the inner Tuhk where they would replenish its supply of explosives.

CHAPTER TWENTY-ONE

After what seemed like several eternities, the distant pinprick of light that was the Tuhk of Istul steadily began grow in size upon the horizon until it was like a dim red blurry splotch set deep in the dark black skies. It continued to grow in stature as the combined forces of elves and men drew nearer. Before long they could make out the distant capitol of the orc-country and the Men of the Isles shuddered at the sight of the malignant stronghold. Even after all that they bore witness to in their travels through the Dead Wood, the Nardic tribesmen were initially struck by awe and terror upon seeing the fortified Tuhk of the orcs. The elves continued to march without slowing or stopping and the tribesmen matched their pace even as they felt all life drain from them.

Ulrich fought to ignore the sickly sinking feeling in the pit of his belly and looked around at his kinsmen to see how they fared. For the most part his fellows gravely marched to what they assumed to be their deaths in absolute silence. None spoke amongst the ranks of battle-hardened veterans as they prepared themselves for what awaited them at the end of their lengthy campaign. They were at the final stretch of their long and arduous journey and soon it would all be over, for better or for worse. No one knew how the upcoming events of the near future would play out, though few amongst them held any faith whatsoever in their sombre ranks.

It was common knowledge throughout the host that the orcs had discovered their presence. They couldn't help but to assume that their enemy had gathered all their remaining forces en masse in preparation for the war that marched upon their doorstep. The assumption turned to fact for them when suddenly Ishtan's distant beacon of light was extinguished one day in their travels. It only served to dishearten them further. The combined forces of the South felt what little hope they'd managed to preserve diminish, leaving them dead and empty on the inside.

They continued their northerly march regardless, seeing that they had no other options. Extermination was, in fact, the only possible outcome for either side. If they were successful, the elves of Gilan would eradicate the orcish race from Aerbon once and for all, though if the orcs prevailed it would likewise spell out the end of Gilan as they knew it. If they were victorious the orcs would ravage the elf-lands, unopposed upon the annihilation of the entire elvish army. So it was that they continued onwards, hoping beyond hope that they could persevere in their efforts.

There were rumours of much worse things than orcs in the North, however, if the rumours of Roman merchants were to be believed. They spoke of necromancers, vampires, and other such demonic creatures. It was said that there was an elvish kingdom in the North who waged war upon those monstrosities, though the Romans who spoke of them knew little beyond that. They gathered the little information they had on the subject in their travels to Legion, where they took the enchanted wildberries of Gilan to a kingdom of men, Legion, in the Northwest. Selling the elvish berries to winemakers in Legion, they occasionally turned their ears to the rumours and news of that land. It was through the Legionnaires that Roman merchants heard the word of fell things in the East plaguing their neighbours, the elves of Aenor.

Though the knowledge of an elvish frontline in the far north comforted Gilan's united forces, the fact that there were more monstrous evils beyond the Northern border of the orc country did little to ease their doubts. As it was, the elves of Gilan did not know much of the world outside their homelands as few travelled far beyond their borders. They knew of the Gorgon Desolation from information they'd gathered via captured orcs and their maps, as well as the occasional scouting expeditions they sent to map out the hostile lands. Their only interaction with the outside world of Aerbon was solely the annual trips of Rome's traders and the no-so-often visits of Nardic sailors who rarely docked in the port of Aereil.

Marching through stagnant darkness of the Desolation, none amongst the ranks of men and elves had the slightest idea that it was the Summer of the one hundred and ninety-eighth year of the First Era. It had nearly been four years since they'd embarked upon their righteous quest, though to the majority it seemed like much more time had passed them by. The wretched fortress of the orcs continued to draw nearer with each passing week; it loomed in the distance like some sort of putrid candle draped in smog. Flames spouted from its chimneys, high above the blanket of darkness that covered those lands. The Tuhk itself glowed a faint reddish brown where the illumination of its exhausts reflected off it, though the light was unpleasant and only made the tower seem all the more sinister.

Nothing could be seen yet of the surrounding city or the ringed walls that protected it, though with the passing days the Tuhk continued to grow upon the horizon. As time went by in their travels Istul's circular city oozed forth from the ground and before long they were upon it. The journey had been a long one, though it was already over and much faster than they would have preferred. If they were totally honest with themselves there wasn't a single soldier, Captain Vasil included, who wanted to be there and even their greatly-revered commander was beginning to see the hopelessness of it all. Captain Vasil was the most widely respected soldier in the whole of

Gilan, as well as their most skilful tactician; in the days leading up to the final battle he racked every last braincell in an attempt to devise a cunning plan.

On the evening of the final day's march the host halted, the highest-ranking officers of each company convened together in the captain's pavilion tent to plot out their course of action the following morning. Meanwhile, elves began unloading the tools and parts of the Nardic war machines they'd purchased at home and lugged all that way in a handful of their horse-drawn wagons. The tribesmen busied themselves about constructing the devices, putting together catapults, trebuchets, battering rams, and the like. Nardic war machines were designed to be portable so that they could even be transported via the smallest of fishing vessels. Their reasoning behind this was that where they were an island nation the need for speed, space, and portability were significant factors in times of war.

As they prepared their camp for the night, just a couple of leagues away from orcish stronghold to the south and east, all eyes watched the malignant Tuhk with unease. Something was terribly wrong. No one could be certain, but they all felt it. The air was as tense as a drawn bowstring and they kept themselves at the ready like a grazing gazelle fully aware of the lion that laid in wait, waiting for the perfect opportunity to pounce upon it. They were potentially marching to their deaths and all around them was the constant reminder of that fact.

The weary faces of Nardic men showed the signs of just how much time had passed in that place, magnified by the stress and worry that wore them down. Though the elves were blessed with unnaturally long lives, even their faces had been aged, careworn, and their hair was even beginning to grey. Only the elves of the Aush Wood were seemingly unaffected by the war; they'd seen much in their seemingly immortal lifetimes and this small chapter of the world was but a passing moment to them. Should they find death at the end of their journey, they would simply embrace it as an old friend and return their life-force to the earth that gave them life.

But if I die here, would my spirit return to Urea*? Egorin futilely fought against the thoughts of doubt, fear, and worry that afflicted him. As a Keeper of the sacred wood, he had been responsible for the deliverance of countless souls and he'd seen and felt first-hand the transference of their spirits. If he died there in the orcish fortress along with the entirety of their army, if they lost, all of their souls would be swallowed up by the demon god they served. Where the host was so close to the capitol, he'd begun to feel the presence of that monstrous creature, as had the rest of the Aush Wood elves. It was faint so far from the source, though they made no mention of the energy that emanated from the capitol for fear of distressing the already beleaguered troops. They were in tune with the spirit world and so only they could feel the demonic force, though they were also the only force capable of dealing with the creature. It would prove no easy task as they all knew; the demon's power was great, greater than any spiritual force they ever felt in the entirety of their lives, like that of a God. Their only goal was to destroy the demon overlord at all costs, even if it meant sacrificing their very souls.

---

*Urea is the world; their planet Earth.

Almardi spent the final night before the battle on the outskirts of their camp beside Namroden, where they sat together staring off into the distant southern darkness in silence. Neither elf spoke, merely enjoying each other's company one last time before they marched to their deaths. They fought to keep their minds empty and carefree, seeing it as their last day together before the End. They'd spent the entirety of their short lives together and they refused to allow death to separate them. Suddenly Namroden broke the silence.

"I love you Almardi."

"And I you Brother." he replied, clasping his dear friend's hand in his own.

"Is that what this is then?" Namroden sighed, withdrawing.

"What's up with you? What is wrong?" Almardi was bewildered by his strange behaviour.

Taking Almardi's face into his hands, Namroden took the stunned elf and planted a kiss upon his lips as they embraced...

The following morning Captain Vasil presented himself before the entire host once everyone had finished eating and preparing themselves for the day ahead of them. He held on to their fleeting chance of victory and explained to them the plan he devised the previous night with the help of his advisers. Five separate contingents would be formed out of their available forces; a frontline force whose task it was to escort the battering rams safely to the outermost wall of Istul and aid them in the penetration of the battlements. A second group, comprised entirely of the Nardic tribesmen, would infiltrate the stronghold through the sewage outlet to the east of city. They would gain entry via the outlet that fed into the wretched sewage canal that flowed straight out from the city, directly to the base of the Iron Teeth where it spilt into an underground well deep in the roots of those mountains.

While the Nardic forces infiltrated the city from the sewers beneath its streets, the third and fourth groups would reinforce the frontlines as they made their way to the market district, where a squad of the Nardic troops would be awaiting them upon opening the inner gate for the elves as they fought their way through the Slums. Last but not least, the fifth company was that of the Aush Wood elves; the spirit keepers and demon slayers. They would join the other half of Nardic tribesmen at the military district where they would come from the north, against the enemy's expectations. From there they would ascend to the highest reaches of the Tuhk and challenge the Master of the Orcs himself. Though the overall outlook of the host was poor they all knew there were no better options available and so they put all of their faith in their renowned commander without question.

CHAPTER TWENTY-TWO
ISTUL, GORGON DESOLATION
Winter, 1E198

The ground shuddered as ballistae fired their explosive arrows past the outer reaches of the city outskirts, firing upon the advancing elf host as well as their battering rams and other siege engines. Gigantic boulders flew crashing down upon the buildings and streets of the orcish stronghold in response; a few of their shots had even managed to smack into the city's inner walls. The battlements refused to yield to the might of the elves, only cracking and chipping when struck by the great rocks launched by the mighty Nardic war machines. Smoke obscured the streets and G'hnak fought his way through the dust and debris, seeking out safety where there was none present. His actions in the midst of the elvish invasion hadn't gone unnoticed however, and before he knew it the scrawny captain found himself staring into the face of his judge.

"Going somewhere?" Rah'shaq lifted the terrified orc by his neck so that his body dangled limply above the ground.

"Release me, you filth!" G'hnak spat back before falling into a coughing fit as his accuser tightened his grip around the young orc's neck.

"Just as I thought; you're no killer." Rah'shaq laughed, carrying G'hnak by his neck to display his shame to the rest of their company.

"Is this who you would take your orders from? The mighty G'hnak Bruh'kulka? Ha! More like G'hnak *Dhurg'ghat*; the Carrion Crow." Rah'shaq cackled as he publicly humiliated the orc before his own crew.

Under normal circumstances, challenging the authority of one's superior was cause for a duel to the death in the orc country. As it was, G'hnak was obviously the weaker of the two and Rah'shaq made the fact known to all who would hear it. That didn't stop the gathered orcs from shouting and chanting in their attempt to further incite a fight, though with a sudden eruption of noise they scurried for cover as the elves invaded and the Slums exploded...

* * *

Ulrich held tight to the haft of his axe, damning Fate and the Gods under his breath as he stacked up alongside his brethren against the outermost wall surrounding the Slums of Istul. Together they braced themselves as the men at the front hacked away at an iron-barred opening situated at the foot of the wall. The gated hole fed a rancid river that oozed from its mouth, following its course in a straight easterly beeline as the orc-made trench led it directly toward its end at the base of the Iron Teeth*. With both arms he joined in as the men nearest to the opening hacked away at the rusty metal bars. The rods shattered upon impact, yielding to the superior might of the Nardic axemen. Upon freeing the opening, the whole contingent of tribesmen present were taken aback by the reality of the obstacle they presently faced.

"*Scheiß!*" Varg exhaled.

---

*Once long ago, sometime roughly between 1E13-28, when the orcs had first developed the capitol's sewage systems, a minor feud between rival goblin and orc factions came to the attention of a greater warlord's clan, who influenced the city's waste management officials to order a trench be dug. They flooded out the homes of the offenders, deep in the underground tunnels beneath the Iron Teeth Mountains, by digging a storm-drain into the base of the mountains into which they pumped their sewage river. It fed directly into tunnels of the goblin kingdom, A'ka'hkus. The flooding almost resulted in the annihilation of their entire kingdom, simply for the sake of a faction dispute. Upon facing their near extinction, the remnants of the goblin race went on to be hunted out and taken in as slaves by the orcs who saw them as an inferior species in the aftermath of their devastation. This is what initially sparked the goblin-orc hostilities; the majority of goblins were unable to forgive them as a race for the terrible offence of the predecessors, even generations after regaining their liberty.

Some of those nearest to the waste river were beginning to cough and spew upon taking in the foul odour that was liquefied orc faeces. As if the scent of the orc excrement wasn't enough to make them sick to their stomachs, they were expected to dive headfirst into it in the hopes that they *might* surface on the other side. The river looked to be a bloody caramelised shade of brown under the illumination of the Tuhk's outpour of flaming smog in the heavens above, though the dim red light only made it all the more repulsive in the warm stagnant air. It had the consistency of refried beans along with a scent worse than rotten eggs and rancid meat magnified several times over. One by one the Nardic men plopped into the fetid faecal stream, swimming under the surface to pass through into the underground tunnel network that comprised Istul's sewage system.

Coughing, choking, gagging, retching, and covered in the abominable excrements of the orcs, the tribesmen surfaced as quickly as they could on the other side. Clambering out of the waste-river, they pulled themselves atop the dual walkways on either side of the underground tunnel they found themselves within. Torches were mounted upon the walls, though they were spaced far apart, lighting the network of underground passages in an eerie light. Shadows danced on the walls and the men could hardly breathe where the wretched odours were so strong. It was warm and humid in that place and the men grew faint as the combined conditions overwhelmed all of their senses.

Ulrich felt as if he were on the verge of losing consciousness and he struggled to push onwards alongside his kinsmen. They struggled to delve deeper into the heart of the underground sewage network beneath the city's streets noiselessly, though occasionally a tribesman's coughing spasms would echo upon the bare cylindrical walls. They were as watchful and wary as they could be given the circumstances, keeping all eyes and ears alert for the slightest signs of activity as they traversed the labyrinth. Water dripped from the rounded ceiling where it splashed in the wretched waste stream that cut through the middle of the tubular tunnels. The men were all on edge as they pushed onwards, fighting back the revolting smell that seemed to emanate from within them as they attempted to stealthily infiltrate the orcish stronghold.

The sound of feet padding along in the distance echoed distantly and the Nardic troop stopped in its tracks. The sound was drawing nearer, heading directly towards them from up ahead a ways. There was an intersection in the passage not far from their current position and the source of the noise seemed to be coming from the right. They prepared themselves and a small four-man squad of orcs crossed the intersection ahead of them on a southerly sprint at full speed. The Nardic archers amongst their ranks fired off a volley of arrows that flew whistling down the tunnel. The arrows took their marks down and the fallen orc crumpled, tumbling into the wretched river comprised of their own wastes with a loud *plop*.

"Where do you reckon they were making for?" one of the men spoke aloud.

"Never you mind; we need to keep pushing forwards." Ulrich replied between choking on his words.

"How much further is it? It reeks down here" one of the younger lads whined.

"How about we actually focus on getting out of here?" Varg sided with his comrade.

As they crossed the intersection, connected by wooden planks serving as a four-way cross-walk, the men saw what the orcs had been making for to their left. There was a great pile of bombs piled up just down the way with a fuse running down the tunnel several metres long. The lengthy fuse would have given the orcish bombers ample time to make their way back to the safety of the streets of Istul's marketplace before their charges detonated. Though it was too late to warn the elves of the danger that laid in wait, the men saw an opportunity to benefit from the destructive power of the orc bombs. A dozen of the tribesmen each took a barrel of the explosives that had been stacked upon a platform spanning both sides of the tunnel. It was made up of a handful of the wooden planks that joined the parallel walkways.

The sewers began to rumble as the elvish assault began. The men ran along on their way to the streets of the Market District as quickly as they could before the elves penetrated the outermost wall. When the elves infiltrated the Slums it would ignite an explosion the likes of which they couldn't even comprehend the magnitude. They carried their stolen cargo along with a firm plan in mind as they made their way deeper west into the Tuhk. Ulrich kept alert as he ran along openly down the passageway alongside his fellows. Adrenaline coursed through their veins as they ran along with the sudden realisation of the pressing need to seek a way out of the sewers as quickly as they could.

*   *   *

Letting loose a foul string of curses, Rah'shaq returned his attention back to the pressing matter at hand even as G'hnak disappeared into the clamorous crowds of orcish soldiers. Following the loss of their captain, G'hnak's former company fell into a disorderly state as they fought amongst themselves over who his rightful successor was. In the heat of the moment Rah'shaq made his way into the heart of the squabbling mass and picked one of the grunts up by his head before crushing the unfortunate orc's skull in his gargantuan hand. The death cry released by his victim gave the hulking orc the attention of his fellow comrades at arms and he took full advantage of the opportunity.

"Are there any here amongst you who would challenge my claim to captaincy?" Rah'shaq roared to the gathered orc mass.

No one had the audacity to challenge his superiority and so order was restored within the rowdy ranks of the leaderless congregation. Though their leadership issues had been resolved, it only allowed them to focus on the more urgent matter that was the elvish invasion of Istul. Shouting out his first command as the new captain of the crew he found himself in charge of, Rah'shaq ordered them to cover even as a massive boulder came crashing down upon them. The orc felt the reverberations of its impact as he was flung off his feet, momentarily sent soaring through the streets before breaking his fall upon the wall of a nearby building. The dilapidated structure gave way as he fell through the wall and rolled upon the floor of the room within like a rag doll before coming to a stop.

Brushing himself off as he brought himself to his feet, Rah'shaq returned to the streets and took in the devastation for himself before calling out to the survivors of the elvish barrage. Catapulted rocks continued to come down upon the stronghold, seemingly at random, though the ground constantly shook whilst boulders fell like rain. The recently-instated orc-captain rallied his remaining troops and found that the casualties had been minimal where he had been so quick to make the call to cover. Across the street he could see as the fellow survivors of his crew rushed to join him in the advance. Leading them away from their current position nearby the Southeast Gate, Rah'shaq led the remnants of his company out of the Market District and into the Slums to take care of whatever was left of the elvish army that beset them.

CHAPTER TWENTY-THREE

G'hnak ducked into the cover of what was left of a former sqat* and took refuge under the ruined remains as another barrage of catapulted rocks came crashing down all around him. Silver arrows rained down as well now that the remaining elves made their advance upon the stronghold. Though the explosive ambush of the orcs had undoubtedly taken its toll on the forces of Gilan, still more of the glowing god-like warriors poured in like ants out of the woodwork. There were fires raging in the city and they were rapidly spreading throughout the Slums as they made their way into the inner marketplace. Even as G'hnak fled further North away from the frontlines a massive boulder came crashing down into the streets and it brought several sqats tumbling down with it.

The way ahead was blocked and even his own people had turned against him upon finding him out for the filthy little rat that he was. Terrified and without any other options, he turned around and fled back the way he'd only just come. Orcs shouted and screamed all around and he could vaguely hear officers barking out orders to their crews amidst the turmoil. Lost and disoriented he struggled to keep his head in the midst of his chaotic mental state; the sheer stress of it all was eating him alive. His head was heavy and all he wanted to do was curl up in a ball and shut out the world.

*Sqat is a term used by the orcs in reference to shared accommodations. In Istul, sqats typically consisted of crudely constructed blocks of flats and apartment complexes.

Running back the way he came G'hnak spotted the deadly silver volleys of the elvish archers as they pushed forwards deeper into the what was left of the ruinous Slum District. Upon breaking free of the closed in streets that kept him trapped on a one-way path, the former orc-captain turned East and made for the outer wall surrounding the marketplace he presently navigated. Even as he sprinted along in his vain attempt at freedom a flurry of arrows whistled past him, though they hadn't belonged to the elves judging by their appearance. One of the unfamiliar pine arrows embedded itself within the thickset iron cuirass he wore upon his chest, flinging him effortlessly whilst simultaneously knocking the wind out of him...

Nardic trebuchets and catapults fired their rounds deep into the heart of the Tuhk and the ground shook as the explosive bolts of orcish ballistae returned fire upon the elves in kind. Captain Vasil leapt out of the way as another such bolt struck a nearby catapult, flinging burning shrapnel in all directions. He'd barely escaped the explosion, though he was already back on his feet and shouting orders even as the orcs reloaded their deadly weapons to fire another volley of the deadly bolts. The grandiose battering ram of the elvish forces continued to crash upon the heavily barricaded entrance into the outermost slums of the malignant orc fortress. There were already gaping holes present in the slum-wall and cracks were starting to show visibly like spider-webs upon the surface of the inner walls.

Standing defiantly against them, the Tuhk continued to oppose the forces set against it without wavering. It stared smugly down upon the elvish legions as it spewed its sickly flames, belching smoke from the iron exhausts that jutted out of it like pores. Explosive bolts fired off from the several tiers of the tower's base as well as from the many ringed walls that divided and encompassed the wretched stronghold of the orcs. Retreating to a safe distance, Captain Vasil rallied the remaining troops of his initial assault even as their war machines continued to weaken the city from afar. Further South, safe and out of sight, there was an elf camp filled with injured, supplies, and the reserves who would take over upon the fall of Istul's outer defences.

An eruption of sound signalled exactly what Vasil had been waiting for as the slum-wall gave way with a resonant *boom*. It was immediately followed by a momentary lapse in fighting, the silence giving away the shock and surprise of the defending orcs. Shouting out the orders to fall back, Captain Vasil sent a messenger back into camp ahead of the retreating elf host on horseback to call to arms the second and third divisions of elves. It was their mission to take the city as he'd planned prior to mounting the assault whilst the initial forces fell back to rest and recover. The returning ranks of the preliminary attack upon the Tuhk passed by their advancing brethren even as they neared the elf camp.

Soldiers from both sides exchanged looks with their kin as each went their separate ways. Only Captain Vasil and a handful of his most faithful lieutenants had remained behind upon breaching the outer wall. They lingered only to lead the frontline forces as they stormed the slums of Istul. Together they joined the approaching ranks of their reserves, taking charge as they poured in through what was left of the southern entrance into the orc capitol. None stood against them upon gaining entry within the sprawling stronghold and so they pushed deeper into the city whilst their war machines continued to fire upon the wretched Tuhk from afar...

Just ahead of him in the formation, Ulrich caught Varg as his friend grabbed the shoulder of a fellow warrior out of the corner of his eye, pulling the man back as the Nardic party neared yet another intersection. Even as the southern men stopped in their tracks there in the sewers, a crew of no more than ten orcs passed them by running a perpendicular track to their own. The archers fired off as they'd done before, leaving none of the orcs alive to make their trek to the designated bombing location. With the way ahead clear once again and their adversaries sinking in a river of their own filth, the tribesmen continued onwards. They ran openly in their desperate plight to escape the powder-keg that was the sewers of Istul before it was set aflame. Time was of the essence and they were quickly running short; the elves were drawing nearer and every man present knew it wouldn't be much longer before they took the outer slums.

Crossing intersection after intersection, the men steadily made their way deeper into the heart of the Tuhk. Struggling to breathe, they pushed on as quickly and warily as they could via the underground labyrinth of interconnected tunnels they traversed with growing anxiety. *It can't be much further now,* Ulrich thought to himself in an attempt to preserve what little hope he still maintained for the meagre band of tribesmen. As they neared the umpteenth intersection since they'd infiltrated the sewage system, the faint sizzling hiss of a pipe sounded from around the corner. Stopping in their tracks the men strained their ears, finding that the source of the noise was not far from where they presently stood. Varg motioned to a handful of archers and together they crept along to the corner of the intersection with their backs to the wall as they stealthily strafed along.

    One archer nocked an arrow to his bowstring and peeked from around the corner. He found that the source of the sound was no more than a lone orc taking massive drags from a strange metal pipe. Though the orc's piece vaguely resembled the pipes of the Nardic Isles, it was very unlike the tobacco pipes of the southern men. The whistle of a lone arrow in the dim torchlit tunnel was the last thing the smoking orc heard before he felt all life drain from the piercing wound dealt to him by the Nardic archer from afar. Upon killing the sentry, the tribesmen continued their advance and found him to be the guard of a ladder leading out of the sewers and into the streets above.

    Whilst his kinsmen made their ascent into the streets of the Market District above, a younger tribesman foolishly picked up the smoking pipe and struck a match. He lit the bowl as he would a tobacco pipe in his homeland. The bowl hissed and cackled ominously even as he milked it, though the young man cleared it in a single hit without thought or regard as to what might be in it. Before the smoke had even had a chance to enter his lungs he was already choking and coughing on the hit he'd so stupidly taken. His nearby fellows shook their heads in disapproval as they awaited their turn to climb out of the stinking hell-hole.

"You imbecile! Could you not wait until we were safely back home to smoke our own stuff out of our own pipes?" Ulrich reprimanded the lad, snatching the pipe out of his hand and tossing it into the stinking river of waste that flowed through all throughout those tunnels.

"Be easy on him; it's been awhile since any of us have had a good smoke." Varg felt sympathy towards the lad. They hadn't had the luxury of tobacco or beer since losing the supply-horses they'd brought with them in their journey through the Dead Woods far to the South, some years ago.

Even as the men rebuked and sympathised with the smoker he collapsed upon the ground. From there he proceeded to seize and convulse, foaming at the mouth. Some of the men rushed to his aid, though it was already too late and there was nothing they could do about it anyway. After a couple of minuted the convulsions stopped and his body grew still. His fellows left him behind as yet another casualty in their war against the orcs as they rushed to make their ascent before the bombs went off and took them along with him. Ulrich took his turn at the ladder and Varg followed directly behind him; together they clambered out of the hole in the streets and rushed away even as a resonant *bang* erupted in the distance to the South.

The men waited expectantly in the safety of a nearby alleyway for the explosion that would ravage the Slums that surrounded the city of Istul. A couple of minuted passed by yet nothing happened. Finally a man by the name of Orin spoke up, dividing the troops into two groups; the first being responsible for taking the stolen explosives of the orcs to the Market Entrance where they would free the way for the advancing elves. The second crew would take the remaining bombs to the Barracks Entrance where they would provide access to the contingent of Aush Wood elves in the North. Ulrich had been assigned to the first group and Varg was put in the second, separating the two and sending them in completely different directions of one another.

"So this is it *freunde*. Though we never had the chance of making our acquaintance back home, it's truly been a pleasure fighting alongside you." Ulrich reached out to shake his companion's hand, though Varg rejected it.

"I doubt we'll ever meet again and I have no hopes of returning home, though I'm glad to consider you a friend." he hugged the bewildered Ulrich and they grasped one another tightly in their final farewell.

"I pray to the gods that you're wrong. If we ever see home again I'd be happy to buy you a pint and tell tales of our bravery in the tavern." with their goodbyes concluded the two joined their respective companies and set out.

CHAPTER TWENTY-FOUR

Covered in blood and mortally wounded, an elf returned from the frontlines clutching at his side as he rode on horseback away from the devastation. He looked to have suffered severe burns and seemed on the verge of collapse even as he entered the camp. Calling out to his brethren the elf delivered news from the frontlines, though it was not good tidings that he brought with him...

The doors that comprised the Slum Entrance creaked and groaned as they were pounded repeatedly by the battering rams of the elves. Still they pushed with all their might against the fortifications of the orcs, slowly but surely wearing away at the heavily barricaded gate that served as the southern entrance into the Tuhk. Further within the stronghold, the ringed walls that encompassed the inner districts were beginning to crumble to the superiority of the Nardic catapults that assailed them. Suddenly a sharp *crack* echoed throughout the Gorgon plains for all to hear as the doors leading into the Slums gave way to the elvish battering rams. With their path unobstructed the elves began to fall back as the main host took over where they left off.

Almardi and Namroden marched alongside the ranks of their brethren, making up the rearguard in the elvish invasion of Istul. From up ahead they could see the forces of Gilan as they poured in through the remains of what had once been the South Gate. Even as they descended upon the city there was a sudden concussive blast of noise as plumes of smoke and fire burst forth out of the very ground surrounding the vile fortress. Almardi, Namroden, and the others amongst the rearguard who were fortunate enough to find themselves outside its range were lifted from their feet and launched backwards through the air from the force of the explosion. To those outside of the Tuhk at the time of the explosion it appeared that a volcano had suddenly erupted.

A mushroom cloud shot up from the base of the stronghold as if an underground geyser had suddenly become active beneath the orcish capitol. It was immediately followed by the screams of elves burning alive in the former sprawling ghetto that was the Slums of Istul. Before the clouds of dust and debris had even had a chance to dissipate the remaining elvish troops outside the city were already pouring in to see what was left of the invasive force trapped within. The outer wall had been wholly destroyed; only a charred archway remained where the South Gate had previously stood and surrounding the devastated streets of the Slums was the rubble and scattered debris of what had once served as its battlements.

The ruined foundations of the sqats that littered Istul's slums were all that remained of the sprawling ghetto that surrounded the great stronghold of the orcs. What was left of the Slums had been drowned in a sea of debris and it was a laborious task to navigate the barren landscape. Ballistae fired their explosive shot down upon the ruins, leaving craters in their wake as they eradicated what was left of the elvish survivors. Liquefied waste started to pool in the holes as the sewage beneath the city began to ooze and seep from where the sewers were exposed and the ground. Looking around Almardi and Namroden could see for themselves that the ground itself was cracked and collapsing upon itself.

Ducking into the cover of a collapsed sqat even as an explosive bolt erupted beside them, Almardi and Namroden fled from their provisional cover up the road a ways before flinging themselves into a tiny foxhole as more of the missiles flew overhead.

Small fires stilled burned throughout the formers Slums, providing the remnants of the elvish assault with some illumination whilst simultaneously lighting them up as targets for the orcish archers upon the Market's outer wall. Using the smouldering pockets of smoke and dust that were still present as cover between the vast expanse of rubble that covered the ruined slum the two lovers made their way to the Market Gate as quickly and stealthily as they could. They were desperate in their plight, hoping beyond hope that the Nardic tribesmen had somehow found a way to free the entrance for what was left of Gilan's army. Their faith was restored somewhat upon the discovery that Captain Vasil had survived the orcish ambush. He was rallying the remnants of Gilan's forces in the southeast just outside the ramp that led up to the Market Entrance and so they answered his call...

The northern reaches of the East End of the Market District were entirely devoid of activity in the midst of the elvish onslaught to the South, leaving the men at peace for the time being. Ulrich made his way down into the heat of the chaos as his squad leader led them to the Southeast Gate Entrance into the former streets of the Slums. Some of their crew carried with them the orcish bombs that were responsible for the devastation, escorted by a band of Nardic archers and axemen. Ulrich ran alongside Orin, their leader, as the company made its way along through the squalid streets. Catapults came crashing down all around as they drew nearer to the South and it grew increasingly difficult to navigate the streets as buildings came crashing down all around them.

From up ahead they spotted a lone orc scurrying through the wreckage in the wake of all the destruction and the Nardic archers all halted and took aim as one body, letting loose a flurry of arrows in his direction. The orc was flung backwards off his feet where he curled up into a ball upon the streets ahead of them. The men rushed towards him, though cautiously just in case he wasn't truly as alone as he'd seemed. Drawing nearer it seemed that he was still breathing, and upon closer inspection it appeared that the arrow hadn't actually penetrated his thickset iron cuirass. Ulrich peered in for a closer look before speaking his mind aloud.

"Look, he still breathes! I see no blood or signs of injury..." even as the words left Ulrich's mouth, the short scrawny orcling warrior hopped to his feet and fled from the band of southern tribesmen. The young warrior didn't make it far however; before long he found his back filled with the pine shafts of Nardic arrows. So it was that G'hnak the Porcupine laid there, dying a coward's death as his life drained out from him, blood pooling around his corpse as his lungs filled with it.

Upon killing the orcish deserter, the tribesmen pushed onwards in the direction of the Southeast Gate where they would place the explosives that would free the way for the forces of Gilan. Orin stopped them a safe distance away from the gate where the area was bustling with activity. Climbing atop the sqals that crowded that place, Orin surveyed the area as he would the pine forests of his homeland. He strategically plotted out the placement of the bombs so as to cause the most widespread devastation that would ultimately result in the demolition of the Market's battlements. Giving his crew the coordinates of the bombing locations they carried out the orders as quickly as they could, igniting the powder-kegs and fleeing for cover out of range of the demolition site.

The bombs went off simultaneously and the uproar of the surprised orcs could be heard from afar by the Nardic men who smiled grimly at the impending doom of their enemies. The towering skyscrapers that filled the South End of the marketplace came crashing down as their structural integrity was compromised by the explosives of its own residents used against them. Taking advantage of the distraction the men made their way through the devastation towards the remains of the Market's battlements, seeking to regroup with whatever was left of the elvish forces in their desperate final stand against the orcs of Istul.

* * *

The fifty metre wall that served as the Military District's outer battlements loomed in the distance to the right as Egorin and his kin made their way east across the rooftop express-ways of Istul's marketplace. Sprinting as fast as their legs would carry them, the Aush Wood elves made their way towards the Northeast Entrance that would lead them deeper into the heart of the orcish capitol in their journey to the Tuhk. They came upon the entrance and found it totally unmanned. There were no doors or gates barring them entry and so they walked through unopposed to find a small contingent of the Nardic tribesmen awaiting them on the other side. Egorin approached one of the tribesmen whom he recognised to be a man by the name of Varg.

The elf shook his head, motioning for all of the Nardic troops gathered before him to stay put when they attempted to join the ranks of the Aush Wood elves. Understanding filled the tribesman's eyes and he yielded to the ancient sentinel of Gilan's sacred spirit wood. Varg stretched out a hand to bid the elf a final farewell, though a look of disgust quickly spread across Egorin's face as he took in a whiff of the orc faeces that coated the Nardic men. Smiling ashamedly, Varg mumbled something incomprehensible to the elf in his native tongue and Egorin returned the grin, assuming it to be an apology. He waved it off and they parted ways upon having concluded the exchange.

Watching as the last of the tribesmen passed under the towering archway that seemed to stretch high up into the skies above, Egorin and his fellows turned their backs upon the outer battlements that surrounded the Barracks before returning their attention to the task at hand. They spanned the vast expanse of barren war-torn plains that covered the lands comprising the Tuhk's

Military District. A varied assortment of armouries, smithies, and factories dotted the landscape alongside the handful of miniature sqals that housed the residents of that place. The length of the orcish training grounds were riddled with foxholes and trenches for use as cover in their constant war-games. As it was, all of their attention was focused in the South where the bulk of Gilan's forced pushed their way into the city.

Egorin and the fellows of his company gravely trekked through the uneven crater-filled fields between themselves and the inner wall of the Tuhk that encompassed the Gardens of the Masters. It was slow going, though they reached their destination without much effort on their part. Just outside of the North Gate a second explosion erupted from somewhere to the South, followed by what sounded like a chain series of buildings collapsing.

Is this yet another orcish ambush? Egorin thought to himself.

He worried for the main host to the South, whom they hoped to still be alive after the decimation of the Slums. The Aush Wood elves had barely survived the whole mess themselves; it took them by surprise even as they infiltrated the Market District through its unguarded northern entrance. Egorin and his fellow elves fled into the cover of some nearby trenches as the uproar of a clamorous group emanated from within the inner ringed wall spanning the Tuhk of Istul itself. They hid within the provisional safety of the trench bunkers as an entire host of Sikha and Shak'hal filed out from within the unholy citadel in the heart of the city. Luckily for the elves, they went unnoticed by the demonic legions who were hell-bent on resolving the disturbance in the South as they marched to reinforce the ranks of their orcish slaves...

*   *   *

Captain Vasil led the advance as the remnants of Gilan's main host surged through the crumbling ruins that had formerly been the outer wall of the Market District. Almardi and Namroden followed their highly-revered commander as they fell upon the orcs who were still recovering from the devastation of the Nardic bombing. It freed the way for the remaining elves who'd been fortunate enough to survive the orcish ambush upon their frontline assault, as well as weakened and scattered the forces of Istul who stood against them. The Nardic siege machines had ceased firing upon the city some time ago and the ballistae of the Tuhk were rendered useless now that the elves were so deep within the heart of that fetid city.

Almardi spotted a handful of the Nardic tribesmen fleeing the ruins of the marketplace, out into the desolate ruins of the Slums. They seemed to be fleeing from Death itself as they fled in terror from some unknown force greater than any they'd yet encountered. Expecting the demonic god of the orcs himself, Almardi braced himself as he charged forward alongside his dearest friend towards what they knew in their hearts to be the End. Word of demons spread nearly as quickly as they fell upon the elves and they found themselves locked in a deadly game of cat and mouse. Mounted archers rode along on horseback, firing their deadly arrows upon the towering Shak'hal officers who marched upon them, whilst the infantry fought back the vast multitudes of Sikha that sought to overwhelm the remnants of the elf host.

The remnants of Gilan's southern forces divided up into three-man cells at the command of Captain Vasil, whom Almardi and Namroden paired with upon receiving the orders. Following the valiant commander of the elf host they took to the back-roads and alleys that cut through the devastated streets of the marketplace as they sought to evade and flank their demonic adversaries. Chaos took root within their ranks as Gilan's surviving warriors desperately fought back against the unholy foes that beset them. Elves cried out as they were brutally hacked down and slaughtered in the streets by the colossal monstrosities of the Masters. Running back out into the open streets that were rife with demonic activity, Almardi and Namroden followed the lead of Captain Vasil as they joined forces with a handful of their fellow elves in flanking the demons.

Coming from the North they fell upon Istul's unholy legions from behind, taking them unawares and slaughtering nearly a dozen of their troops before the hostile host became alerted to the attack on their rearguard. Some of the Shak'hal officers turned their attention to the ambush that had taken a minor toll on their forces, seeking to eliminate the nuisance that was led first and foremost by the renowned commander of Gilan's army. Almardi fought to match the pace of his comrades though it grew difficult as they began to clash with the Sikhan host that rushed to meet them under the command of the gruesome Gorgon captains. Statuesque Shak'hal marched against Captain Vasil and his rag-tag band, engaging the elves in a brutal bloodbath where they met on the field of battle in those cramped and squalid streets. Shrieks and death cries emanated from both sides like the chatter of birds on an early summer morning as the elves fought back against the foul abominations who opposed them with all of their remaining strength.

CHAPTER TWENTY-FIVE

The black cast-iron gates that served as the doorway leading into the unholy Church of the Masters were wide open, allowing Egorin and his band of demon-slaying spirit keepers entry into the horrid structure that was the base of that city's towering citadel. As they spanned the surrounding gardens between themselves and the abominable base of the Tuhk they hacked their way through the Pah'kan priests who were rife in that courtyard, slaughtering them in a spray of blood and gore. Wretched black plants sprouted from the cracked and barren soiled that covered the bleak expanse Egorin and his companions flew across in their pursuit of the orc priests. The Pah'ka withdrew into the safety of their hallowed church, though even the malignant Tuhk couldn't hold off the wrath of the elves who poured through the abhorrent archway that served as its entrance. Egorin and the Aush Wood demon slayers charged through the sanctuary of the Tuhk's church, hacking down the orcs and priests who fled before them even as they passed the abominable creatures.

Making their way into the heart of that circular citadel, they pushed past orc guards who futilely sought to escape their fury to no avail. Countless corpses of the dead orcs who stood against them laid in the wake of the Aush Wood elves as they sought out the lift that would take them to the antechamber of the Masters, somewhere in the highest reaches of Istul's malignant Tuhk. None could escape the divine retribution of elvish steel as the Aush Wood elves sought to end the accursed existence of that land's inhabitants. Though the spirit keepers generally only armed themselves with the preferred bows of their kind, they had replaced their ranged weapons with the dual daggers that they carried with them. Rarely used, they kept the weapons close at hand in the event that they found themselves locked into close-quarters combat with their adversaries. For this reason the Aush Wood elves were a terrible force to be reckoned with, both at long-range and up close and personal. The orcs knew of those holiest crusaders amongst Gilan's forces sheerly by the reputation they'd made for themselves as demon slayers, having been responsible for the majority of Shak'hal deaths and disappearances prior to the war.

Egorin and his fellows pushed deeper into the heart of the Church that served as the colossal citadel's foundations and finally found what they were looking for, painting the walls of the halls leading up to it red with the blood of the orcs who defended it. They came upon a circular room without a ceiling and found it unguarded by the residents of that unholy place. A large round elevator pad attached to ropes, gears and pulleys sat in the centre upon the cold stone floor and it was completely unadorned but for a single lever that served as its switch. The room itself was no more than an elevator shaft and looking up they could see that all of the rooms on each floor opened out to the circular shaft. So it was that the pad served as the floor upon ascending to each level, as the elves saw for themselves...

* * *

Turning into the cover of an alleyway, Almardi followed Captain Vasil alongside Namroden and a handful of their fellows only to find the way ahead barred by a Shak'kal overlord and his Sikhan crew. The elves fell upon the Sikhan troops who rushed to meet them at the command of their Shak'kal lieutenant and the clamorous clashing of steel echoed off the tins walls of that alley like thunder. A shadow shot past Almardi and he saw it strike a fellow elvish soldier in the chest out of the corner of his eye. The elf was flung aside by the force of the blow and devoured whole by the darkness before he even had a chance to land. Almardi spotted what was responsible for the devastating strike; a demonic archer was firing charged bolts of darkness that enveloped their mark and swallowed them whole.

Captain Vasil fought his way through a slew of Sikha on his way towards the abominable foe whilst Almardi flanked the creature from the side. His fellows fought back the Sikha and provided Almardi with the distraction he needed to slaughter the archer unawares. The creature let loose a death shriek and flung Almardi helplessly in the force of the blast as it imploded. Brushing himself off as he regained his senses, Almardi stumbled to his feet, only to find his companions dying all around him as the fought back against the Sikha who were steadily pouring into that cramped alleyway. He swung his sword, beheading a Sikha that charged towards him, and rushed towards Namroden even as the elf matched himself against the Gorgon lieutenant in a one-on-one fight to the death.

The Shak'kal officer wielded a giant broadsword whose blade was taller than the elf was himself, though Namroden refused to back down. Almardi called out his friend's name even as the elf rushed to meet his adversary on the field of battle, only to be hacked in two by the hulking Gorgon mammoth. The elf watched as his dearest friend's torso parted from his legs, flung by the force of the blow only to crumple lifelessly upon the ground where they laid frozen in their grotesque state of death. Namroden's death had been so quick that it hadn't even registered to Almardi, who could barely believe his eyes. Though the Gorgon lieutenant had merely swatted the elf aside with his cleaver, it had the force of a train as it came crashing down upon him.

Tears welled in his eyes and stained his face as Almardi mourned the loss of his partner. Sinking to his knees as he the hopelessness of it all sank in, he wept whilst the battle raged on around him. The grief and despair quickly turned to anger and hate; picking himself up Almardi charged the Shak'kal officer and let loose a battle-cry as he flung himself at the colossal titan. He lunged at the creature's chest with his sword outstretched as he fell upon it with all of his might. The hulking beast swung its gargantuan sword too late, the massive arc barely missing Almardi as his elvish blade plunged into its heart. Stumbling backwards even as he imploded in a mini-supernova of demonic energy, the explosive death of the Shak'kal lieutenant disintegrated Almardi's sword-arm in the process and flung him like a rag-doll across the alley. He crumpled to the ground and lost consciousness even as he landed, the Darkness threatening to consume him...

*　*　*

The holy elves of the Aush Wood gathered themselves aboard the lift that would take them to the highest reaches of that most wretched tower of evil they found themselves within and Egorin pulled the lever that activated it. Gears began to grind and the platform started to ascend gradually. The elevator rose quickly enough, though shortly after they had passed the halfway point an alarm was raised as they were spotted by an orcish patrol. Enemy forces began to leap down from the rooms that opened up to the elevator shaft. Sikhan bone spites and Shak'kal officers flooded the lift and engaged the Aush Wood elves as it ascended.

The antechamber was within sight; they only had to hold off a little longer. Egorin dodged the blow of a Gorgon captain that felled two of his brethren, quickly firing an arrow from his bow into the demonic creature's heart, causing it to implode as it swallowed itself up like a black hole before bursting in an explosive blast of dark energy. The elvish forces were overwhelmed by the demons that beset them from all sides. They desperately fought back as they awaited their arrival at the final destination. It wasn't much further, they only had a few more floors to go before they reached the antechamber. Egorin rolled out of the way of a great Gorgon cleaver and lunged out of the path of a Shak'kal mace as it came crashing down upon him.

Firing another arrow into the skull of a Sikha, Egorin darted out of the way of yet another Shak'kal officer and took aim at two more Sikha before replacing his bow with the dual daggers he also carried. The lift was overflowing with demonic warriors and the air was thick with the presence of the Masters. They could feel the dominating will of the orcish overlord and its aura was terrifyingly powerful. Reaching its destination the lift came to a sudden stop and the fighting ceased momentarily. Twenty wraith-guards filled the circular room and a pedestal stood at the head of the room upon a great pedestal. The pedestal was a crude black tree, liken to a budless guaka-guaka plant with tendrils as thick as a man's waist, and the tree wrapped like a snake around the satanic skull that sat within it. A powerful force resided within that skull and it left all those in its presence spellbound and awestruck.

The skull was seven feet wide and nearly twelve feet long; its hound-like jowls were the humongous gaping entrance into Hell itself. Two gnarled ram's horns jutted from the base of the skull and it had the facial structure of a pit-bull crossed with a ghastly dragon. The Gorgon God of Chaos had once been a mighty colossus, terrible to behold, though those were in the times of Myth, long before the recording of time and long since forgotten in the mortal world. All around the demonic skull was swathed in black waves of dark energy that flowed around its pedestal like and electric current or a magnetic field. Breaking the enchantment and shattering the silence, Egorin let loose a valiant battle-cry as he charged forwards.

His comrades pushed back the hulking Gorgon brutes back, allowing Egorin to break their defences and run unopposed towards the skull of the dead god where it sat within the unholy Tree of Discord. Knowing in his heart what he had to do Egorin threw himself at the skull, breaking the barrier of the foul aura that encased the skull and pushing through the demonic waves of energy with both daggers outstretched in front of him. He shove both daggers simultaneously into the forehead as he planted both feet the bridge of its nose. He kicked off even as it imploded and the explosion blasted him off into the nothingness of nonentity as the whole antechamber was devoured by the implosive demonic blast. The Tuhk swallowed itself up and the remains of the fortified tower-temple came crashing down upon itself.

CHAPTER TWENTY SIX

Swinging his axe, Ulrich brought it down in a sweeping arc that severed the heads of two Sikhan warriors even as they fell upon him. Their skeletal remains collapsed upon the ground as they were exorcised of the demons that possessed them, allowing the bones to return to their restful peace. Ulrich leapt over the bone pile of his defeated adversaries and regrouped with his fellow tribesmen as they fought their way towards the advancing elvish frontlines who pushed their way deeper into the heart of Istul's marketplace. Shrieks of dying orcs, elves, and bone spites filled the air along with the whistling of arrows and clang of steel as both sides threw themselves at their enemies without thought or regard for their own lives. The clamour was only occasionally interrupted by the deafening explosion of Shak'kal officers as they were defeated in the cramped and squalid streets, though the occurrences were few and far between.

Falling back towards the elvish front, Ulrich spotted Captain Vasil even as the elf divided his nearby comrades into three-man cells. The captain's specialised squads followed his lead as they diverted from the path of the greater elf host, seeking to flank their unholy enemies from the rear. Ulrich did his best to ward off the Sikha that assailed him, joining the elf host in providing their captain with the distraction his crew needed to fall behind the enemy lines. In his peripheral vision Ulrich spotted Almardi and Namroden as he fought off another wave of the Sikhan forces. The pair of elves followed their captain around the corner of a street, out of Ulrich's line of sight, and he returned his attention to the brutal bloodbath that was unfolding before him.

The majority of Istul's orcish inhabitants were beginning to see the futility of it all; they fled from the elves and their Gorgon overlords alike, realising that neither side truly represented their interests. Death and oppression were their only options and there were few who found either appealing. Escape was their only hope and so the cowardly majority took to it. Arrows jutted out of their backs as the deserters were shot down mid-flight whilst the bold who stood their ground were steadily hacked down by elvish steel. Gilan's forces pushed deeper into the orcish stronghold as Istul's demonic reinforcements rushed out to quell the advancing waves of elves. Ulrich continued to fight alongside the Nardic tribesmen and elves who stood with him in the final battle of their long and arduous campaign.

A Shak'kal lieutenant rose up and roared a challenge to any who would hear him. Men cowered before the demonic creature as it struck down the bold few who dared to opposed it. Ulrich retreated back a ways and regrouped with the advancing elvish host as they rushed to meet the satanic beast in battle. The Shak'kal stood nearly five metres tall and each swing of the mace it carried had a force capable of tearing down entire sqals. Arrows pelted the gargantuan mammoth, though they were as harmless as flies to the Gorgon titan. Dodging the devastating blow of the Shak'kal mace, Ulrich took a dive and launched himself at the hulking abomination, severing its ankle by swinging his axe deep into the tendons. Stumbling to its knees the creature collapsed and struggled to regain its footing. From behind him an entire squad of elves charged towards the wounded demon and launched themselves at the kneeling wretch, decapitating its arms, legs, and head in a flurry of blows. Upon the total decapitation of its vessel, the remains of the lifeless Shak'kal disintegrated into the void of nothingness from whence it came.

Dismayed by the loss of their commander at the hands of their enemy, the Sikhan forces shrieked in grief, terror and wrath. Ulrich took advantage of the momentary shock and used it as a distraction to slip out of the heart of the chaos. He took to a back-road in an attempt to regroup with a nearby elf company, closer towards the inner wall of the Market District, in the direction of the Northeast Gate. He fell into formation amongst their ranks even as they were assailed by more Sikha from behind and ahead, closing them in upon the three way intersection they now found themselves entrapped within. Ulrich led them back the way he'd just come and they darted into the cover of an adjacent alley heading north, only to find the way ahead barred by a Gorgon behemoth leading his Sikhan troops against none other than Captain Vasil and his small band of elves.

Ulrich heard Almardi's piercing cry as he screamed out his lover's name and he saw as the fair elf was cleaved in two by the great cleaver of the Shak'kal he so foolishly challenged. The Nardic man couldn't believe his eyes as the elf he'd come to know as a friend toppled in two pieces to the ground where he laid dead. Even as the reality of it all sank in Ulrich stopped dead in his tracks, as did all those gathered in that cramped alleyway, as Almardi charged towards the Shak'kal lieutenant and lunged at its chest with the grace of an arrow. The Gorgon beast swung his sword in an attempt to deflect the elf, though Ulrich could see the elvish scimitar protruding from its back as the demonic mammoth burst forth in an intense explosion of demonic energy. Almardi was flung across the alley from the force of the blast and it looked as if he'd been blown in half by the implosion as blood sprayed from his flying lifeless body.

The tribesman watched in dismay as his elvish friend crumpled to the ground. All around the Sikhan troops stood motionless in sheer horror at the destruction of the Shak'kal overlord. Captain Vasil rallied the friendly forces and the Sikha snapped out of their trance; the fighting resumed and the Sikha began to flee in terror at the wrath of the elves. Ulrich fought alongside the elves who fought back against the Gorgon menace with renewed intensity as they fell back into formation in the frontline advance. They pushed deeper North towards the entrance into the Military District and the enemy forces began to withdraw deeper into the hear of their stronghold.

From ahead Ulrich spotted his only friend, Varg, as the fellow Southerner made his way towards Ulrich's position. Varg called out to him and they made their way towards each other, fighting their way through the orcs and Sikha that stood in their way. The shouting had also attracted the attention of yet another Shak'kal officer, though the monstrous beast before them was a mighty Gorgon General, spanning nearly ten meters tall and pushing buildings themselves out of its way as it walked unopposed. Sikha fled before it and elves dared not challenge it. Ulrich grabbed his friend by the shoulder and together they fled back South as Varg took the lead.

"*Scheiß!*" Varg screamed as the creature chased them through the alleys and back-roads they took to in a futile attempt to lose it.

"News! What tidings do you bring!?!" Ulrich cried out as he ran with all of his might.

"The Aush Wood elves have taken the Tuhk! Where are Namroden and Almardi?" Varg replied as Captain Vasil took the lead.

"*Tot.*" Ulrich shouted bluntly above the clamour and they both fell silent at the news as they ran for their lives in those cramped streets.

Suddenly an explosion erupted behind them and the colossus ceased in its pursuit, stopping in its tracks and looking towards the heart of the city as a chain of smaller explosions erupted. Everyone ceased their activity as one body and turned their attention towards the malignant Tuhk of Istul itself as the structure fell apart and collapsed out of the sky upon itself. Smoke rose in a ghastly mushroom cloud of putrid smoke over the rubble of the former citadel and it spread outwards into the outermost reaches of the orcish stronghold around what once had been its mighty base. The smoke poured over the Market District and covered the streets in a thick blanket of soot, smoke, and ash. The air was thick with the scent of death and destruction and it became difficult to breathe.

"*Scheiß!* What was that?" Ulrich shouted, coughing and sputtering as he choked on the rancid smog that obscured the city.

"The elves! They did it! They destroyed the Tuhk!" Varg exclaimed with glee.

The Sikha screamed in monumental horror at the devastation of their Master's tower-temple. Anarchy took root within their ranks as the Sikhan forces gave in to the overwhelming terror that engulfed them. Ulrich and Varg regrouped with Captain Vasil and together they launched an attack against the Gorgon General even as he recovered from the shocking destruction of the Master's Tuhk. The death of the Gorgon God of Chaos only renewed the might of the demonic behemoth and he burst into flame as his wrath manifested itself. His sword drew ablaze and he swung it with devastating force, bringing sqat toppling to the ground in flames that spread throughout the streets. The elves pelted him with arrows and the spearmen threw their pikes and spears in a last-ditch effort at bringing the monster down, though to no avail.

Captain Vasil ordered a retreat and the remnants of the elvish host fell back along with the tribesmen who aided them. The titanic monstrosity swatted elves out of the way by the dozens and everyone fled for cover before its might. The orcs were all long-gone, either dead or having fled the city, and the bones spites were all fleeing into the outer reaches of the Tuhk where Gilan's reserves were at work covering the rear guard of the elvish assault. They slaughtered the terrified Sikhan masses effortlessly whilst the remnants of Gilan's frontlines engaged the only remaining Shak'kal within their ranks. Captain Vasil rallied his troops against the unholy Gorgon General. Varg and Ulrich fell back as the elvish demon-slayers took charge. Leading them first and foremost was Captain Vasil, racing towards the gigantic Shak'kal at full-speed in his divine wrath. The Gorgon General matched his pace as it charged towards him and his company of elves and Ulrich watched from afar alongside his only friend in the world.

The elf captain leapt from wall-to-wall in an alley and made his way to the third-story rooftops where he lunged at the General's chest. The Gorgon titan swatted him aside with the ironclad palm of its hand, sending him through the wall of a sqat. A handful of his kin had also attempted their own attacks simultaneously, though the gargantuan abomination had sidestepped them all. None could get near him from the ground where his body was ablaze and the ground around him burned in his wake. Plotting to himself, Ulrich grabbed Varg by the should and led them around the hulking creature to flank it from behind. Upon realising his comrade's plan Varg put up an argument, though Ulrich quickly quelled any resistance with his calming reassurance and determination.

Together they made their way behind the great Gorgon General even as he marched upon the remaining forces of elves that futilely stood against him. They rushed from behind and threw themselves at the behemoth's ankles, severing the tendons and bringing it down to its knees where in sank in an uproar of grievous pain. Captain Vasil reappeared from the wall he'd fallen through and out of the corner of his eye Ulrich saw as Vasil leapt down in a divine dive, straight into the chest of the Gorgon General. His sword plunged straight through it's heart and the beast keeled over. It imploded as it collapsed, blasting Ulrich and Varg down the street; they lost consciousness from the force of the explosion before they'd even hit the ground...

The remnants of the elvish campaign gathered themselves together with their Nardic allies and they left that place, having finally won the war. With the orcs all either dead or gone from those lands the war was won and their god was dead. Turning their backs on the ruinous wreckage that remained of the former orcish stronghold, they gathered their dead and wounded kin as they could and brought them back to the elf camp far to the southeast away from the sprawling capitol. When Ulrich awoke he found that Varg was still unconscious, though much to his surprise he also found his fallen friend Almardi aboard their wagon. Looking closer he saw that the elf still breathed, though Almardi was comatose in his deathlike state, halfway between the world of the living and the dead. His arm seemed to be severed at the shoulder, though it was heavily bandaged and a black resinous oil seeped through his wrappings. Black veins stretched across his entire right-half and the elf shivered in a cold sweat.

Ulrich held little faith in the elf making a recovery and he mourned his loss. Varg on the other hand seemed to be in relatively healthy condition, sound asleep aboard the wagon that drove them West, back towards Gilan in the long journey home. Ulrich turned his attention back towards the Tuhk and watched as it shrank back in the distance. The sun shone through a small hole in the black blanket that covered those lands and Ulrich wondered to himself just how long had passed since he'd embarked upon that fateful journey. Alas, the war was won and he was a hero, as were all those aboard the wagons in that caravan, along with those who walked beside it, and the countless dead who fell fighting for the righteous cause.

EPILOGUE

BAIERN, DUSSELDORF

Summer, 1E198

"Hans, go out and fetch some fish and potatoes in the marketplace for tonight's dinner!" Aeryn was a beautiful brunette with big brown eyes and a good figure for a mother of two. She handed her son a silver piece to take with him into town even as she made the request.

The family lived in a small log cabin on the outskirts of town near the woods where their father, Aeryn's husband, worked as a lumberjack. He was away in the mainland to the North, fighting in foreign wars with elves and goblins. Meanwhile at home, Hans and his mother took up what work they were able to keep their family fed and healthy. Hans worked in the woods as his father did before him, and his mother stitched leather armour for a living to get by; strange men were at their home at all hours buying and having their armour repaired. Occasionally Hans got in fights with the burly Nardic men when some would chat with his mother and present themselves as potential suitors to the beautiful soldier's wife. Hans ran along down the road with the silver piece clenched tightly in his fist; the fish would cost three coppers and the potatoes would be four, and that left him with three copper pieces to buy himself and his brother Frank a cheap toy from one of the market stalls as well as a gift for his mother.

Hans was thirteen and his brother, Frank, was seven; their mother was thirty and their father was thirty two, married to their mother at the ripe age of 16. He walked along the bare golden-brown dirt path in the wooded grassy hills of Dusseldorf, the largest of the chain of islands that comprised the Nardic Isles in the Sumatran Ocean south of the vast continent of Aerbon. The weather was fair in the southern climate for a summer day; the Nardic Isles were a warm country and the days were hot year round, though it was notoriously hot in the summer. The enormous pine trees native to the country provided some shade from the hot summer sun, however it only took a few minutes of exposure to the weather outside before Hans was drenched in sweat. Once he reached the town centre of Baiern he found a fisherman's stall; there were flies buzzing around the great heaps of fish piled in buckets around the stand, the stench wafted in the hot summer breeze and Hans held back the vomit as he retched after catching a whiff.

"Have you got anything fresh Master Fisherman?" Hans asked as innocently as he could, trying not to be rude in the face of such of foul and repugnant odour.

"Ah, young Hans! Why, how is your mother Aeryn doing on this fine day; only the freshest for such a fine woman, would you tell her I said that? Ah, but don't go telling her I say it to all the young ladies, because I don't!" the fisherman stammered, grabbing the finest fillets he could find amongst only the best of his personal supply from the catch.

Hans thanked the man and ran off even as the fisherman inquired about the lad's mother. He approached the potato vendor, a farmer's wife, and she sold him a small sack of decent sized potatoes for the fair price of four copper pennies. With the day's shopping finished he browsed the selection of dolls and figurines for his brother Frank who would be very pleased indeed with his brother's choice. For himself, Hans bought a slingshot in secret; his mother would never let him have such a device, saying it was a crude toy for naughty boys. He stowed it away in his leather breeches before buying his mother a sweet roll with the last copper penny he had of what his mother had given him.

The port town of Baiern was a rather small thriving community in the Northeast of the main island in the Nardic Isles, Dusseldorf. The town had a thriving lumber mill and the southern waters were rich with southern flounder and bass which the Nardic fishermen caught along with Sumatran Mackerel. There were hunters who made a good living off the hide and meats procured from the hulking elks* that roamed the wooded hills of the Nardic countryside. The Chief taxed the lands and everyone paid a percentage of their year's income to the great Warlord in Sehnshult. The houses were all made of wood and the town was rather small, as were most of the towns that dotted the island, and there were farmlands in the south of the country. Each town was ruled by a chief and each had their own independent militia; the Warlord of Dusseldorf reigned over all of the Nardic Isles from his throne in Sehnshult and all of the minor chieftains were subject to his rule.

The trek home was pleasant and peaceful; birds chirped in the trees and bees buzzed through the woods, Hans gaily trotted home to his mother with the sweet roll in one hand and a pack containing the fish and potatoes in another. When he arrived home the door was ajar and he could hear muffled sounds of choking within the house. Not knowing what to expect, Hans dropped everything where he stood in the road outside his family home and rushed in to investigate the source of the sound. He raced frantically through the small cabin to his mother in her bedroom where she was curled up sobbing with her back towards him and his brother. His brother Frank stood in the doorway choking on his tears trying to form sentences but failing. Hans tried to figure out what had happened but Frank just kept pointing at their mother and trying to talk whilst crying incoherently.

---

*In the Isles, moose are referred to as elk, a term used by the Aerbonean people for large deer, as the Nardic moose bore a resemblance to the red deer of Southern Aerbon and the caribou of the North.

Aeryn was entirely unaware of the world around her, lost in her own sadness, and there was nothing Frank or Hans could do or say to make her acknowledge their presence. Suddenly Hans saw what Frank had been pointing at; in between Aeryn's arm and her side a letter stuck out as if she'd been reading it but had tucked it into her arm to curl up and cry. Hans reached for the letter and ignored his sobbing mother as she coughed and heaved from crying her heart out as he gently tugged at the parchment slip. With some effort on his part the letter finally came free and he opened it up to read it's contents. His eyes scanned the first few lines and he saw that it was address to his mother, or his father's immediate family at least. The letter was from the Warlord of the Isles; it spoke of his father sailing abroad to the Northern lands and of ship wrecks off the coast. Furthermore the letter went on to say that there were no recorded survivors from the accident and that the elves had betrayed the Nardic Tribes. The letter apologised for the needless deaths of all the soldiers sent abroad and asked for the allegiance of all men able to bear arms in an effort to wage a righteous war against the elves who betrayed their trust.

My father is dead by the will of the elves, and now my mother has lost her will to live, Hans thought to himself.

He felt a great sadness overwhelm him and waves of rage washed over him. The elves had destroyed his family and taken his father from him; he swore an oath to himself that he would not let the elves live without penalty for their treason against his people. Hans left the house in which he'd spent the entirety of his life and walked down the wooded road towards the decadent Nardic fortress in the heart of the the island, Sehnshult. The chief island of the Nardic Isles, Dusseldorf, was the largest of the islands, though it was not too large as one could span the length of the island on foot in just over a week with ample time for stoppages. It wasn't even that far, however, from the young lad's home in Baiern to the capitol of Dusseldorf in the heartlands. Once he arrived in Sehnshult he would enlist in the Nardic army even as they prepared to sail to war against the elves. His father's death would not be in vain as Hans sought to avenge him in the campaign against the elvish kingdom of Gilan, somewhere North across the water...

Made in the USA
Lexington, KY
26 November 2019